It took a little more work and ingenuity to assemble the props he needed for his show. If everything worked as he planned, he'd be able to leave the slave fields. It all hinged on Crampatch's spoiled daughter, if she showed, and he impressed her, he'd have his meal ticket punched to Crampatch's mansion.

He went through his tricks. The slaves were loving it; but to Jack's increasingly worried annoyance, the audience he'd really hoped for was nowhere in sight.

He kept the show going for over an hour before privately giving up, and was on his last few lines of patter when he turned casually back to the table spotted an approaching car.

And in it were Crampatch and his spoiled daughter. Here to pick up a new toy.

This was his chance. For his grand finale, he launched into his most complex juggling routine, following it with his best card and rope tricks. The audience exploded into a wild racket of applause, cries, hoots, grunts, whistles, and squawks.

Crampatch's right-hand man bulled his way through the dispersing crowd.

"Crampatch's daughter wants a new toy. You're it."

"I'm honored," Jack said.

"Don't be," the man warned. "You think you're treated badly out here, just wait until you get into the house."

"Zahn has always managed to tell an enthralling story in the past, and this one is no exception. Ignore the young adult label if you're older and read it anyway."   —*Chronicle*

Books by Timothy Zahn

Dragonback Adventures (Starscape Books)
*Book 1: Dragon and Thief**
*Book 2: Dragon and Soldier**
*Book 3: Dragon and Slave**
*Book 4: Dragon and Herdsman**

The Blackcollar
A Coming of Age
Cobra
Spinneret
Cobra Strike
Cascade Point and Other Stories
The Backlash Mission
Triplet
Cobra Bargain
Time Bomb and Zahndry Others
Deadman Switch
Warhorse
Cobras Two (omnibus)

Star Wars: Heir to the Empire
Star Wars: Dark Force Rising
Star Wars: The Last Command

Conquerors' Pride
Conquerors' Heritage
Conquerors' Legacy

Star Wars: The Hand of Thrawn
Book 1: Specter of the Past
Book 2: Vision of the Future
Starwar Wars: Outbound Flight

The Icarus Hunt
*Angelmass**
*Manta's Gift**
*The Green and the Gray**
*Night Train to Rigel**

*Denotes a Tom Doherty Associates Book

DRAGON
and SLAVE

THE THIRD DRAGONBACK ADVENTURE

TIMOTHY ZAHN

A TOM DOHERTY ASSOCIATES BOOK
NEW YORK

For Pam and Barry:
For their faith and trust in the midst
of their own battles

DRAGON AND SLAVE: THE THIRD DRAGONBACK ADVENTURE

Copyright © 2005 by Timothy Zahn

Edited by James Frenkel

A Starscape Book
Published by Tom Doherty Associates, LLC
175 Fifth Avenue
New York, NY 10010

www.starscapebooks.com

ISBN 0-765-34041-0
EAN 978-0-765-34041-2

First edition: June 2005
First mass market edition: June 2006

Printed in the United States of America

0 9 8 7 6 5 4 3 2 1

With a slight change in engine pitch, and a small ripple of vibration through the deck, the *Essenay* came off the ECHO stardrive.

They had arrived at the planet Brum-a-dum.

Stretched out on his belly on the dayroom floor, Draycos hunched himself up onto his front paws and looked around. Over by the wall, fourteen-year-old Jack Morgan was seated at the narrow table, his elbows on the edge, his chin propped up in his hands. He was peering down at the table's surface, moving his lips silently. Concentrating on his studies, the boy had apparently missed the fact that the *Essenay* had returned to normal space.

Draycos turned his attention toward the camera/speaker/microphone setup that allowed the ship's computer to monitor the room's activities. In the dark lens of the camera he caught a distorted glimpse of his own long, triangular head and the spiny crest starting between his glowing green eyes and extending down his long back. Like a dragon the size of a small tiger, Jack had said at their first meeting.

The description had intrigued Draycos, and he'd spent several hours over the past two months researching the topic of dragons in the *Essenay*'s library. Some of the stories he'd found had been rather flattering. Others had definitely not been. "Well?" he called toward the camera.

"Well what?" Uncle Virge's voice came back, sounding grumpy.

"I thought perhaps you would like to announce our arrival," Draycos said mildly.

Jack looked up from the table. "We're here?" he asked. "Uncle Virge?"

"Yes, we're here," the computerized voice confirmed reluctantly. "Don't get excited—I'm still scanning the area. That could take awhile."

Jack threw a knowing look at Draycos. "Come on, Uncle Virge, quit stalling," the boy said. "We already know where the Chookoock family estate is. Just plot us a landing course and take us down."

"It's not that simple, Jack lad," Uncle Virge protested. "There are airway lanes to be located, arrival procedures to be observed, Brummgan customs documents to be filed—"

"And you can do all of that with your eyes shut," Jack interrupted. "Just take us down, okay?"

There was an audible sigh from the speaker. Uncle Virge was a sort of ghostly echo of Jack's Uncle Virgil, the conman and safecracker who'd raised the boy after his parents' deaths when he was three. Before Uncle Virgil's own death a year ago, he'd somehow managed to implant a version of his personality into the *Essenay*'s computer. With only that personality to keep him company, Jack had continued on, taking odd shipping jobs to support himself as he flew alone between the stars of the galaxy's Orion Arm.

Alone, that is, until Draycos, poet-warrior of the K'da, had crashed unexpectedly into his life.

Uncle Virge didn't like Draycos. He didn't like Draycos's warrior's ethic, or his continued presence aboard the *Essenay,* or the fact that he had dragged Jack into his private mission.

And he *certainly* didn't like this plan. "Jack, lad, really now, this is just plain crazy," he said, his voice soft and earnest. "Even by *my* standards. Can't we take just a little more time to think about it? There *has* to be a better way to find these mercenaries of yours."

Jack looked back down at the tabletop, his eyes avoiding Draycos's. He was trying hard to hide his feelings, but Draycos could see the tension in his face. Jack didn't like the plan any more than Uncle Virge did.

Which made it unanimous, because Draycos didn't much like it either.

But they were running out of choices. More importantly, they were running out of time. In four months the main fleet of K'da and Shontine refugee ships would reach the Orion Arm after their long, weary voyage across space. Their final goal was the uninhabited planet of Iota Klestis; but first they would be stopping at a rendezvous point known only to the fleet and the commanders of the advance team.

Except that all of those advance team commanders were dead. Their ships had been attacked as they arrived at Iota Klestis, and everyone aboard except Draycos had been killed by the unstoppable Death weapon of their enemies, the Valahgua. The attackers had then taken control of the ships, and by now had surely discovered the location of the upcoming rendezvous.

All Draycos and Jack had to go on was the fact that the Valahgua had picked up some allies among the various human and alien beings of the Orion Arm. A mercenary group, almost certainly, one which they already knew employed Brummgas. If they could identify that group, they might have a chance of locating the rendezvous point themselves before the refugees arrived.

If they couldn't, the fleet would fly straight into an ambush . . . and the K'da and Shontine peoples would cease to exist.

"Maybe there *is* a better way, Uncle Virge," Jack said. "But I'll be stripped, sanded, and varnished if I can come up with one."

"You could still take this to StarForce," Uncle Virge said.

"We've been through all this," Jack reminded him sourly. "StarForce, the Internos, and every other government agency is out because we don't know who we can trust."

"Then how about Cornelius Braxton?" Uncle Virge persisted. "He owes you big-time for pulling his marshmallows out of the fire the way you did during Arthur Neverlin's big power grab."

Jack shook his head. "You don't create a megacorporation like Braxton Universis without a lot of brains and a lot more ruthlessness," he pointed out. "Grateful or not, ten to one he'd try to twist all this to his own advantage." The boy's lip twitched. "Besides, I don't think Neverlin's given up, and I'd rather not be standing anywhere near Braxton when he makes his next move. No, for right now it's got to be just you and me and Draycos."

"But to throw yourself into a slavemaster's lap?" Uncle Virge protested. "What if he doesn't go for it?"

"He will," Jack assured him. "Slavemasters are in the business for the money. All we have to do is make sure the offer is too good to pass up."

"And if you can't get out afterward?"

"What, with my trusty K'da poet-warrior at my side?" Jack threw a strained smile at Draycos.

"I'm sure he'll be a big help," Uncle Virge said, his tone making it clear he wasn't sure of that at all. "But why go in as a thief? Why not as a soldier looking for work?"

"I've tried being a soldier," Jack said. "You saw how well it worked."

"You lived through it," Uncle Virge countered. "That says a lot."

Jack snorted. "Not really," he said. "Anyway, what do you suggest I use for references? Ask them to get in touch with the Whinyard's Edge?"

"Besides, the Chookoock family already has many mercenaries to hire out," Draycos put in. "That is why we chose this particular slave dealer, after all."

"Yes, I remember the logic, thank you," Uncle Virge said icily. "I just don't think it's going to be easy for a slave to get into their personnel records."

"It'll be a lot easier from in there than it would be from out here," Jack said. "Look, it's not that big a deal. A quick flip-and-dip into their computer, you swoop the *Essenay* in, and we all fade together into the sunrise."

Uncle Virge sniffed. "You make it sound so easy."

"Easier than the job we did aboard the *Star of Wonder*," Jack said. "At least here I'll have you and the *Essenay* on hand to back me up."

"Maybe," Uncle Virge said ominously. "Maybe not. Slavemaster estates aren't the easiest places in the world to break into, you know. When push comes to shove comes to a poke in the snoot, I may not be able to do much from the outside. In which case, you and your K'da poet-warrior will be on your own."

"We've been on our own before," Jack reminded him. Still, Draycos could see the boy's throat muscles tighten a little more. "Quit stalling. Let's get to it."

Uncle Virge sighed. "If you insist," he said. "I suppose you'll want a look at the place before we land."

"That would be nice," Jack said dryly. "Pipe it back here, will you?"

The display screen on the dayroom wall had been showing a pleasant, peaceful scene of a sunlit mountain pass. Now it changed to a view of a cloud-mottled, bluish-green landscape far below. "How soon till we can see something?" Jack asked.

"Give me a chance, Jack lad," Uncle Virge huffed. "We've only just reached the planet."

"Okay, okay, don't pop a port," Jack said soothingly. "I can work on this awhile longer."

"What help may I offer?" Draycos asked, padding across the room to Jack's side and looking down at the table. Jack had turned the surface transparent, and on the displays beneath it were rows of what looked like wiggled tracks made by extremely startled worms.

"It's a group of common Brummgan words, written in Brummgan script," Jack said. "Most Orion Arm computers have automatic translators built in, so I shouldn't have any trouble reading their data lists once I'm in. But there might be other stuff along the way I'll need to be able to read."

"Very likely," Draycos agreed. "How may I help?"

"That screen over there shows the translations," Jack said,

pointing to the far end of the table. "I'll mix these up and then try to read them. You see if I get them right."

They went through the drill twice, with Jack missing only seven words the first time and four the second. By the time they were finished, the dayroom display was showing a high-resolution image of the ground below them.

"You'll have to settle for an angled view," Uncle Virge said as the image shifted direction a little. "We're heading for the Ponocce Regional Spaceport, at the southern edge of Ponocce City and about three miles from the Chookoock estate itself. Given our current vector, it would look suspicious for us to fly directly over them."

"Just do the best you can," Jack said.

"Right," Uncle Virge said. "Anyway, that's it coming up on the left, pressed right up against the eastern edge of the city. That white line there—see it? That's the estate's outer wall."

Stretching out his long neck, Draycos studied the image scrolling slowly across the display. The estate was a huge one, covering nearly as much territory as the city alongside it. The ribbon of white that Uncle Virge had identified as the outer wall snaked across the landscape, disappearing here and there behind low hills or tall bushes until it finally vanished completely behind the trees of a thick forest. Along with the forest, the estate also included neat rectangles of cropland, areas of bushy undergrowth, a rock quarry, several ponds, and a small river.

The wall itself was deceptively plain and simple-looking, with no signs of guard towers or patrolling aircraft. It was almost as if it was there just for show.

Draycos didn't believe it for a minute. Neither, obviously, did Jack. "So what's the story on that wall?" the boy asked.

"Some kind of hardened ceramic, looks like," Uncle Virge said. "Shape-wise, it seems to be a sort of X cross section. That means you have an overhang to deal with no matter which side you start climbing from."

"That ought to discourage casual visitors," Jack commented. "What about non-casual ones?"

"Not sure," Uncle Virge grunted. "It looks like there may be a set of lasers running along the groove at the top, nestled down into the center of the X and aiming upward. There may be some flame jets mixed in, too."

Draycos felt the tip of his tail making slow circles. Lasers and flame jets, firing straight up out of the top of the wall. The Chookoock family was serious about keeping people out.

Or, perhaps, serious about keeping people in. "How many slaves do they keep inside the estate itself?" he asked.

"Hundreds," Uncle Virge said grimly. "Humans and several other species. A lot of them are working the cropland and quarry, plus there's a big group in the forest."

"Logging?" Jack asked.

"I don't know," Uncle Virge said. "Most of that batch are gathered around a particular line of bushes. Don't know what that's all about."

"What about buildings?" Jack asked.

"There are several." On the display, a red rectangle appeared, outlining a group of brown-and-green-speckled buildings that blended smoothly into their surroundings. "The long buildings here and here are probably slave quarters," Uncle Virge said, marking them with red blips. "We've also got service buildings—kitchens, laundry facilities, washrooms."

"A complete community within the wall," Draycos commented.

"Two communities, actually," Uncle Virge said, sounding disgusted. "The slaves' area; and *this*." The image shifted again, centering on a huge brown-roofed building. "The Chookoock family mansion."

Draycos leaned a little closer to the display. The mansion was set about half a mile back from the western edge of the estate, with an extensive parking area in front and a long, winding drive connecting it to a wide gate in the white wall. On both sides of the drive were formal gardens, complete with flower beds, shrubs, and occasional clumps of small trees.

To the north of the mansion was a large open area where the grass had been marked with a series of lines and circles. Some sort of sports ground, probably. A tall grandstand sat facing the field at the south end, with tall flagpoles at its corners. Further to the north, between the open ground and the slave areas, was a thick line of brown and green that was probably another wall.

He turned his attention to the mansion itself. The structure was four stories high, judging from the window placement. It was composed of a central section with a number of small wings jutting out at odd angles. There was no particular symmetry to the design, but the final result was nevertheless not unpleasing to the eye.

The structure was built of irregular pieces of stone in shades of brown, tan, and gray. Probably stone from the estate's own quarry—he'd noticed similar shades of rock there. Overall, the whole thing reminded him of a rocky section of cliff from which the soil had been scraped or eroded away. Perhaps that had been the designer's intent.

"Cozy," Jack said. "Ideal for you and three hundred of your closest friends. So, back to the perimeter wall. Any idea how high it is?"

Draycos looked at the wall. By comparing its shadow to that of the house, which he'd already estimated to be four stories tall . . . "I would say about thirty feet high," he offered.

"It's actually thirty-two," Uncle Virge said.

Draycos felt his tail twitch with annoyance. Typical. With access to the *Essenay*'s sensors, Uncle Virge had probably had that number several minutes ago. But instead of saying anything, he'd let Draycos make his own estimate first.

And had then showed him to be wrong. Not very far wrong, but enough. Just one more subtle attempt to sow seeds of doubt and distrust toward Draycos in Jack's mind.

From the very beginning, Uncle Virge had tried to get the boy to see things in his own, self-absorbed way, to persuade him to wash his hands of the K'da poet-warrior and this mission to save a people Jack didn't even know. Clearly, he hadn't given up that effort.

"Well, we already knew we weren't going to go in over the wall," Jack said. "Anything *outside* the wall that can help us?"

"Precious little," Uncle Virge said. "There's the gatehouse, of course—"

"Gatehouse?" Jack asked.

"To the left of the main entrance," Draycos said, flicking out his tongue to touch the edge of a small shape almost hidden beneath the wall overhang.

"Right," Uncle Virge said, sounding a little annoyed that Draycos had noticed it. Another small red rectangle appeared to mark the image. "Probably someone in there checking passes and invitations and keeping the riffraff out."

"Though the actual defense positions are here and here," Draycos added, indicating a pair of camouflaged and virtually invisible huts nestled into two groups of trees in the formal gardens flanking the drive. "The guard outside is merely for show."

"And there are bound to be more guards inside the house, as well," Uncle Virge said. "You *sure* you don't want to try a different plan?"

"What about the employees?" Jack asked, ignoring the question. "They don't all live in the mansion, do they?"

Uncle Virge sighed. "No, I'm sure there are some with homes in the city."

"Good," Jack said briskly. "Get busy and find one."

CHAPTER 2

The Ponocce Regional Spaceport was confusingly laid out, overloaded with paperwork-pushers, and just plain badly run. It was also staffed entirely by Brummgas, which, in Jack's opinion, was another way of saying the same thing. The big, wide aliens had a reputation across the Orion Arm for being as strong as giant oaks and just about as smart.

But for all that, he found himself breezing through the entry procedure in remarkably quick time. Even more surprising, his hiker's backpack with its load of disguised burglar tools didn't even rate a second look. Perhaps, he thought, a spaceport located near a major slave dealer had learned not to look too closely at visitors or their luggage.

Night had already wrapped the sky in stars as he pushed through the double doors—which were supposed to open automatically but didn't—and stepped out onto Brum-a-dum soil. "Another day, another dustball," he quoted the old saying, taking a careful sniff of the air. Every world, he'd discovered over the years, had its own unique set of aromas. Most of the combinations, in his humble opinion, stunk.

Brum-a-dum was no different. But he'd smelled worse.

Just outside the spaceport building was a small parking

lot. Beyond that was a street with a luminescent walkway running along its edge. The road itself was humming with vehicles, and there were enough pedestrians that Jack didn't feel too conspicuous.

He walked another ten minutes before deciding he was alone enough to risk checking in. "Uncle Virge?" he murmured toward his left shoulder. "You there?"

"Where else would I be?" the computer's voice grumbled from the comm clip fastened to his jacket collar.

"Have you got a mark, or haven't you?" Jack asked, ignoring the sarcasm. Uncle Virge always got crabby when Jack was about to do something he didn't like. "Come on—I don't want to stay on this rock any longer than I have to."

"The chief gatekeeper has a house facing the main gate," Uncle Virge said reluctantly. "Two stories, lime green with purple trim. A popular color combination here, unfortunately."

"Don't be snobbish," Jack said. "Any other possibilities?"

"A few, but he's definitely your best bet," Uncle Virge said. "Certainly he's the most likely to have access codes stashed away at home."

And because of that, he would also probably have the best security system in town. A definite challenge, even for someone with Jack's training and experience. "Sounds good," he said, trying to hide his own misgivings about this whole thing. "What about a high-level family official?"

"We've got two possibilities on that one," Uncle Virge said. "First is a Brummga named Crampatch. He's Chief Steward, in charge of most of the household operations. Second choice is Gazen, the man in charge of the slaves themselves."

"The man?" Draycos spoke up from his usual place on Jack's right shoulder. "Do you mean a human male?"

"Isn't he clever?" Uncle Virge said with a sniff. "Those language lessons are really paying off."

Draycos's head rose off of Jack's skin, his snout bulging against the shirt and jacket as he shifted from his two-dimensional form to full 3-D. His tongue flicked out toward the comm clip—"Knock it off, Uncle Virge," Jack said quickly. The K'da was under enough pressure without Uncle Virge going out of his way to irritate him. "How was he supposed to know the Chookoock family had non-Brummgan employees?"

"Even Brummgas are smart enough to know they need help with a business this big," Uncle Virge muttered.

"Good thing, too," Jack said. The sewer-rat tricks Uncle Virgil had taught him for sneaking into other people's computers probably wouldn't work on Brummgan-designed systems. But with a human in charge of the slaves, there should be at least a couple of human-designed computers around to keep track of the paperwork.

Jack could only hope that those same computers also kept track of the Chookoock family's brisk trade in Brummgan soldiers-for-hire. "So which one do we want?" he asked Uncle Virge. "Crampatch or Gazen?"

There was a sound that might have been a sigh of resignation. "Gazen," the computer said. "Crampatch might not be smart enough to follow the logic we're going to present him."

"Fine," Jack said. "You ready to go into your Buffalo shuffle?"

"Maybe we should let you get a little closer first," Uncle

Virge hedged. "We don't want to give him too much time to think."

"We don't want him in a last-minute panic, either," Jack pointed out. "Do it now."

Over the evening breeze he heard another sigh. "Whatever you say," the computerized voice said. "Here goes."

There was a series of soft clicks as he keyed the number. Jack continued walking, wondering if the Brum-a-dum phone system would be as badly run as the spaceport equipment had been.

Apparently, the Brummgas had imported their phone experts, too. There was one final click—"Yeah; talk to me," a human voice answered.

Jack caught his breath, his mind flashing back to his encounter nearly two months ago aboard the *Advocatus Diaboli*. The man who had ordered him to steal a metal cylinder from the starliner *Star of Wonder* had had a snake-like voice very much like this one. Could it be the same man?

On his right shoulder, Draycos hissed softly. "It is not him," he murmured.

Carefully, Jack let out his breath. No, it wasn't Snake Voice. But even the dragon had noticed enough similarities to wonder about it.

Or maybe it was just the personality of the man behind the voice that was coming through. A man, like Snake Voice, who cared about nothing and no one except himself.

"My name is Virgil, Mr. Gazen," Uncle Virge said. "I called to offer you a deal on a very special slave."

There was a brief pause. "How did you get this number?" Gazen demanded.

"Oh, I'm something of an expert at digging out confidential information," Uncle Virge said smoothly. "As is my partner. My *former* partner, I should say."

"What you *should* say is good-bye," Gazen said, his dark voice going even darker. "You've got three seconds to explain why I shouldn't track this call and have some Chookoock family enforcers show you why playing phone tricks on me is a *really* bad idea."

"By all means, go ahead and send them," Uncle Virge said. "Just make sure they're bringing money. As I said, I'm offering you a deal on a very special slave: an expert thief and safecracker."

Gazen snorted. "Sorry. I only deal in land and household slaves."

"*And* mercenaries," Uncle Virge reminded him. "Brummgan soldiers for hire."

There was another short pause. "So, which merc group are you connected with?" Gazen asked.

"None of them," Uncle Virge said. "But it occurred to me that a man who deals in hired guns might also be able to find a home for a boy of Jack McCoy's skills."

"A boy?"

"Only fourteen, but already one of the best in the business," Uncle Virge boasted. "I trained him myself."

"And you *are* the best, I suppose?" Gazen said sarcastically.

"Of course."

For a moment the line was silent. Jack kept walking, staring out into the crisscross of muted streetlights marking his way. Gazen was hovering over the bait, eyeing it and wondering if it was worth a taste. If he decided it was, they were in.

If he decided it wasn't, Jack was going to be toast. Jelly side down.

"And I'm supposed to take your word for all this," Gazen said at last.

"Not at all," Uncle Virge assured him. "I've arranged a demonstration."

"Really. What sort?"

"Your chief gatekeeper has a house across from the Chookoock estate," Uncle Virge explained. "I've sent Jack to burgle it."

"And what exactly did he steal?"

"Nothing, yet," Uncle Virge said. "I assumed you'd want to watch him in action before we discussed price."

"If he's as good as you say, why are you dumping him?"

"Because he's getting too old for what I need," Uncle Virge said. "I like to work against people's assumptions. You see a ten-year-old kid walk into a millionaire's mansion, you don't expect him to be casing the place. By the time he hits fifteen, though, people start paying attention."

"So you've decided to sell him?"

"Like you, I'm a businessman," Uncle Virge said. "I spent a lot of time and effort training this kid. Why not get all I can out of my investment?"

"Why not indeed," Gazen said dryly. "All right, I'll play along. I presume I don't have to tell you what happens if I find out you're running a scam here?"

"Not at all," Uncle Virge said. "In fact, I believe your enforcers are already gathering outside my landing bay."

"Excellent," Gazen said with satisfaction. "Brummgas are as dumb as dirt soup, but they're efficient enough with the things that matter. Where's the boy now?"

"Approaching the gatekeeper's house from the direction of the spaceport," Uncle Virge said. "But he's still at least half an hour away. Plenty of time for you to set up observers."

"His instructions?"

"To find the access codes for getting into the Chookoock estate."

There was a long, stiff silence. "Really," Gazen said at last, his voice suddenly silky smooth. "What for?"

"As I told you: a demonstration," Uncle Virge said.

"You sure you didn't have anything else in mind?" Gazen asked. His voice was still smooth, only now it was the smoothness of a bed of quicksand. "Like maybe selling any codes he happens to find?"

"If I wanted to do that, would I have called you up in advance?"

"Not unless you were stupid," Gazen conceded. But the darkness was still in his voice. "What do you want for the boy?"

"Let's make it sporting," Uncle Virge suggested. "Fifty thousand auzes, plus another ten for every minute less than half an hour that it takes him to get through the house alarms, find the gatekeeper's safe, and crack it. What do you say?"

"Fine," Gazen said. "Let's see how he does."

"Excellent," Uncle Virge said. "I'll be in touch."

There was a double click, and the connection went dead. "It appears to be working," Draycos commented.

"So far, anyway," Jack said, grimacing into the darkness. "Let's try not to disappoint him."

CHAPTER 3

The windows on the street side of the gatekeeper's house were dark when Jack arrived. It looked like everyone had already gone to bed, but he took the time to walk around the entire block first just to make sure.

All the windows were dark, all right. And at nine o'clock. "They sure roll up the walkways early around here," he muttered to Draycos as he stopped in the shadow of a bushy tree.

"Pardon?"

"They close down shop and go to bed," Jack explained, eying the gatekeeper's house. So far he hadn't seen or heard anyone, not even on his walk around the block.

But they were there. He could feel it in the prickling of his skin. Gazen and his people were watching to see just how good a thief this kid was.

And if they decided he was good enough, they would buy him.

Not hire him, like he and Uncle Virgil had sometimes been hired to break into safes. Not even indenture him, like the Whinyard's Edge mercenaries had.

They would *buy* him.

He shivered. On the human-controlled Internos planets, slavery had been banned long ago. But on Brum-a-dum, as well as on many other worlds in the Orion Arm, it was perfectly legal. In some places, it was even common.

He hated this, he decided suddenly. It was one thing to sit in the cozy comfort of the *Essenay*'s dayroom concocting grand and complicated schemes. It was something else entirely to be standing here a few minutes away from becoming a slave.

Or, if he failed the test, those same few minutes away from being dead.

But he had no choice. That brief look from space had shown there was no other way into the Chookoock estate, at least not without a couple of divisions of StarForce Marines. The only way in was to be invited.

For a fourteen-year-old thief, this was the only way to get that invitation.

"What is a consular adjunct?" Draycos asked.

Jack frowned. "A what?"

"There," Draycos said, and Jack felt the dragon's tongue slide across his collarbone toward the house he was standing in front of.

He turned to look. Like the rest of the houses in the area, it had the darkened windows of a place that had shut down for the night. But on a decorative post by the front walkway was a small glowing sign:

INTERNOS CONSULAR ADJUNCT

DAUGHTERS OF HARRIET TUBMAN

"You got me," Jack said, frowning at the sign. "Some kind of official Internos office, I guess. But I don't know what an adjunct is. Or what a Harriet Tubman is, either."

"Why would an Internos office be placed so close to a slave dealer's territory?" Draycos asked. It wasn't easy for a whisper to sound suspicious, but the dragon managed it without any trouble. "You told me the Internos does not condone slavery."

"It doesn't," Jack said. "Keep your voice down, will you?"

"I am sorry." The dragon didn't sound sorry, but he did lower his voice. "Could the Daughters of Harriet Tubman be a pro-slavery faction?"

"I've never heard of any pro-slavery factions in the Internos," Jack told him. "Look, can we skip this until we get back to the ship? We've got a job to do."

"Of course," Draycos said, sounding subdued. "My apologies."

"Okay." Jack turned back to the gatekeeper's house, slipping his backpack onto one shoulder and pulling out what looked like a portable music player. "Let's do it."

The house was surrounded by a modest lawn consisting of tall, cactus-like plants rising up out of a tightly meshed, clover-like ground cover. A quick scan with the sensors in the music player showed that there were no field-effect or laser-grid alarm systems guarding the surface of the lawn. It took a more cautious, step-by-step check to make sure there were no hidden tripwires or pop plates lurking underneath the clover itself.

But the lawn was clean, and he made it across without trouble. "I presume we are not going to try the front door?" Draycos murmured as Jack slunk along the side of the house toward one of the rear corners.

"Not the front door, the back door, or the side door," Jack agreed, still watching for tripwires as he edged his way along. "See that second-floor bay window up there?"

"The window that sticks out from the wall?"

"Right," Jack said. "The species profiles say that Brumm-gas like to soak in their bathtubs for hours at a time, staring out a window and thinking whatever deep thoughts Brumm-gas have at a time like that. Probably, they mostly wonder where the soap has gotten to."

"We wish to enter through his bathing room?"

"It beats going through a bedroom window and landing on someone trying to sleep," Jack pointed out, crouching down and checking his bearings. He was right under the edge of the bay window. Perfect. "I did that once," he added. "I thought he and I were going to have a joint heart attack right there."

Tucking the music player back inside his pack, he pulled out a pair of six-inch-long cylinders. Each cylinder had what looked like a suction cup at one end and a thin, four-foot-long rope wrapped around it ending in a loop-stirrup. Officially, these things were mountain-climbing tools called step-lifters, designed to help a climber work his way up smooth cliff faces.

In Jack's business—his former business, that is—they were known as bootstraps, and had been adapted for less innocent climbing purposes.

He unwrapped the ropes and got his feet snugged into the stirrups. Holding the cylinder in his left hand horizontally, he lifted it a couple of feet up the wall. The attached rope pulled his left leg up as he did so, rather like a marionette's string. He pressed the cylinder end firmly against the wall, and there was a faint hiss as the suction cup secreted quick-set glue and locked itself in place. Pulling down on the cylinder with his hand as he pushed down with the foot in the stirrup, he rose a couple of feet up the side of the wall.

Balancing on the stirrup, he lifted the cylinder in his right hand a couple of feet higher than the left-hand one and pressed it against the wall. The glue cup attached, and he again pulled himself up to its level. That left his left-hand cylinder down at about waist height. Pressing the release, he snapped the glue cup off, leaving it fastened to the wall. Another glue cup popped out of the cylinder from behind to take its place; lifting the cylinder and his left foot, he fastened it to the wall again and continued up.

The disadvantage of the bootstrap was that it left a trail of glue cups pointing straight at the thief's entry point. The saving grace was that, most of the time, Jack was long gone by the time anyone was awake enough to notice them.

The bay window consisted of small panes of plastic set into a spiderweb framework made of curved bars of metal-clad hardwood. The two outer sections of the window could be opened for ventilation, though they were currently locked shut.

There were also three separate alarms on the window. One was on each of the movable sections, guarding against unauthorized opening from the outside, while a third protected against breakage of any part of the window.

Again, no problem. A quick but careful wiring of the metal edges of the framework to another of Uncle Virgil's gadgets, and the breakage alarm was history. From his backpack, Jack retrieved a tube of goop whose label identified it as antibiotic first-aid cream. Attaching another glue cup to a strategically located window segment, he unscrewed the tube and squeezed a thin line of the stuff around the edges.

The acid ate silently through the plastic, sending up thin tendrils of brown smoke as it went. Crinkling his nose against the stink, Jack hung onto the wall like a giant spider and waited. The acid finished its work, and Jack pulled the section free. Easing a hand inside, he disabled the alarm on the nearest window section. Then, releasing the catch, he pulled the window open and squeezed through.

As he'd predicted, he found himself easing himself down into a wide, deep bathtub designed to look and smell like a Brummgan swamp. The tub was empty, fortunately, though he made sure to hang firmly onto the edge as he crossed, in case it was still wet and slippery.

The bathroom door led, logically enough, into a bedroom. At the far end of the room, to one side of another window, was a bed built on the same scale as the bathtub. Even for a Brummga, Jack decided uneasily, this gatekeeper must be an unusually large specimen. Keeping a wary eye pointed that direction, listening for any change in the rhythm of the snoring, he stepped carefully out onto the thick bedroom carpet and began to sidle crab-style toward the bedroom door. The office and safe, he knew, would most likely be on the first floor.

"Stop," Draycos murmured in his ear.

Jack froze in midstep. "What?" he whispered back.

"There—in the carpet ahead," Draycos said, his voice so faint it couldn't have been heard more than two inches away. "A glint of metal."

Jack frowned, his foot still raised. What in the world was the dragon seeing?

And then he spotted it. A glint of metal, all right, resting along the top of the carpet.

A tripwire?

Carefully, he set his foot back onto the floor. Just as carefully, he eased down into a crouch for a closer look.

It was a tripwire, all right. In fact, it was a set of five tripwires, running not quite parallel to each other along the floor, directly across the path from the bathroom to the bedroom door.

Jack smiled tightly. No one put tripwires in their own bedroom. Not even Brummgas were that stupid. This had to be something Gazen had thrown together in the half hour since making his deal with Uncle Virge. A bonus challenge, something the average thief would never expect.

Luckily for Jack, he wasn't an average thief. Stepping carefully between the wires, he continued on.

The doorknob was gimmicked, too. A fairly sloppy job, really; but then, Gazen hadn't had *that* much time to play with.

No sonics or laser-grids or field-effect alarms greeted him as he eased the bedroom door open. Stepping out into the corridor, he closed the door silently behind him and headed for the stairs.

He ran into three more alarms along the way, including two motion detectors and another set of tripwires. Now that he knew the score, though, he spotted them easily and had them neutralized in a couple of minutes.

The safe was "hidden"—though Jack hesitated to even use that term—behind a decorative wooden slab mounted on the wall. One end of the slab held a Brummgan-style clock, with all twenty-six hours of their day marked off, while the other sported a dozen military-style ribbons.

Gazen had missed a bet: the slab itself wasn't wired. Either the slavemaster had run out of time to set his booby-traps, or else he hadn't expected Jack to get this far.

The safe was a standard keypad type, thought by many to be impossible to break into. Not exactly a piece of cake, but hardly a plate of stale cabbage, either. Pulling out his equipment, Jack set to work, resisting the urge to see how much of Uncle Virge's promised half hour he had left. He wasn't supposed to know about the deal, after all, and if Gazen noticed him looking at his watch he might wonder why.

Maybe that had been the real reason for putting all those extra alarms in the gatekeeper's bedroom and hallway, in fact. Maybe Gazen wasn't so much worried about testing Jack's abilities as he was in trying to cheat Uncle Virge out of that extra ten thousand per minute.

If that was his goal, the safe itself was going to be a disappointment for him. It might look like a top-class system, but under a spark-catcher stethoscope it turned out to be as electronically noisy as any Jack had ever cracked. Less than five minutes after he started, he set down his equipment, worked the handle, and swung the safe door open.

And as he did so, the darkened room suddenly blazed with light.

CHAPTER 4

Jack spun around so fast that he almost lost his balance, remembering to look startled and terrified. "Wha—?" he gasped, his voice breaking off into an astonished squeak.

That last part didn't take any acting at all. Suddenly, it seemed, the whole room was filling up with Brummgas. Each of them wore a close-fitting helmet and a sort of armored tunic done up in a bright pattern of red, black, and white. Some of them were waving slapsticks his direction; others had handguns out and pointed.

There was only one thing to do when facing that many weapons. Jack froze into a statue, making sure his hands were open and in full view of everyone.

The next few minutes were a swirling tangle of movement and noise and confusion. The two Brummgas who got to Jack first grabbed him and pulled him away from the safe. They ran their large hands over his whole body like breadmaking machines gone crazy, pulling off his jacket and comm clip, emptying each pocket, even tearing off his belt with the hidden money pockets on the inside.

Then they passed him off to another pair behind them and began gathering up his backpack and the rest of his equipment. His new handlers searched him again, then handed him off to the next in line, who passed him to the ones behind them. Jack wondered if he was going to make it all the way around the room before someone figured out what exactly to do with him.

But then this last pair of Brummgas spun him around, and Jack found himself face to face with a human male.

He was a big man, muscular, with shoulders nearly as wide as those of the Brummgas standing around him. His face was lined and unshaven, his hair cut short in military fashion, and his clothes looked like they'd been thrown on hastily in a very dark room. The effect was almost comical.

Until Jack looked into his eyes.

They were cold eyes. Hard eyes. Eyes that held no mercy, no kindness, not even a hint of human feeling.

An eerie sensation tickled between Jack's shoulder blades. He'd seen eyes like that before, on some of the most vicious criminals Uncle Virgil had known. A man with eyes like that was hardly even human anymore.

"Well?" the man asked softly.

It was the slavemaster himself. Gazen.

Jack took a deep breath. He'd had a whole spun-rainbow excuse all set up and ready to go, a tangly story full of tears and panic about a bet with school friends, and how he would never, ever do it again if they let him go. It was the sort of story a professional thief would be able to launch into on a second's notice, just that much more evidence that he was worth the price Uncle Virge was asking for him.

But as he stared up into those eyes, it suddenly didn't feel like a good idea to spin such an obvious lie for this man. "I guess I picked the wrong house," he said instead.

Gazen's lips might have twitched. "I guess you did," he agreed.

His eyes flicked to Jack's Brummgan handlers. "Bring him," he ordered.

Without waiting for a response, he turned his back and headed for the door. Wrapping their hands around Jack's arms, the two Brummgas dragged their prisoner after him.

After the crowd that had burst in on him inside the house, Jack had rather expected the yard to be crawling with Brummgas, too. But aside from a pair of long, squat cars parked in front of the house everything looked the way Jack had left it. Apparently, Gazen had decided there was no point in waking up the whole neighborhood over this.

The Brummgas stuffed Jack into the back seat of the first of the cars, wedging him between them. Gazen got in the front beside the driver. They made a tight U-turn, and with the second car following closely behind they headed toward the white wall.

Jack had caught glimpses of the wall on his way to the gatekeeper's house. But it had been dark, and the wall was set far enough back from the street that he hadn't gotten a close look.

Sitting pinned between two Brummgas, his view wasn't that much better. Still, it was the best he was likely to get, at least from the outside. Slouching down as far as he figured he could get away with, he peeked out the window.

The wall was more impressive at ground level than it had been from several thousand feet up. For one thing, its thirty-two-foot height seemed taller now that he was looking up at it. For another, although Uncle Virge had been right about the wall's X-shape, he'd missed the fact that the top part curved over and downward, nearly circling up underneath itself again.

The effect was like facing a huge, mile-long wave that was getting ready to break over the approaching car. Not the most pleasant image Jack could think of.

The gate was as impressive as the wall itself, made of more of the wall's white ceramic and laced with gold-colored metal straps. Six more armed Brummgas were waiting there, all dressed in the same red/black/white as the group in the gatekeeper's house. The Chookoock family colors, he decided. As the two cars drove up, the gate swung open.

"Stop the car," Gazen ordered sharply, sliding down his window.

The vehicle braked to a hard stop beside the guards. "Who ordered the gate opened?" Gazen bit out.

"I did, *Panjan* Gazen," one of the Brummgas said, taking an eager, lumbering step forward. "I knew you were in a hurry—"

"You opened the gate without checking identification?" Gazen demanded.

The Brummga stopped short. Too late, his walnut-sized brain was starting to realize that Gazen hadn't stopped to compliment the staff. "But—"

He ground to a halt, whatever excuse he was about to make apparently getting lost somewhere between brain and mouth. Gazen stared at him in silence for a few more seconds, long enough for even a Brummga to work out that he was in big trouble. "You will check my ID," Gazen continued, his voice quiet. "You will check the IDs of those in the car behind me. You will then secure the gate. After that, you will report to the Guard Master."

The Brummga's mouth was hanging slightly open now, his breath coming in heaving surges like a drowning man coming up for the third time. "Yes, *Panjan* Gazen," he managed. "Uh . . . your identification?"

Gazen waited another two seconds, then slid a wallet from his inside pocket and handed it over. The guard opened it, looked inside, then handed it back. "Thank you, *Panjan* Gazen," he gulped. "You may proceed."

Still staring at the guard, Gazen gestured the driver forward. The car pulled through the gate and headed down the winding driveway.

Jack studied the terrain carefully as they drove, looking for the hidden guard stations Draycos had pointed out from the air. With only muted accent lights scattered around the garden, though, they were completely invisible.

"And what about you?" Gazen asked, half turning to look at Jack.

"Sir?" Jack asked.

"You like our wall, do you?" Gazen said. "You were studying it on our way in."

Jack had thought he'd been subtle enough in his examination that no one in the car would have noticed. But even from the front seat, Gazen had caught on.

That made him both very observant and very smart. Not a good combination to go up against.

Definitely not a good combination to lie to. "It's very impressive," he said. "Kind of looks like a really big ocean wave. I don't think I've ever seen anything like it before."

"And just like a really big ocean wave, it will kill you if you try to challenge it," Gazen said pointedly. "Remember that."

"Sure," Jack said. "What . . . uh . . . what are you going to do to me?"

Gazen turned back around to face front. "We'll discuss it inside."

Like the wall, the main house was more impressive at ground level than it had looked from the sky. Earlier, Jack had noticed that the place had been designed to look like a section of rocky cliff face. Now, up close, he could see that it had also been designed to be a fortress. The front door was flanked by armed Brummgas, most of the windows were protected by thick rock overhangs, and a dozen gun barrels peeked out from slits just below the roof line.

Either the guards at the door were smarter than the ones at the gate, or else the word had been hastily passed ahead of the incoming cars. Whichever it was, Gazen and his whole group were made to show their IDs before they were allowed inside.

The entryway was huge, extending two stories up, with nearly enough floor space for a small freighter like the *Essenay* to fit inside. The walls and angled ceiling were covered with paintings, layer-portraits, light-twists, and other works of art. Sculptures and elaborate decorated pillars were scattered around the floor, their weight sinking into a thick blue carpet. At the far end a double-curved wooden staircase led up to a second-floor balcony.

He caught glimpses of other expensively decorated rooms leading off the entryway, but Gazen didn't pause long enough for him to get a good look at any of them. He led the boy across the room, up the staircase and across the balcony, and down a corridor that was only slightly less elaborate than the rooms downstairs. Coming to a plain, unmarked door, he pushed it open and gestured Jack inside.

The room was just as plain as its door. A small desk, a padded desk chair, a metal guest chair facing the desk, and that was it.

That, plus a pair of rings set in the floor for anchoring a prisoner's legs. The whole place had the unpleasant look of an interrogation room. "Sit," Gazen ordered, circling the desk and sitting down.

Gingerly, Jack sank into the other chair. "The rest of you wait outside," Gazen added to the guards, his eyes steady on Jack.

The Brummgas obeyed without comment. Gazen waited until he and Jack were alone, then leaned slightly forward, his arms resting on the desktop. "Well," he said, his tone almost casual. "I don't suppose I have to tell you the kind of trouble you're in. Breaking and entering is a serious crime on Brum-a-dum, good for five to twenty years in a penal colony."

His eyes hardened. "Breaking and entering Chookoock family property is even more serious," he went on. "That one can earn you an immediate death penalty."

"I didn't know," Jack said in a low, pleading voice. So here he was, all alone with Gazen. No leg cuffs, no handcuffs. And as far as he could tell, Gazen wasn't even armed.

Of course, the big man *did* outweigh him by at least two to one. Still, a panicked, desperate kid might still take the chance.

Which meant that this was a test. Gazen was trying to see just how cool under pressure Jack could be.

"Of course you knew," Gazen said calmly. "Don't play

stupid. Your partner sent you there specifically to try to steal the gate codes."

"No," Jack protested. "No, he didn't tell me what I was supposed to get. He didn't tell me any of that. He just said to get whatever was in the safe. He never even told me whose house I was breaking into. It's his fault, not mine."

Gazen's expression didn't change, but Jack could see a slight tightening at the corners of his mouth. First Uncle Virge had offered to sell Jack to him, and now Jack was trying to shoot all the blame straight back at Uncle Virge. Both of them perfectly willing to sell out the other at the drop of a biscuit.

It was exactly the way Gazen should expect a couple of self-centered criminals to behave. Probably the way he would behave himself in the same situation.

At least, Jack hoped so. This whole thing hinged on Gazen believing the situation was exactly as Uncle Virge had presented it. The minute he suspected there was something more going on, Jack was dead.

"It doesn't really matter who knew what," the big man said. "You were the one caught with your fingers in the fudge mix. That makes you the one skip-dancing on eggs."

Jack swallowed hard. "Is there anything I can do to, you know, make things right?"

"Such as?"

"Well—" Jack shrugged slightly. "Maybe I could . . . you know, work off my punishment?"

"And how exactly do you propose to work off twenty years worth of prison time?" Gazen countered. "Are you suggesting you work for me for the next twenty years?"

Jack grimaced. "I was hoping I could pay it off a little

faster than that," he said. "Maybe I could help you with a job or two?"

Gazen lifted his eyebrows. "Are you suggesting I hire you to commit crimes for me?"

"No, no," Jack said hastily. "I just thought I could maybe help you out in some way."

Gazen leaned back in his chair again, studying Jack's face. "All right," he said at last. "Perhaps there is something you can do. I'll look into it."

He got to his feet. "And while I do, let's put you somewhere safe. Guards?"

Jack slowly let out a breath he hadn't realized he'd been holding. So it had worked, exactly the way he'd told Uncle Virge it would. Gazen would now lock him up somewhere, he and Draycos would escape and get to one of their computers, and with luck they would be able to track down the mercenary group they were looking for.

Behind him, the door swung open. "Yes, *Panjan* Gazen?" one of the Brummgas asked.

Gazen gestured to Jack. "The boy needs a lesson," he said. "He needs to know the cost of crossing the Chookoock family."

He looked back at Jack . . . and for the first time since the two of them had met, the big man smiled.

Not a pleasant, cheerful, human smile, but something dark and vacant and as cold as a penguin's footprints. "Take him," he ordered softly, "to the slaves' hotbox."

CHAPTER 5

The Brummgas led Jack out the back of the house to a row of open-topped cars. They shoved him into one, three of them piled in around him, and they turned onto a smooth road built of dark stones fitted neatly together like pieces of an extra-long puzzle. With the soft clicking of stone edges beneath their tires, they headed off away from the mansion.

And suddenly this plan wasn't looking nearly so good anymore.

The road wound its way through another section of formal garden, then past the open sports field they'd seen earlier from the air. Beyond the field a ten-foot-tall hedge stretched across the grounds, as far to both sides as Jack could see in the backwash from the headlights. The road led them through a narrow gap in the hedge, just barely wide enough for the car.

Beyond the hedge, the landscape was rougher and wilder, with none of the careful maintenance he'd seen in the grounds near the house. The fancy stone road ended at the hedge, too, turning into a more ordinary stone-embedded blacktop.

They had left the Chookoock family's personal compound. Now, they were in the working areas of the estate.

The slave areas.

Jack stared out into the glow of the headlights, trying to remember the layout he'd seen from the *Essenay*. But it was all rather vague in his mind. His plan had always been to get into the main house, and once it was clear he wasn't going to get there by going over the wall he'd mostly lost interest in the grounds themselves.

But Draycos would have paid attention, he knew. The K'da warrior was very good at details like that. That would help.

He only hoped it would help enough.

They were coming up on the edge of a forest when the headlights finally picked up a group of buildings ahead. At first glance, the setup reminded Jack of the Whinyard's Edge training camp, with a couple of long barracks-style buildings mixed in with a few other structures of different shapes and sizes.

But at second glance, it was clear this was a very different sort of place. The paint on the buildings was peeling badly, and in many of those spots the bare wood was discolored and rotting. The steps leading up to the various doors were rough and unfinished, some of them with the bark still attached to the wood.

The overall construction was poorly done, too. Not all the boards seemed to fit right, and there were gaps in places where the boards had been too short, or else had rotted away.

The car turned a little to the left as they approached the cluster of buildings. Its headlights swept across and then steadied on a group of what looked like three metal packing crates set out in the middle of a wide circle of sand.

One of the Brummgas sitting behind Jack tapped his shoulder with a finger the size and weight of a wrench. "Pick a number," he said.

Jack frowned. "Two hundred seventeen."

The Brummga made a disgusted sound. "Pick a number from one to three."

In the privacy of the darkness, Jack made a face. Like he was supposed to have known that. "Three."

"Number three," the Brummga told the driver.

The car angled a couple more degrees, and a moment later came to rest with its headlights centered on the packing crate on the far left. "Get out," the first Brummga ordered.

Jack obeyed, the aliens piling out alongside him. While the other two stood guard, the driver stepped to the box and crouched down. There was a large handle near the bottom of the crate, just above a narrow horizontal slit, with a keyhole at one end.

The Brummga fumbled a key into place and turned it. Getting a grip on the handle, he straightened up again, swinging the whole front of the box upward. "Get in," he ordered, gesturing inside with his free hand.

Steeling himself, Jack did so.

From the outside, the box had seemed pretty small. From the inside, it seemed even smaller. He had to duck low to keep from whacking his head on the ceiling as he stepped in, and if he'd tried waving his arms around he would have dislocated both elbows. There was a small pan in one corner; from its lingering aroma, it probably served as the toilet facilities.

The driver didn't give him much chance to study his new quarters. Jack was barely inside when the wall swung shut behind him, throwing a brief gust of air at the back of his neck and plunging him into darkness. There was another click from the lock, the sound of plodding footsteps in the sand, and the hum of the car as it pulled away and headed for home.

Leaving him alone in the darkness.

Well, not entirely alone. "Are you all right?" Draycos asked quietly from his shoulder.

"Oh, just dandy," Jack growled as he turned around to face the door and carefully sat down. The floor was plain sand, gritty against the palms of his hands, and through his shirt the metal wall felt icy cold against his back. Odd for a place that Gazen had called a hotbox. "This wasn't exactly how I'd planned to spend the evening. You have any idea where we are?"

"We are in the slave colony nearest the river," Draycos said. "Approximately one-half mile from the edge of the Chookoock family grounds, within the edge of the forest and near a large patch of the bushes Uncle Virge noted."

"How wonderful it is to be here, too," Jack said, digging at the sole of his left shoe. The molded rubber looked solid enough; but a little prodding at the proper place found the secret catch and popped it open.

There was a soft thud as the spare comm clip he had hidden inside dropped onto the sand. His eyes were adjusting now, enough to see a sliver of starlight seeping in through the crack beneath the door. Retrieving the comm clip, he clicked it on. "Uncle Virge?"

"I'm here," Uncle Virge's voice came back instantly. "Careful, lad. Not too loud."

"Don't worry, no one's going to hear me," Jack told him. "They've got me stashed out in the slave quarters."

There was a brief silence. "Not in the mansion?"

"The echo you're hearing isn't from a walk-in closet," Jack said. "They've got me in a tin room the size of the *Essenay*'s freezer."

"Very strange," Uncle Virge said, his voice frowning. "Gazen just transferred a hundred and ten thousand into my service account at the spaceport."

Jack blinked. "That much?" he asked, feeling oddly pleased at the number.

"That much," Uncle Virge assured him. "For a sum that size, he ought to be taking better care of you."

"Maybe not having me beaten to a pulp qualifies as gentle handling in his book," Jack said. "What do you mean, he transferred it into your service account? He didn't fork over real cash?"

"No, but that's okay," Uncle Virge said. "It's not like we were planning to actually spend it. But I'm a little concerned about your situation. This was supposed to be a quick up-down hop, with you in the main house the whole time."

"I guess Gazen didn't read the script," Jack said with a grimace. At his right shoulder, Draycos's snout rose up from his skin, poking into the air like a submarine periscope. "Just means we're going to have to find a way back, that's all. I figure another day or two—"

"Quiet," Draycos cut in suddenly. "Someone is coming."

"I'll call you back," Jack whispered, and clicked off the comm clip. He hadn't heard anything himself, but after two months of living with Draycos he knew better than to question the dragon's ears. Tucking the comm clip back into its hiding place, he hurriedly smoothed over the sole.

He could hear the footsteps now, sloshing through the

sand around the hotboxes. They seemed slow and lumbering, rather like a Brummga's. Uneasily, he wondered if Gazen had decided to send someone to beat him to a pulp after all. A shadow crossed the light coming in from under the door.

"Hello?" a gravelly voice called softly. "Anyone there?"

Not a Brummgan voice, he decided. That was a hopeful sign. And despite the low pitch, he also had the odd impression it was female. "Yes, I'm here," he called back. "Who are you?"

"My name's Maerlynn," the voice answered. "I'm sort of the welcoming committee."

"I've already met the welcoming committee, thanks," Jack said sourly, rubbing his shoulder where the Brummga had tapped him. "Large, friendly sorts with big fingers."

"Are you hurt?" Maerlynn asked. "I may be able to get you some bandages or salves."

Jack frowned in the darkness. Who *was* this person, anyway? "No, I'm all right," he said. "What are you? I mean, what's your connection here?"

There was soft sound like a glob of mud being thrown against a wall. A chuckle? "Noy's parents used to call me the Den Mother before they died. A human term, I suppose. You *are* human, aren't you? Greb couldn't see very well when they brought you in, but he thought you were. He said he thought you were young, too. Are you?"

Draycos's head rose again from Jack's shoulder. "Move to the side wall," the dragon whispered into his ear.

Jack nodded and started to ease himself around. "Yes, I'm human," he acknowledged. "And I'm fourteen. I don't know if you count that as young or not. Who's Greb?"

"One of my children," Maerlynn said. "He's sixteen, so he probably does consider fourteen to be young."

"Yeah, I've known some sixteen-year-olds," Jack grunted. "What about you?"

"I'm Maerlynn, as I said," she said. "I'm an Ysanhar. Female. And I'm not going to give you *my* age."

"I wasn't going to ask," Jack said. He was in position now, with his back pressed against the side wall of his prison. In their two-dimensional forms, K'da had a handy trick of being able to see through walls, provided the barrier was thin enough. From his angle, Draycos might not be able to see Maerlynn where she was right now, but she should come into view as soon as she headed back to the slave buildings.

Assuming she *did* go back to the slave buildings. He still wasn't convinced this wasn't some trick of Gazen's to get him talking. "Are you a slave?" he asked.

"Everyone on this side of the thorn hedge is a slave," Maerlynn said, an odd sadness in her voice. "You, too, it would seem. Here—take this."

Something poked at Jack's feet through the crack under the door. He reached down a hand, being careful not to pull his back away from the wall. He didn't know what would happen to Draycos if he moved while the dragon was looped over the wall that way, but it wasn't something he wanted to find out the hard way.

His fingers touched an edge of rough cloth. "What is it?"

"A blanket," Maerlynn said. "It's going to get pretty cold in there tonight."

Colder than this? Jack wondered, suppressing a shiver. "So how come Gazen called it a hotbox?"

There was a slight pause, just long enough for Jack to wonder if he'd said something wrong. "You'll find out about mid-morning," Maerlynn said. "How long are you in for? Do you know?"

"He didn't say," Jack told her. "He just said I needed a lesson about what it meant to cross the Chookoock family."

"I see," Maerlynn said. "Do you need anything else right now? Food? Water?"

"No, I'm all right," Jack said.

"Get some sleep if you can," Maerlynn said. "I'll try to come talk to you again later."

"Okay," Jack said. "Thanks."

"You're welcome." There was another slight pause. "By the way . . . if any of the Brummgas ask, I'd rather you not tell them I came and talked to you. We're not supposed to go near people in the hotboxes."

"I won't," Jack promised. Though how she expected him to explain the blanket he wasn't sure. "Thanks again."

"Sure," Maerlynn said. "Good-bye."

The shadow vanished, and there was the sound of fading footsteps. The feel of the dragon shifted again, and his head rose from Jack's shoulder. "Well?" Jack asked.

"She is medium height and of a somewhat round build," Draycos reported. "Her skin looks rough, somewhat like the outer coating of a pineapple. Her head was covered with tendrils of a white substance. Similar to human hair, but it did not look precisely the same."

"They're called featherines," Jack said. "Yeah, that's an Ysanhar, all right. What were her clothes and shoes like?"

"Her clothing was well-worn and patched in several places," Draycos said. "Her shoes were in similar shape."

"And she headed back to the slave quarters?"

"Yes."

"One of the slaves, all right," Jack concluded.

"Was there doubt?"

"There's always doubt when you deal with people like Gazen." Jack shook his head. "She isn't going to have a very pleasant night."

"I do not understand."

"She's probably wondering if *I'm* some kind of plant," Jack explained. "I shouldn't have mentioned that I'd talked to Gazen. Most of the slaves in here have probably never even heard the name, let alone talked to the guy." He shivered, a violent shake that ran through his whole body. "Geez, it's cold."

Draycos cocked his head. "Put the blanket behind you," he suggested. "Drape it between you and the wall."

Jack did as instructed, folding the blanket in half first to provide the thickest insulation possible. Now his chest was exposed to the air, but at least he wasn't leaning up against the cold metal wall anymore. "Good," Draycos said. "Now hold still."

And with a surge against Jack's shirt, the dragon leaped off his skin. Twisting around in midair, he managed to avoid whacking his head on the low ceiling and landed on Jack's chest and hips.

"Oof!" Jack grunted. Draycos had come down with his paws straddling Jack's chest and legs, but even with most of his weight supported that way there was enough left over for Jack to feel it. "What did you have for breakfast? Cement omelets?"

"I am sorry," Draycos murmured, his breath warm on Jack's cheek. "I was hoping I could help you keep warm."

"I appreciate it," Jack said. Having the dragon three-dimensional certainly made the packing crate more cramped.

But on the plus side, the K'da was radiating a fair amount of heat. Already he could feel the chill starting to leave his skin. "Matter of fact, I appreciate it a lot," he added. "Thanks."

"You are welcome," Draycos said. "I agree with Maerlynn, that you should sleep if you can. It will help pass the time, and the temperature may become much colder later."

"Good point," Jack said, swiveling his shoulders and hips into the most comfortable positions he could. "See you in the morning."

CHAPTER 6

Between all the preparation, the long walk from the spaceport, and the burglary itself, it had been a long, hard day. Despite the uncomfortable position the hotbox forced on him, Jack soon fell into a deep sleep.

Sometime in the middle of the night he woke up again, shivering, to find that his gold-scaled K'da blanket had vanished. Draycos had reached the end of his six-hour limit and had returned to two-dimensional form against Jack's skin. Wrapping himself in his blanket, thinking unkind thoughts about K'da endurance, he huddled in the cold and tried to get back to sleep.

He awoke again to find a bright edge of sunlight streaming in under the hotbox door. The chill of night was gone, and the temperature in his prison had become quite comfortable.

But that relief turned out to be as short-lived as Uncle Virgil's temper in a card game. Within minutes, or so it seemed, the hotbox went from cozy to warm to uncomfortably warm.

And it got worse. Soon the thin metal behind his back grew hot enough to burn skin that lingered against it for too long. Once again he pressed Maerlynn's blanket into service, folding it between his back and the wall.

Sometime around noon he drifted off into a restless

sleep, full of strange and feverish dreams. Old memories mixed with images from past and present. He saw Uncle Virgil, tall and arrogant, wrestling with Draycos as he shouted out safecracking lessons to Gazen and a group of Brummgas.

The dream faded away and was replaced by another, this one featuring some of the mercenaries he'd met in the Whinyard's Edge. Under Sergeant Grisko's shouted direction, Jommy Randolph and Alison Kayna recited one of Draycos's poems, getting half the words wrong.

At one point he was back aboard the *Star of Wonder*, only it also seemed to be the *Essenay*'s dayroom. Seated across the table from him, Cornelius Braxton and his wife were arguing about Orion Arm history, the future of Braxton Universis, and the price of mangoes in Sumatra. On the table between them was a huge pitcher of water, an inch out of Jack's reach.

Once, he thought he woke to hear voices calling to him from outside the box. But by then his brain was so blurred that he couldn't tell what was real and what wasn't.

It was all so foggy, in fact, that when the hotbox door finally swung open and a Brummga ordered him out he assumed it was just another dream. He had slogged across the sand, and was stumbling through a patch of clover-grass before it finally dawned on him that he really was out.

"How do you feel?" a familiar voice asked quietly from his side.

Jack blinked the sweat out of his eyes and looked at the pineapple-skinned Ysanhar walking beside him. That was why his arm felt odd, he realized suddenly. Maerlynn was walking beside him, holding that arm in a steadying grip. "I'm okay," he croaked, trying to pull away from her.

"Just relax," she told him, not loosening her grip in the slightest. "You're not in any shape to walk on your own."

"I can do it," Jack insisted. Privately, though, he had to admit she was right. Hazy patches were chasing each other across his vision, and every couple of steps he briefly lost track of which way was up and which was sideways. The sun had disappeared behind the trees of the nearby forest, and he shivered violently every time a breeze cut through his sweat-drenched clothes.

But he was human, and he had his pride. More than that, he was Jack Morgan. He could do this on his own.

Maerlynn was having none of it. "Oh, come on," she chided. "Give your pride a rest, all right? Besides, if you fall on your face I'm the one who'll have to pick you up."

Jack's knees buckled briefly, and the flicker of pride faded away. "Yeah," he muttered. "Okay."

She led him into one of the long buildings. Just as the outside had looked like a broken-down version of a Whinyard's Edge barracks, so too did the inside. Most of the space was taken up by a single room, with rows of narrow cots lining the walls on both sides. At one end, in the direction Maerlynn was leading him, there was a small open area with a couple of dilapidated tables and a few rickety chairs. At the other end was what appeared to be a small washroom.

And packed into the room were slaves.

Jack found himself staring as Maerlynn led him between the rows of beds. There were at least a dozen different species represented, he saw, from thick-scaled Doloms to feather-covered Jantris to even a handful of humans.

Most of them were on their beds. Some were sitting on the edges of the cots, talking quietly with their neighbors or fiddling with cards or small trinkets. A couple were whittling with what seemed to be homemade knives.

But the majority of the slaves were lying down. Lying stretched out on backs or sides, or lying curled around themselves in postures of fatigue or hopelessness.

A few of them looked up as he and Maerlynn passed. Most didn't even bother.

"I've made you up a bed with my other children," Maerlynn said as she led him to the open area and sat him down at one of the tables. "You'll want to sleep soon—a session in the hotbox drains a person more than you might think. But first we need to get you something to eat and drink."

"This him?" an eager young voice asked from Maerlynn's other side.

Jack tilted his head to look past the Ysanhar as the newcomer came into view around her. It was a human boy, maybe six or seven, short and thin. His hair was carrot-colored, with a faceful of freckles behind the deep tan.

"This is him," Maerlynn confirmed as she pulled up one of the other chairs and sat down diagonally from Jack. "This is Noy, one of my children. And I believe I heard the guard call you Jack when he let you out?"

"That's right," Jack said, frowning. A human boy was one of an Ysanhar's children? "Jack McCoy."

"Nice to meet you, Jack," Maerlynn said. "Officially, anyway. Noy, where's the pitcher?"

"We've got it," another voice said.

Jack turned his head, fighting a fresh wave of dizziness as he did so. Coming toward them from the other end of the room were two Jantris, their greenish-purple feathers glistening in the low glow of the overhead lights. One of them was carrying a battered metal pitcher carefully in front of him, while the other held an equally battered metal cup.

"Thank you," Maerlynn said. "Jack, these are Greb and Grib. Greb was the one I told you about, who was watching out the window when the Brummgas brought you in. Be careful with that, Greb."

"I am," the Jantri with the pitcher said as he set it down in front of Jack. As he did, a few drops of water sloshed out onto the table.

"They're twins, by the way," Maerlynn said, taking the cup from Grib and filling it halfway from the pitcher. The sound of the splashing water made Jack's mouth feel even drier. "Now be careful," she warned as she handed him the cup. "You don't want to shock your stomach with too much all at once."

The water seemed a little oily, with a variety of mineral and chemical flavors and odors. Jack had never tasted anything so good in his entire life. He gulped it down, spilling some of it over the edge of the cup and down his cheeks in his haste.

He set the cup down, panting slightly. "Can I—?"

"Of course," Maerlynn said, already starting to refill it. "Just be careful."

He drained three more cups before Maerlynn called a halt. "All right, that should do for a bit," she said. "Let that get into your system, then you can have some more."

She beckoned. "In the meantime, you're probably pretty hungry."

Noy popped into view at Jack's elbow, holding a rectangular piece of wood with a fat, folded green leaf on it. "It's stuffed cabbage," the boy told him as he set down the board. "We saved it for you from dinner."

"For me?" Jack asked, his stomach growling. Between the fatigue and thirst, he hadn't realized just how hungry he really was. His mouth would probably be watering if he'd had any liquid in his body to spare. "How did you know I was going to be let out tonight?"

"We didn't," Noy said. "But if you were, Maerlynn wanted to be ready."

"We don't have any flatware or plates, I'm afraid," Maerlynn said. "We have to leave all that in the meal hall. But I'm sure you won't mind eating with your fingers just this once. Well, go ahead—eat up."

Cautiously, Jack tried a bite. The cabbage leaf was a little soggy, and the rice and diced vegetables inside were of course stone cold. And like the water, it tasted better than anything he'd ever eaten in his life.

Also like the water, it vanished quickly. "Thanks," he said. "I needed that."

"I knew you would," Maerlynn said. "The Brummgas don't take very good care of people they put in the hotboxes."

"Of course not," Jack said with a snort, retrieving the three grains of rice that had escaped onto the table and licking them off his fingers. "What's the point of punishing someone if you're going to pick them up and dust them off afterwards. I'm surprised they even let you save me some food."

The twin Jantris exchanged glances. "Well, they didn't exactly *let* us," Noy said. "We sort of sneaked it out."

Jack blinked. "How?"

"That's enough talking for now," Maerlynn said before Noy could answer. "Jack needs to drink a little more water, then get himself to bed. Morning starts early around here, Jack, and I imagine you'll be put out on the line tomorrow."

"Out on what line?" Jack asked, pouring himself another cup of water.

"Picking rainbow berries with us," Maerlynn said. "They grow on thorny bushes along the edges of the forest."

Jack grunted as he drank. Probably the bushes he and Uncle Virge had seen on the flight in. "Sure, why not? They've got all these slaves anyway. Might as well give us something to do."

Below the mop of white featherines, Maerlynn's forehead wrinkled. "You're wrong if you think it's just make-work. Rainbow berries are a valuable commodity, and you can't use robotic harvesters on them."

"You have to look at the colors to see if the berries are ripe," Greb explained. "Machines can't read it good enough."

"*Well* enough," Maerlynn corrected him. "Actually, you probably could make a robot harvester that could do it. But even if you did, you'd have the problem of giving it a soft enough touch to pick them without damage. *And* you'd have to make the whole thing small enough and flexible enough to get between the branches without knocking off all the unripe ones."

Jack nodded as he poured himself more water. "In other words, if slaves can do it, why bother trying to come up with a machine?"

Grib made a sniffing sound. "One of *those,*" he muttered to his brother.

Greb nodded. "See you tomorrow, Jack," he said, taking Grib's arm. Circling the table, they headed to a pair of empty cots that had been pushed together and lay down on them.

Jack frowned toward Maerlynn. "One of those what?"

She shrugged, looking uncomfortable. "They were born here," she said. "Slavery is the only life they've ever known."

"So was I," Noy spoke up.

"That's different," Maerlynn said. "Your folks never accepted this life the way Greb and Grib and their parents did. Yours never gave up hoping for freedom."

"Are they still here?" Jack asked, glancing over his shoulder at the other slaves.

"No," Maerlynn said gently. "They're . . ."

"They're dead," Noy said, an odd note of defiance in his voice. "My dad was beaten to death after he tried to escape. After that, my mom got a fever and she died, too."

Jack grimaced. "I'm sorry," he said, wishing he'd kept his mouth shut. "I didn't know."

"Of course you didn't," Maerlynn said. "No need to apologize. Would you like to clean up any before you go to bed? I'm afraid the only showers in here are cold water."

Jack shivered. "Thanks, but I'll pass. I think I'd rather sleep anyway."

"I understand," Maerlynn said. "Noy, would you show Jack to his bed?"

"Sure," Noy said. "What about his clothes?"

"There's a sackshirt on his bed," she said, getting to her feet. "He can sleep in that."

"Okay," Noy said. "Come on, Jack."

He led the way down the line of cots to an empty one beside the two where Greb and Grib were lying, talking quietly to each other. "This one's yours," Noy said.

"Thanks," Jack said, nodding to the two Jantris as they looked up at him. They nodded back and returned to their conversation.

"Oh, and this is Lisssa," Noy said, pointing to the cot on the other side of Jack's.

A Dolom girl lay there, her thick, tile-like scales looking dull and dingy in the dim light. She was curled up on her side, her back to Jack and the Jantris, her attention on a crudely carved stick she was turning around in her hand. "She's a Dolom," Noy added.

"Yes, I know," Jack said. "Hello, Lisssa. My name's Jack."

Lisssa turned her head halfway around. "Hello, Jack," she said, and turned back to her stick.

"She's kind of quiet," Noy explained. "Sorry."

"That's okay," Jack said. "Quiet is good. Where's this sackshirt Maerlynn mentioned?"

"Right here," Noy said, pulling a wad of cloth from under the pillow. "Go ahead and get undressed."

Jack glanced back at Lisssa. He hadn't had much privacy back in the Whinyard's Edge, either. But at least there he hadn't had any girls in the barracks. Even if most of the girls here were aliens, the whole thing felt a little uncomfortable.

Noy must have seen something in his face. "Don't worry about it," he said, very quietly. "No one looks at anyone else here. You learn not to."

"Yeah," Jack said. On the other hand, he doubted anyone here had a full-body tattoo of a dragon plastered across his back.

Still, there was nothing for it but to go ahead. He shook

out the sackshirt and laid it out on the bed. It was exactly what he would have expected from the name: a sack, open at the bottom, with arm and head holes cut out at the top.

Noy seemed to be studying a section of floor near the head of Jack's bed. Bracing himself for the inevitable reaction, Jack pulled off his soggy shirt.

The boy didn't even look up. Jack glanced around the room, frowning, as he picked up the sackshirt.

Nothing. No one jumped to their feet, no one stared and pointed, no one gasped or whistled or snorted or even breathed extra hard. As far as he could tell, no one even saw him.

He slid the sackshirt over his head, covering Draycos again. So they really *didn't* look at each other. He pulled off his shoes and socks, and was working off his jeans when Maerlynn arrived with a basket. "Put your clothes in here," she instructed, holding it out. "I'll have them ready—"

"Five minutes!" a loud voice called from the doorway, cutting her off.

Jack looked that direction. A large, ugly, deeply tanned man with a thick gray-black beard was standing just inside the room. He was wearing the same slightly shabby clothing as everyone else, but with a bright red sash running from shoulder to waist.

The man glanced around the room, and his eyes fell on Jack. For a couple of seconds his gaze lingered, as if he was sizing up the newcomer. Then, without another word, he turned and left.

"That's Fleck," Maerlynn said. "He's what we call a trustee."

"He helps the Brummgas keep us in line," Noy added contemptuously.

"Now, now," Maerlynn said soothingly. "He's a slave just like we are. We all have different jobs and duties, and that one's his. I was starting to say, Jack, that I'll have your clothes ready by morning."

"What, in five minutes?" Jack asked.

"That just means lights off," Maerlynn said. "I've been here long enough to know my way around in the dark. Now, you get yourself some sleep. You too, Noy."

"Okay," Noy said, moving toward a cot on the far side of the Jantris. "G'night. G'night, Jack."

" 'Night," Jack said. "And thanks."

He pulled down the thin blanket and got into bed. The mattress and pillow were lumpy, like they'd been stuffed with wood shavings or irregularly shaped beans. Still, the cot was long enough for him to stretch all the way out. That already put it two steps above the hotbox.

He was still trying to hammer out the major lumps when the overhead lights went out.

The sounds of activity stopped at the same time. Clearly, the rest of the slaves knew the routine well enough to be ready when bedtime came.

Ready, and probably eager. After a few days laboring out in the fields, Jack thought glumly, he would probably be the same way.

Jack had planned to stay awake long enough for the rest of the slaves to get to sleep, and then discuss the situation with Draycos. But the hotbox had drained him more than he'd realized, and he found he simply could not keep his eyes open.

Within seconds, he was fast asleep.

Draycos waited until everyone in the long hut was asleep. Then, sliding off Jack's arm, he dropped to the rough wood of the floor. Senses alert, he padded silently between the rows of cots to the door.

The door had been left open a few inches for ventilation. He looked carefully at the door jamb, mindful of the sorts of alarms and tripwires he and Jack had found in the gate-keeper's house. But there was nothing like that here.

He poked his head halfway through the gap and stood motionless for a minute, watching and listening and tasting the outside air. There were no guards or patrols nearby, at least none he could detect. Shouldering the door open, he slipped down the steps and out into the night.

There were no outside lights, either. But between the starlight and the glow in the sky from the city to their west, there was enough light for K'da eyes to see by.

There was an even brighter glow coming from the direction of the slaveowners' mansion. Draycos bared his teeth toward it, the tip of his tail twitching with contempt and disgust. Every thread of his being longed to take on the Chookoock family and their despicable slave trade.

But this was not the time to bring justice to these people. His task tonight was much simpler: to learn the enemy's territory.

He began with the slave colony itself, circling each of the two long sleeping huts and then briefly nosing around the other buildings. In one of the smaller structures he could hear running water and the sounds of someone moving around. Maerlynn, he decided, sacrificing some of her precious sleep time to wash Jack's clothing. The other buildings all seemed to be deserted.

Next, he extended his search beyond the buildings, moving out in a standard spiral pattern. Remembering their aerial survey from the *Essenay,* he made a point of watching for concealed guard posts, especially in the forest areas.

Again, nothing. He ran across an occasional hut nestled into the trees along the way, each one about three times the size of last night's hotbox. But there was no scent of Brummga near any of them. It was as if the Chookoock family, having purchased these people's bodies and minds and souls, simply expected them to stay where they'd been put.

On the other hand, he had to admit, where else was there for them to go?

The nearest section of the perimeter wall was to the northwest. He set off through the forest in that direction, running lightly across the matted leaves, dodging around trees and bushes. Every hundred paces he stopped to listen and smell for patrols or guard stations. But still there was nothing.

The ground near the wall included several rolling hills. Choosing one that would give him a good view, he moved to the edge and climbed the tallest tree he could find. If his estimate was correct, he should now be high enough to look *down* on the wall and into the center of the curving X-shape.

Moving carefully out onto one of the upper branches, he pushed aside the leaves.

And got his first really good look at the barrier he and Jack were going to have to cross.

It was every bit as impressive as he'd expected. The anti-aircraft lasers Uncle Virge had warned them about were there, all right. He could see the larger lenses of long-range weapons set into the white ceramic every ten feet or so, with the smaller lenses of shorter-range lasers arrayed between them. Between the lasers were long, narrow grooves that were most likely the flame jets Uncle Virge had also mentioned.

Long-range lasers for high-flying aircraft. Short-range lasers for smaller, lower-flying vehicles that might try to slip through the ten-foot gap between the larger weapons. And flame jets to kill anyone who tried to simply climb over the wall.

The Brummgas seemed to have covered all their bets here. But as Uncle Virge might say, that only meant it was time to cheat.

Because if the fire from the flame jets could be blocked, even for a single minute, Jack might have time to scramble over without harm. And in a forest, the obvious candidate for such a barrier was a tree.

He worked his way around to a different side of his tree and studied the edge of the forest. But no. The Brummgas had been smart enough to cut back the forest along the whole length of the wall.

Not very far, but far enough. No one would be able to chop down a tree and have it fall across the wall.

A pity, too. Barely a hundred yards away he could see a

hill that was actually taller than the wall. A tree cut from there would have been perfect.

Or could it still be done?

For another minute he studied the tall hill. If he and Jack cut down one of the trees and rolled it to the base of the wall . . .

But again, no. Any tree thick enough to block the fire would be too heavy for him to lift to the top of the wall. If Jack still had the climbing gear he'd used at the gatekeeper's house, they might have been able to rig something up.

But Gazen had taken that away with the rest of Jack's burglar equipment. And Draycos somehow doubted he and Jack would have time to search the mansion for it.

Could Uncle Virge do something, then? Use the *Essenay* to haul a tree trunk or ceramic bar to the top of the wall to block the flame jets? But that assumed the Chookoock family had no defenses against an attacker who was too clever to simply try to fly over their wall. Surely they'd planned for something like that.

Regardless, he couldn't risk the *Essenay* to find out. So the wall was a dead end. But then, he reminded himself as he climbed head-first down the tree, he'd expected it to be. Time to try a different approach.

Maerlynn had called the barrier between the slaves and the Chookoock family grounds a thorn hedge. With the darkness, and his own limited viewing angle beneath Jack's shirt, Draycos hadn't noticed any thorns as they were driven through the gap the night before. But as he approached the hedge this time he could see that the name was quite accurate.

In fact, the hedge was almost an encyclopedia of thorn types. There were rows and rows of tiny ones, the kind that would snag and tangle clothing. There were extra-long ones, sturdy enough to stab all the way through Jack's palm should he be careless enough to hit it hard enough. And there was just about every other length in between.

Draycos arched his tail as he studied it, marveling at the design. Either the Brummgas had interwoven several different types of thorn bushes and vines together to create the hedge, or else they'd genetically combined all the various thorn types into a single, incredibly nasty plant. Either way, it made for a serious barrier.

He followed the hedge to where it ended against the wall, then traveled its length all the way in the other direction. There were, he discovered, only three openings in the thorns. Two of them were wide gateways, clearly designed for cargo vehicles. They straddled roads that headed into the lumbering and mining areas. Both of those gaps were protected by smaller versions of the metal-and-ceramic gate Gazen had brought them through into the Chookoock family grounds. The third was the smaller gap the Brummgas had driven through on their way to lock Jack into the hotbox.

A gap with no guards and no gate. Open, inviting, and apparently unprotected.

Right.

He eased toward the gap with the same caution he would use in approaching a dozing Valahgua assault battalion. Twenty feet away, he spotted the sensor disks along the sides, half hidden behind clumps of leaves. Another five feet, and he was able to see the connecting wires woven in among the branches. Another five, and he could hear the faint hum of the electronics.

He didn't dare go any closer. Clearly, the opening was a

trap, designed to lure in any slave who might be thinking of sneaking into areas where he wasn't supposed to go.

But then, a poet-warrior of the K'da hardly needed to use an opening to get over a ten-foot hedge. Neither did a human boy with a K'da warrior as an ally.

Moving away from the gap, he headed eastward. A hundred yards in that direction was a low bush a few feet from the hedge. Draycos maneuvered his way carefully between bush and hedge, fully aware that the longer thorns might be able to slide between his golden scales and draw blood. Rolling onto his side, he extended his claws and began to cut his way into the hedge.

It was a slow, delicate operation. The hedge was a confused tangle of branches and vines, and he often had to cut each one in three or four places to free the piece he needed to move.

Even trickier was the need to work behind the first layer of branches, leaving that group intact. It might be days before he and Jack were ready to move, and he couldn't afford some sharp-eyed Brummga noticing a growing hole in the hedge.

He couldn't even cut the front layer away, work behind it, then wedge the branches back into place. Most plants changed color or texture after they'd been cut, and that would be as much of a giveaway as an open hole.

He worked for about an hour, until the tingling in his scales warned him that the time was approaching when he would need to return to his host. Stuffing the pieces of hedge he'd cut under another bush, he headed back to the slave colony.

All was as he'd left it, except that the sounds of washing

had ceased. Slipping through the open door of the long hut, he returned to Jack's cot.

The boy was sleeping soundly, his mouth hanging slightly open. Stepping to his side, Draycos touched a forepaw to his hand and slid up his arm in two-dimensional form. He traveled along the arm, toward his usual position across Jack's back, arms, and legs.

And as he did so, there was a soft grunt from the next cot.

He froze in place, his eyes darting that direction. The Dolom girl, Lisssa, was propped up on her elbow. Staring into the darkness in Jack's direction.

Draycos felt his breath catch like ice in his lungs. Had she seen him come in? Worse, had she seen him climb onto Jack's body?

He held still, silently cursing his carelessness. Yes, he was tired and hungry; but that was no excuse. He had a duty to his people to survive, and to keep his existence a secret.

For a long minute, Lisssa didn't move, either. Then, blinking twice, she lowered herself back onto her cot. A minute later, her slow breathing showed she was again asleep.

Carefully, Draycos finished positioning himself across Jack's back. He still wasn't sure what, if anything, the Dolom had seen, but it now seemed unlikely she had seen anything too obvious. Surely she would have screamed the hut awake if she had.

Wouldn't she?

On the other paw, she was an alien, of a type he had never met or studied. Perhaps screaming simply wasn't in her species' makeup.

He gave up the effort. Whatever came of this, if anything,

it would probably wait until morning. He and Jack would deal with it then.

Nestling himself against Jack's skin, feeling the renewing energy flowing from his host, he fell asleep.

CHAPTER 8

"Listen up," Fleck said, glaring down at Jack. "I'm only going to explain this once."

"Yes, sir," Jack said, using the meekest voice and manner in his repertoire. Up close, Fleck was even uglier than he'd looked across the sleeping hut. His tanned face had tiny pockmarks all across it like the craters on an asteroid, his eyes were bulging and bloodshot, and his beard seemed to be going bald in spots.

He was also bigger than he'd seemed. It would probably be smart to stay on his good side.

"All right." Fleck waved along the line of bushes, which were growing so close together that they were practically a hedge all by themselves. "These are the rainbow berry bushes."

He reached to the nearest of the stubby branches and swung it up, exposing the neat row of fingernail-sized berries clinging to its underside. "And this," he said, pointing to one of them, "is a ripe berry. You see the color pattern, the way the red at the stem blends into yellow, and then into green and blue?"

"Yes," Jack said, trying hard not to be sarcastic. It was pretty obvious, actually.

"Yeah, I know—it's obvious," Fleck growled. "But *this* part isn't."

He turned the berry over in his thick fingers. "Look here in the middle of the blue. See that little dot of purple? That's *very* important."

He turned the berry back around. "So is this ring of little bumps right where it connects to the stem. You don't have both of those, you don't have a ripe berry, and you leave it be. Got it?"

"Got it," Jack said, nodding. Okay; so it wasn't quite as simple as it had first looked.

"I hope so," Fleck said warningly. "Because if you mess up, the Brummgas *will* catch it. And then you'll be in trouble."

"Like I'm not already," Jack muttered under his breath.

"What was that?"

"I said I got it," Jack said aloud. "This isn't exactly brain surgery, you know."

"And you're not exactly a brain surgeon, are you?" Fleck pointed out. "Here's your bowl."

He handed Jack a container that looked like an extra-deep pie pan with a long leather strap strung between two points on the rim. "You want me to show you how to use it?"

"I think I can figure it out," Jack said. He looped the strap around his neck, letting the container rest against his stomach. "Close enough?"

"I guess maybe you *are* a brain surgeon," Fleck said sarcastically. "Just one more thing."

He plucked the berry he'd identified as ripe and set it down gently into Jack's bowl. "Don't just toss it into the bowl. You do that, you're likely to crush the ones on the bottom. Damaged berries get you in trouble with the Brumm-gas, too."

He took a step closer to Jack, looming over him like an es-pecially unfriendly rain cloud. "And if you're in trouble with the Brummgas, you're in trouble with me. Got it?"

Jack grimaced. Staying on Fleck's good side might be harder than he'd thought. "Got it."

"Then get to work."

Turning, he stalked away. "Don't worry about Fleck," Maer-lynn said, stepping over to Jack's side. "He talks grouchy, but mostly he's all right. Go ahead and get started—I'll watch and see how you do."

She watched for ten minutes before she seemed convinced he did indeed have the hang of it. "You're doing fine," she said. "I'll be down the line over here. If you have any ques-tions, just ask."

"I will," Jack said. "Thanks."

She headed away along the edge of the bushes, toward where Jack could see Noy and Lisssa picking. "I still think you could build a robot to do this," Jack muttered, turning back to his bush. "You could at least make a scanner to help out."

"Perhaps it is a hammer problem," Draycos suggested from his shoulder.

Jack turned one of the berries over. No purple spot. "What's a hammer problem?" he asked, moving on to the next berry in line.

"It is from one of the sayings Uncle Virge has quoted to me," the dragon said. " 'When the only tool you have is a hammer, every problem looks like a nail.' "

"Yeah, he quotes that one to me, too," Jack said. This one

had both the purple spot and the bump pattern. Plucking it from its stem, he put it in his bowl. "If you've got a whole bunch of slaves, everything you're doing looks like it ought to be done by slave labor. That's more or less what I said yesterday."

"I am merely confirming your reasoning," Draycos said. "I went out and examined the wall last night."

"Great," Jack said. "I was going to suggest that, but I fell asleep before I could talk to you. How's it look?"

"Every bit as dangerous as our examination from the *Essenay* indicated," the dragon said. "I do not believe we will be able to escape that way."

Jack shrugged. "No problem," he said. "I was expecting we'd have to go out through the gate anyway."

"True," Draycos said. "On the other hand, you also expected we would be leaving by today at the latest."

"Thanks for the vote of confidence," Jack growled, glaring down his freshly-washed shirt at the dragon's snout, draped across his collarbone. "This is just a little setback."

"Of course," Draycos said.

"And sarcasm won't help, either."

"I was not being sarcastic," the dragon protested. "The good news is that there do not seem to be any patrols in the slave area. That means we will have freedom of movement."

"That could be handy," Jack agreed. "Anything else? Wait a second," he interrupted himself softly. Out of the corner of his eye, he had picked up movement.

"Hey, Jack," Noy's voice came from that direction. "How are you doing?"

"Okay, I guess," Jack said, turning around. "It's not that hard."

"No," Noy said doubtfully, peering into Jack's bowl. "But you're going to have to work faster than that if you want to eat tonight."

Jack frowned. "What?"

"You have to fill your bowl by dinnertime," Noy explained. "Otherwise, no dinner. Didn't Fleck tell you?"

Jack looked off to the left. Fleck was off in the distance, pacing back and forth behind a group of Jantris. "No, he didn't tell me," he growled. "How full does it have to be?"

"Up to here," Noy said, pointing to a line about half an inch below the rim of the container.

"Got it," Jack said, a sinking feeling swirling in the pit of his stomach as he stared into the nearly empty bowl. "Then what?"

"You take your bowl over there," Noy said, pointing to a pair of tables set up in the shade of a tall tree. "The Brumm-gas show up between five-thirty and six. You bring them a full bowl, and they give you a meal ticket."

"A what?"

"A meal ticket," Noy repeated. "It's a little metal square you can trade in for dinner in the meal hall."

"And no ticket, no dinner?"

"Right," Noy said. "So I'd better let you get back to work. I just wanted to say hi."

"Thanks," Jack said. "And thanks for the warning."

"No problem," Noy said, moving away. "See you later."

He wandered off toward another spot in the tangle of bushes, stopping every few feet to check the nearest branches. "That was awfully nice of Fleck, wasn't that?" Jack muttered toward his shoulder as he turned back to his work.

"Perhaps there was no malice intended," Draycos suggested. "He may merely have forgotten to tell you."

"You don't even believe that one yourself," Jack said. "The guy just thought it would be funny for me to listen to my stomach growl all night."

He stopped short, a jolt of conscience suddenly hitting him. "Which reminds me . . . I didn't save you any of my food last night. I'm sorry."

"That is all right," Draycos assured him. "There was no practical way you could have done so with Maerlynn and the others watching."

"I know, but . . ." Jack ran out of words.

"Do not worry about me, Jack," Draycos said into the awkward silence. "I am a poet-warrior of the K'da. I am accustomed to hardship in the line of duty. You must not worry about me, but keep your full attention on the task at hand. Agreed?"

Jack sighed. "Agreed."

"Good," Draycos said. "I am working on a plan that I believe will allow us to move undetected into the Chookoock family grounds. From that point, it will be up to you."

"Okay," Jack said. He'd finished the upper branches of this particular bush; kneeling down on the soft ground, he started checking the lower ones. "From that I assume the hedge is wired?"

"Yes," Draycos said. "The gap we were brought through has many sensors attached. How did you know?"

"Because an open gap like that is about as obvious as an elephant at an anteaters' tea party," Jack said with sniff. "These Brummgas are not exactly mental giants. I hope you aren't going to try to disarm them by yourself."

"I am not going to disarm them at all," Draycos said. "I

have begun carving a tunnel through the base of the hedge at a secluded location."

"There'll still be all the rest of the grounds to get through after that," Jack pointed out.

"True," Draycos said. "As I said, that part is up to you."

Jack snorted. "Thanks. Loads."

CHAPTER 9

There were two breaks that morning, each one a big fat five minutes long. Most of the slaves took the opportunity to sit down and stretch tired muscles. Jack, in contrast, worked straight through both.

A longer, twenty-minute break came at noon, accompanied by a cup of what Maerlynn called nutrient broth. To Jack, it seemed more like flavored water with delusions of souphood. But it tasted all right, and he had to admit he felt better after drinking it.

He worked through most of that break, too, holding his soup cup with one hand and sipping from it as he picked.

It was midafternoon, and Fleck had just called another five-minute break, when he first heard the music.

He paused and looked around. It was a delicate sound, clear and precise and clean. Ethereal, even, if he was remembering that word right. The kind of music that would fit perfectly with a movie scene of a tropical paradise.

Which made its presence in the middle of a slave colony like a sweetly smiling kick in the teeth.

"Where is that music coming from?" Draycos murmured.

"I don't know," Jack said, straightening up and looking around.

And then, an old man came into view from around a curve in the bushes. He walked slowly, as if his knees were tired or stiff or both, and on his head he wore an amazingly wide-brimmed hat.

And in his hands he carried a musical instrument like nothing Jack had ever seen before.

Jack blinked, wiping the sweat off his forehead. The instrument was mostly metal; that much he could tell from the glints of sunlight off its surface. Sections of it looked familiar, too, as if the old man had put it together from pieces of a half dozen other instruments. The part he was blowing into seemed to have come from a flute, but there were also valves from a trumpet and possibly a tuba. Other parts Jack didn't recognize at all.

He glanced around. The only other slave nearby was Lisssa, leaning half into her bush as she strained to reach some berry deep inside the tangle of branches. "Hey, Lisssa," Jack said, stepping over to her. "What's with the musician?"

She made a sound like a horse snorting. "It's the Klezmer."

"What's a Klezmer?"

"I look like an encyclopedia to you?" she retorted. "That's just what he calls himself."

"Okay, okay," Jack said soothingly. "I was just asking."

"And I'm just telling," Lisssa said sourly. "Probably means 'leach' in some human language."

Jack frowned. "Leach?"

Lisssa snorted again. "Take another look."

Jack turned back. The Klezmer was walking slowly along the line of berry pickers now. Each of the working slaves turned toward him as he passed.

And to Jack's surprise, each dropped some berries into the container looped around the Klezmer's neck.

"Okay, I give up," Jack said. "What are they doing?"

"Like I said, he's a leach," Lisssa growled. "Story goes his eyes have gone too bad for him to pick berries. My eyes so cry over him."

"But don't the Brummgas have some kind of . . . ?" Jack floundered.

"What, retirement plan?" Lisssa asked scornfully. "Don't be ridiculous. We don't work, we don't eat. Period."

She shrugged in the Klezmer's direction, the thick scales of her shoulder scratching against the branches with the movement. "So he's got this scam going. He plays music and pretends he's not begging. And everyone else gives him berries and pretends it's not charity."

Jack studied her right ear, about all of her face he could see through the branches and leaves. There had been an odd emphasis on the last word. "You don't believe in charity?"

Reluctantly, he thought, she pulled back from the bush and turned those dark eyes on him. "Are you that naïve?" she asked bitterly. "Or are you just stupid? We're slaves. *Slaves*. The bottom of the bottom of the stack. Charity is for people who have something extra to give. Not us. Here, no one looks out for you but yourself."

"What about Maerlynn?" Jack asked. "Seems to me she's trying to look out for us."

"Oh, right," Lisssa countered. "Maerlynn. She helped Noy's parents, too. They both ended up dead. She helped Greb and Grib's uncle. He wound up dead, too."

Her eyes flicked over Jack's shoulder. "And let's see what good all her good intentions do for anyone now."

Jack turned around. Coming up behind the Klezmer was another of the open-topped cars like the one they'd used to bring him to the slave colony. Inside, he could see two Brummgas: one an adult male, the other much smaller and younger. The car coasted to a stop and both of them got out.

"Quick—look busy," Lisssa warned, sticking her face back into the bushes.

Jack took a long step to the next bush over and got back to work, watching the two Brummgas out of the corner of his eye. They began walking slowly along the line of working slaves, the younger one jabbering to the older.

And suddenly the air seemed full of tension.

"What is it?" Jack murmured toward Lisssa. The Klezmer, he noted, had stopped playing and was standing off to the side, stiff and silent. "An inspection?"

"Worse," Lisssa hissed from inside her bush. "Crampatch's spoiled brat of a daughter is back for a new toy."

Jack frowned. *A toy?*

The two Brummgas kept walking, the younger one pointing here and there and making questioning noises, the older one answering her back. Lisssa was right, Jack realized: it was exactly like she was a kid in a toy shop. A kid trying to talk her father into buying her one of everything.

And then, the daughter stopped suddenly, her jabbing finger becoming insistent. Her father answered; she pointed all the more violently. He shrugged and said something.

And from the line of bushes stepped one of Lisssa's fellow Doloms. The older Brummga gestured, and taking his daughter's arm he turned back toward the car. Setting his collection bowl carefully onto the ground, the Dolom followed.

Behind him, Lisssa hissed something vicious sounding. "May her body swell up and burst," she muttered.

"What's she going to do with him?" Jack asked.

"Probably paint him," Lisssa said, biting out each word like it was a piece of bad-tasting gristle. "That's what she usually does when she takes Doloms. She thinks our scales look like a paint-by-number mosaic, just waiting for her to decorate. May she and her family be cursed forever."

She made a deep rumbling noise that seemed to echo in her chest and throat. "Or maybe she'll decide to try carving designs in him again. She did that once."

Jack winced. "Sounds painful."

"It is if you get too deep," Lisssa said. "She did. After she got bored and sent him back, like she always does, he got sick from infections in the cuts. It took him six days to die."

"Nice kid," Jack murmured, hunching his shoulders. Draycos was sliding restlessly along his skin, and he could practically feel the dragon's anger.

He didn't blame him. If things like this were why the K'da hated slavery so much, he was ready to join the club himself. "What about this one?" he asked Lisssa. "Do you know him?"

It was a stupid question, he realized too late. Of course she would know all the other Doloms among the slaves.

But her answer surprised him. "Not really," she said. "I think his name's Plasssit or Plusssit. Something like that."

Jack frowned at her, but the thick tile-pattern of her face as she stared at the Brummgas was unreadable. "You don't know?" he asked. "I mean . . . he's one of your people."

Her eyes shifted back to Jack. "What was your name

again?" she asked pointedly. Just as pointedly, she turned her wide back to him and went back to her work.

"Right," Jack murmured. The message was clear. Lisssa didn't want to know any of them. They were slaves, and she was a slave, and the only place to hide from that reality was inside herself.

And so that was where she would stay.

The Brummgas and the Dolom drove away, and for a moment there was silence. Then, the Klezmer resumed his music, and the slaves returned to their picking.

Later, when the Klezmer came by, Jack put a handful of berries into his bowl. The old man murmured some thanks; and on a sudden impulse, Jack put in a second handful.

For a long time afterwards he wondered why he'd done that. It had probably surprised him more than it had the Klezmer, especially considering that his own dinner or lack of it was on the line. Perhaps it was his reaction to Lisssa's selfish attitude that had sparked such unusual generosity.

Or maybe it was just knowing that Draycos was watching. Draycos, and his blasted pain-in-the-neck K'da warrior ethic.

He did notice that when the Klezmer went past Lisssa, she ignored him completely.

As it turned out, his generosity didn't end up costing him anything after all. By the time the Brummgas set up at their tables, he had filled his bowl to the line. In fact, he'd continued past the line and loaded berries all the way to the very top. He turned in his bowl, collected his meal ticket, and joined the line of slaves heading to dinner.

The meal hall looked about the way Jack had expected:

long tables with plain wooden benches on both sides. The meal itself was actually better than he'd expected. It consisted of another of the cabbage rolls he'd had the night before, plus a bowl of the nutrient soup they'd been given at noon, plus a piece of multigrain bread of some kind, plus a small slab of real meat.

The cabbage roll didn't taste quite as good as it had when he'd been starving. But it tasted good enough. He drank the soup, too, wiping the bowl with his bread to make sure he got every drop.

The meat went quietly into a pocket to give to Draycos later.

When the meal was over, each slave cleaned his utensils at a long tub of water and returned them to the cooking slaves. After that, Jack's plan had been to take a quiet walk off by himself, where he and Draycos could talk without being overheard.

But during the meal he'd found his muscles tightening up from the strain of the day's work. Some of them were muscles he hadn't even known he had. By the time he hobbled out of the meal hall on stiff legs, the thought of doing anything but going straight to bed was long gone.

He changed into his sackshirt, laying out his other clothing neatly over the end of his cot. Maerlynn came by once to see how he was doing, and left again after he assured her he was fine.

She didn't offer to wash his clothes this time. That was probably something he would have to do on his own from now on. Tomorrow, when he wasn't so tired, he would ask someone how he went about doing that.

He forced himself to stay awake for a few minutes after the lights went out, hoping that everyone else in the hut would get to sleep quickly. "Draycos?" he whispered when he judged he'd waited long enough.

"They are all asleep," the dragon confirmed softly. "Are you all right?"

"I'm pretty tired," Jack admitted, sliding the meat out from under his pillow where he'd hidden it. "Otherwise, I'm okay. Got some food for you here. Sorry it's not more."

"It is quite adequate," Draycos assured him. His head rose up from Jack's chest, his crest pushing up the thin blanket. "I am not very hungry."

"Yeah," Jack said, watching as the dragon wolfed down the meat in a single bite. "Right."

"Truly," Draycos insisted. "You should sleep now."

"No argument there," Jack agreed. "You going back to the thorn hedge?"

"Yes," Draycos said. His head flattened again onto Jack's chest, and Jack felt him slithering along onto his right arm. He picked up the cue and turned onto his left side, draping the arm over the cot toward the floor.

The dragon slid off his wrist, landing on the wooden floor without a sound. "See you later," Jack whispered. "Don't get caught."

"I will be careful," Draycos said.

"Good." Jack snorted gently. "I was just thinking. Remember back at the Whinyard's Edge recruiting center, when Jommy Randolph made that snide comment about the training being like summer camp?"

"I remember," Draycos said. "And?"

Jack made a face in the dark. "Compared to this," he said, "it was."

Draycos brushed Jack's arm with his forepaw. "Good night, Jack," he said. "I will return soon."

CHAPTER 10

The next few days settled into a simple if unpleasant routine. Jack got up at daybreak with the other slaves and trudged out to the rainbow berry bushes. He worked, drank his noonday soup, worked some more, turned in his bowl, ate dinner, and trudged back to his bed.

At first his muscles ached all the time. After a couple of days, as he got used to the work, they mostly ached at bedtime. A few days after that, they almost stopped aching at all. Almost.

Every other day the Klezmer came by. Each time he did so, Jack made sure to give him a good handful of his berries.

At first he tried to tell himself that he was just trying to blend in. Almost all the other slaves except Lisssa, he'd noted, seemed to give the old man something from their own bowls. Even Fleck, who didn't have to do any picking at all, usually had a handful ready to slip into the Klezmer's bowl.

Jack also tried to convince himself he was just doing it to show up Lisssa's defiant selfishness, or that he just liked the music. But after the third time he finally had to admit the truth. Very simply, he enjoyed helping out the old man.

It was a new experience for him, and it gave him a lot to think about in his long hours under the hot sun. Uncle Virgil had occasionally made back-scratching deals with other criminals or corrupt police, deals where he'd done a job in exchange for something else. But he would have fallen on the floor laughing if anyone had ever suggested he give away anything for free.

His computerized alter ego, Uncle Virge, was of course incapable of falling on the floor. But Jack knew that if he ever heard about this he would certainly deliver a stern lecture on why Jack should be looking out strictly for himself.

Which made Jack wonder just where the whole idea had come from in the first place.

Was Draycos's warrior ethic starting to rub off on him? That was certainly possible. After two months of hearing about high-minded K'da ideals, anyone would start believing in them. Or was this coming from Maerlynn and the way she was always scurrying around helping her adopted children?

That was it, he finally decided. Maerlynn. He wasn't really giving the Klezmer anything for free. All he was doing was passing on the good deeds he'd already gotten from Maerlynn. It was a back-scratch deal after all, except that he wasn't paying back Maerlynn directly.

It made him feel better to think of it that way. Better, and a lot safer. He wasn't going off the deep end of the pool like some junior K'da warrior. All he was doing was paying back a debt.

He probably would have felt even better if he'd really believed that.

On the fifth day at work, he found himself so unbelievably grubby that he finally couldn't stand it anymore. There were a couple of cold showers in the washroom at the end of his sleeping hut, and that evening he postponed his bedtime long enough to give himself a quick rinse. It helped some, but with his clothes still dirty the feeling of being clean didn't last very long. When he asked Maerlynn about laundry, she told him the slaves usually waited until Tenthday, when they were given a day off of work.

Tenthday, to his annoyance, turned out to be another two days away. Still, he'd lasted this long. He could certainly hold out until then.

It was Ninthday when the routine fell apart.

He was heading for the line at the tables with his bowlful of berries when a sudden shadow fell across his face. He looked up to find Fleck glowering down at him. "Hello, Fleck," he said, making a smooth sidestep around the big man. "How's tricks?"

Fleck's own sidestep wasn't nearly as smooth as Jack's. But it did the job just fine, planting him squarely in front of Jack again. "You got too many," he said.

"I've got too many what?" Jack asked. He was tired and hungry, and not in a mood for games.

"What do you think?" Fleck growled, jabbing a finger at Jack's chest. "Berries. You got too many berries."

Jack looked down into his bowl with astonishment. "What in the world are you talking about?"

"You're only supposed to fill to the line," Fleck said. "Not all the way to the top. What, you think the Brummgas are going to give you a bonus?"

"What, you don't like a kid my age doing better than the rest of you?" Jack shot back. Without waiting for an answer, he started to walk away.

Fleck's rough hand on his arm made it clear the conversation wasn't over. "I'll tell you what I don't like, kiddy-face," he said. "I don't like you poking your stick into the bug hill. If you keep showing the Brummgas you can pick more berries in a day, they'll make *everyone* pick that many."

It was, Jack realized later, a perfectly reasonable argument. He certainly wasn't interested in giving the Brummgas ideas for working their slaves any harder than they already were. And if Fleck had just given him a minute to think it through, everything would have been fine.

Unfortunately, Fleck didn't. "So you stop now," he insisted.

And reaching into Jack's bowl, he scooped out a handful of berries.

"Hey!" Jack snapped. He grabbed the other's wrist and shoved it away, then jumped back, trying to get out of reach.

Once again, the big man showed he was faster than he looked. He took a long step forward, slapped Jack's hand aside, and grabbed the strap that held the bowl around his neck. With a tug that seemed to snap Jack's head back against his shoulders, he yanked the boy toward him. "You don't do that," he said, very quietly, from three inches away. His breath smelled like stale nutrient broth. "Not to me. Not ever."

Jack stared straight into that ugly face. There was a punch Uncle Virgil had taught him, he remembered, a punch he'd guaranteed would drop any bully flat on his rear. Out of sight at his waist, he curled his right hand into a fist and braced himself.

And then, he felt the warning touch of K'da claws against his arm. He hesitated—

"Stop," a flat Brummgan voice ordered.

Jack turned his head, letting his hand drop back to his side. One of the Brummgas standing guard over the berry collection process was striding toward them, a slapstick clutched in his hand. "You," he said, jabbing the slapstick toward Fleck. "Release him."

Fleck did so. Jack reached up and rubbed the back of his neck where the strap had dug into his skin. "It's all right," he said. "We were just—"

Without a word the Brummga slashed the slapstick across the side of his face.

Jack spun around and tumbled to the ground, a flash of pain arcing through him. His bowl bounced against his chest as he hit, spilling the berries all around. "Wait!" he managed as the Brummga lowered the slapstick toward him. "I didn't—"

The end of his protest bubbled into a groan as the tip slashed across his chest, this second tingle rattling his teeth. The weapon was on its lowest setting, without enough juice to knock him unconscious. But it had more than enough to hurt.

"You not argue with Red Stripe," the Brummga growled, pointing at Fleck's red sash. He raised the slapstick for emphasis; in spite of himself, Jack winced back in reaction. "You understand? You not argue with Red Stripe."

"I understand," Jack said, his teeth chattering together with pain and shock and fury.

The Brummga waved the slapstick again, apparently just to see Jack's reaction. "Good. Don't forget."

He looked at Fleck and pointed the slapstick at Jack. "Hotbox," he ordered.

"Yes, Your Commandary," Fleck said, bowing his head. Reaching down, he grabbed Jack's arm and hauled him to his feet. With his free hand, he unlooped the now nearly empty bowl from around his neck and handed it to the Brummga. "How long?"

The other eyed Jack as if measuring him. "One night," he decided. "He will work tomorrow."

Fleck glanced at Jack. "Tomorrow is Tenthday, Your Commandary," he said.

"He will work regardless," the Brummga said. "He will bring a full bowl, or he will not eat."

Fleck bowed again. "Yes, Your Commandary. It shall be done."

For a moment the Brummga continued to watch Jack, as if expecting an argument. Maybe even hoping for an argument.

But Jack had learned his lesson, and remained silent. With a rumble from his chest, the Brummga turned away and plodded back toward the collection table.

As he did so, something else caught Jack's eye. Another car was approaching the slave colony, carrying two Brummgas and a wildly painted Dolom. Lisssa had been right: Crampatch's daughter got bored quickly with her private slaves.

"Come on," Fleck growled, turning Jack around and giving him a shove toward the hotboxes.

"What about my berries?" Jack asked, looking back at the berries lying on the ground, many of them smashed. A hard, tiring day's work, all gone.

Fleck gave him another shove. "You didn't want dinner tonight anyway, did you?" he asked sarcastically. "Think of it as a lesson learned cheap."

"The guy with the big stick is always right," Jack murmured. "I already know that one."

Five minutes later, he was back in the hotbox. "Here we go again," he muttered. "Our home away from home. Looks just the way we left it, too."

"I am sorry, Jack," Draycos murmured from his right shoulder.

Jack shrugged. "It's not like there was a lot you could have done to help," he pointed out reasonably. "Besides, you already did. If you hadn't stopped me from decking that big jerkface, I'd probably have drawn a week in here."

"Still, I am sorry I could not prevent it," Draycos persisted.

"Forget it," Jack said, trying not to let his anger at Fleck and the Brummgas spill over onto Draycos. "Tell you what. As soon as your people get settled in on Iota Klestis, we'll bring a few of your buddies in and make Fleck pick up every berry he spilled. And eat them. How's that sound?"

Draycos seemed to think that one over. "You are joking, of course."

"Mostly," Jack said. "But it's still kind of nice to think about."

"But not very productive."

"Maybe not," Jack said. "But there's not a whole lot of productive I can be at the moment."

"Still, it is not good for your mind to dwell on such things," Draycos said. "It can have a negative effect on your judgment."

"You didn't seem to have any trouble killing that guy aboard the *Star of Wonder*," Jack said.

"That was different," Draycos said, a little stiffly. "That was justice. It is not at all the same as revenge."

"I know," Jack conceded. He really shouldn't toy with Draycos and his warrior ethic this way, he knew. But it was just too easy sometimes to hot-start the dragon's buttons and play a little tune on them. "How much longer will it take you to get through that hedge?"

"Not long," Draycos said. "Perhaps two days. Three at the most."

"And then?"

"Once we are both at the hedge, I will cut through the last few branches," Draycos said. "We will then be clear to enter the Chookoock family areas."

"And from then on it's up to me," Jack said, nodding. "Then you'd better get to work. The sooner we get out of here, the better."

CHAPTER 11

They waited until the camp was dark and quiet. Then, Jack slid his hand under the door, and Draycos slipped out into the night.

The trip to the thorn hedge had become a familiar one over the past few days. Draycos moved silently along the uneven ground, habit and experience keeping him to shadows and cover wherever possible.

His mind, though, was a million restless leaps away. The injustice of what had just been done to Jack still throbbed in his brain like an angry percussion master with a full set of concert drums.

For that matter, this whole situation was beginning to get beneath his scales. This was an important mission, and part of his job was to keep personal feelings from affecting his judgment.

But in this case, knowing that and doing it were two very different things. This was a slave colony, and it was simply not possible for a poet-warrior of the K'da to completely suppress his anger and contempt.

And as to Jack's idea about coming back to make Fleck regret his actions, it was sadly short of the mark. What this place needed was not a few of Draycos's friends, but six assault squads of K'da and Shontine warriors. Three squads to free the slaves, the other three to burn the entire place to the ground.

He flicked his tail sternly. That was not a proper thought for a warrior, and he knew it. Justice was a vital part of the K'da warrior ethic. Vicious, bitter vengeance was not.

And any chance for justice was still a long way in the future. Jack could claim that everything beyond the hedge was his job if he wanted to, but Draycos knew better. There was a large expanse of ground they would have to deal with before they even reached the mansion. Worse, much of that ground was open, without any cover to speak of.

No. Before he could allow Jack through the hedge, he would have to do a thorough check of the area on his own. He would have to examine the grounds, search for hidden guard posts, and study the outside of the mansion itself. His task was far from over.

And perhaps it was because he was thinking too much about the task ahead that he made it to within sight of the thorn hedge before he noticed the faint taste of Brummga in the air.

He stopped abruptly, dropping flat into the shadow of a bush, silently cursing his lack of attention. A well-known route, a routine duty—that was where a warrior faced the greatest threat of trap or ambush or simple mistake.

It was a good and timely reminder. He could only hope it hadn't already been a fatal one.

For a long minute he lay in the shadows, his nostrils and tongue sampling the air. There was definitely a Brummgan presence nearby; the scent was too strong to be simply left over from the day's activities. But the light breeze kept switching directions, hindering his efforts to pin down a location.

And then, as he strained every sense, he heard a soft cough.

Soft, but loud enough. His pointed ears twitched onto the direction, his eyes probing the darkness.

There he was, sitting beneath the same type of bush Draycos himself was hiding beside. A Brummgan soldier, complete with infrared-view detectors and a short but nasty-looking automatic weapon.

Sitting where he had a perfect view of the spot where Draycos had been digging his tunnel through the hedge.

Slowly, carefully, Draycos gave the rest of the area a complete check. He spotted two more Brummgas, similarly equipped, one in another shadow, the other beneath a sheet of camouflage webbing.

One of them Draycos could have handled, had he decided that such a move would aid their goal. But with three of them in widely spaced positions, an attack was out of the question. Slowly, carefully, he began to crawl back the way he'd come, his belly pressed tightly against the ground. Not until he was a hundred yards out of the watchers' sight did he finally stand fully upright again.

The taste of defeat on his tongue.

So all his work, all his cleverness, had been for nothing. The Brummgas had spotted his tunnel, and had set a trap for him. It was only the fact that they couldn't possibly have anticipated the arrival of a K'da warrior that had prevented them from nailing him on the spot.

What they *were* expecting, clearly, was one of their slaves.

And if they were smart enough to watch one end of the darter's hole, they were probably smart enough to be watching the other end, too.

Earlier, he had left Jack and the hotbox without much more than a quick and casual check of the area. There hadn't been any alarm, which meant he must not have been spotted.

He didn't know yet how they'd managed to miss him. But however it had happened, he knew he couldn't count on being that lucky twice in a row. This time he approached the slave colony like the warrior he was supposed to be: slow, alert, and flat on his belly.

He hadn't noticed anything odd when he'd left, and now he discovered why. For one thing, the enemy observer was off to the side, where he could watch the doors into the two sleeping huts but didn't have a clear view of the three hotboxes. For another, the observer wasn't a Brummga. It was a human.

Not just any human, either. It was Gazen himself.

Draycos looked across the starlit patch of ground, watching Gazen idly fingering his rifle. Under normal circumstances, he could easily tell one human scent from another. But having just spent an hour in the hotbox with Jack, and a particularly strong-smelling Jack at that, he hadn't noticed the taste of Gazen in the air.

He twitched his tail in annoyance. First he had wasted time with thoughts of vengeance. Now he was wasting equally precious time making excuses.

For two months he had been trying to gently push Jack toward the path of a K'da warrior. He had tried to teach the boy to think and behave with a sense of justice and honor, instead of reacting like the selfish thief his Uncle Virgil had raised him to be.

Now, he wondered if perhaps some of the training had ended up going the other way.

He twitched his tail again. More rationalization. More excuses.

More wasted time.

All right, he ordered himself firmly. So Gazen himself was here. That meant he was taking this attack on the thorn hedge very seriously. And given that Jack was the newest arrival, he might have expected that Gazen's suspicions would immediately have turned his direction.

But apparently, that wasn't the case. If it had been, Gazen should have found a place where he could watch the hotboxes as well as the sleeping huts.

Unless he didn't know Jack had been kicked out of his bed for the night.

Draycos let his jaws crack open in a wry smile. So all unknowingly, Fleck had in fact done him and Jack a huge favor. If he hadn't gotten Jack in trouble, Draycos might very well have strolled out of the sleeping hut tonight straight into Gazen's waiting hands.

Carefully, he began backing up again. They'd been saved by the thinnest of eyelid scales, the kind of luck every warrior hoped for. But that didn't mean there was any reason to throw a congratulatory party, either. Their main escape plan had just been discovered and neutralized. That meant they would have to fall back on Plan B.

Unfortunately, as far as he knew, they didn't have a Plan B.

Jack was asleep when he reached the hotbox, his hand

jammed under the door to give Draycos a way in. The boy didn't wake up as Draycos slipped up his arm and settled into his usual position across his back. The two of them had a lot to talk about; but the hotbox still held some of the day's heat, and he might as well let Jack sleep while he could. There would be plenty of time to talk later when the growing cold drove him awake.

That point arrived two hours later, when Jack began shivering in his sleep. Draycos managed to postpone it another half hour by returning to three-dimensional form and using his body to help keep the boy warm. But eventually, even that wasn't enough.

Jack listened in silence as Draycos related the night's activities. "That was a close one, all right," he commented when the K'da had finished. "Thanks to Fleck and his low-rent friends. A shame we can't ever tell him—I'd love to see the expression on that ugly slap-catcher face of his."

"It would be interesting," Draycos agreed. "I presume, then, that you no longer wish to make him eat the spilled berries?"

Jack waved a hand. "The bugs have probably gotten to most of them by now, anyway."

He shivered violently. "I just wish I'd thought to bury that blanket Maerlynn gave me in the floor here. It would have come in handy."

"As a matter of fact, I did bury it," Draycos told him. "I thought it would be bad for Maerlynn if you were found with it. Unfortunately, it is no longer here."

"Maerlynn must have dug it up afterward," Jack said with a sigh. "Too bad."

"The point is that we now have a serious problem," Draycos said. "I would have no difficulty myself jumping over the hedge. But I could not carry you over without risking injury to you."

"That just means we'll need another way over, that's all," Jack said. "Over, or through."

Draycos felt his ears twitch. "You have an idea?"

"I think so," Jack said. "It'll take some fancy timing, but if I can pull that part of it off it should work."

"May I ask what you have in mind?"

"Sure." In the dim light, he saw Jack smile tightly. "You remember Greb mentioning a couple of days ago that his and Grib's hatchday was coming up in three weeks? I thought we might throw them a little hatchday party."

"In three weeks?" Draycos asked, frowning.

Jack shook his head. "Life is uncertain," he said. "Let's do it now."

CHAPTER 12

The Brummgas let him out of the hotbox an hour or so after sunrise, just about the time the place was starting to warm up to a decent temperature. The rest of the slave colony was quiet, with everyone no doubt taking advantage of their day off to catch up on some sleep.

All except Fleck. The ugly man was waiting with the Brummgas, a bowl in his hand. Without a word he held it out toward Jack and jerked a thumb over his shoulder. Sighing to himself, Jack looped the strap around his neck and trudged off. It was, he knew, going to be a long, lonely, tiring day.

He reached the rainbow berry bushes to find he'd been wrong on all three counts.

He wasn't going to be alone. Maerlynn was already there, along with Greb and Grib and Noy and a half dozen others.

All of them already with small piles of berries on the ground beside them.

"What's this?" Jack asked, blinking in surprise as he looked around. "I thought this was Tenthday."

"Good morning, Jack," Maerlynn said cheerfully. "Yes, it is. Better get these piles picked up right away, before someone steps on one of them."

"I'll help," Noy offered. Stepping carefully over his own

pile he trotted over to Jack and put in the few he still had in his hands. "Grib's pile is the biggest—we'll get those first."

"But—" Jack said, still bewildered as he let Noy lead him over toward the twin Jantris. "Isn't this your day off?"

"Sure," Noy said. He turned his head away from Jack and coughed. "But it's your day off, too. We wanted to help you."

"We saw what happened," Maerlynn explained as Noy carefully scooped up Grib's pile of berries and laid them gently in the bowl. "It isn't fair to punish you for a rule you didn't know."

Jack stared down at Noy as the boy moved to Greb's pile and started gathering the berries into his hands. Selfishness between thieves and con men was something he knew very well. Help between soldiers he could sort of understand— after all, their lives might depend on each other.

But none of the slaves working here had a single thing to gain by helping him out. In fact, it could well be exactly the opposite. "Won't you get in trouble?" he asked. "I mean, that Brummga wanted *me* to sweat all day."

"Maybe that's what he *wanted*," Maerlynn said. "What he *said* was that you had to bring in a full bowl of berries if you wanted to eat. He never said you had to fill the bowl yourself."

"But that's what he meant," Jack argued. "Don't get me wrong—I appreciate the help. But I don't want to get you into trouble."

Maerlynn smiled, an oddly sad look on her face. "We're already slaves, Jack," she said gently. "How much worse trouble could we be in?"

Lots worse, the obvious answer flashed through Jack's mind. But for once in his life, he had the sense to keep his mouth shut. These people all knew the risk they were taking for him. They were taking it anyway. "Thank you," he murmured instead.

"We have to stick together," Maerlynn said quietly. "If we don't look out for each other, who else will?"

"No one, I guess," Jack said, thinking about what Lisssa had said once about charity and looking out for yourself.

Lisssa herself, naturally, was nowhere to be seen.

"So let's get a move on," Maerlynn said firmly. "It's our day off. Let's get this finished and go relax."

With all those hands, and with only one bowl to fill, they were done in less than half an hour. "And that's that," Maerlynn said as Jack dropped in the final handful. Right to the line, he confirmed with a sort of guilty satisfaction, and not a single berry over.

"Now we'll put them inside the hut, under your bed, until the Brummgas come to pick them up," Maerlynn said as they all trooped back to the colony. The place was starting to come alive, Jack noted, with several of the slaves moving about. "And then we'll be done for the day."

"So what does everyone do on Tenthday?" Jack asked. "Aside from laundry, I mean," he added as he spotted a pair of Compfrin females carrying grimy-looking bundles.

"In the morning we mostly just rest," Noy said, pausing to cough. That cough had been getting worse all morning, Jack had noted uneasily. It was starting to sound wet, too, as if fluid was gathering in his lungs. "In the afternoon we usually play games," the boy went on. "Some of the grownups like to carve or make things out of wood."

"There are often repairs that need to be attended to," Maerlynn said. "Beds sometimes fall apart, or some of the cooking or serving equipment breaks. The Brummgas aren't very good about maintaining this end of their land."

"You like chopball?" Greb asked. "We're going to play some later."

"Haven't ever played," Jack said. "But I had an idea for something else we might do. You said you and your brother had your hatchday coming up, right?"

"Right," Grib said. "We'll be sixteen. Almost adults."

"We're already molting," Greb added proudly, running a finger across his chest. "We should have all our adult feathers before we're seventeen."

"A lot of Jantris don't even start getting their feathers until they're seventeen," Grib said. "That's what Maerlynn said. She reads a lot."

"She said that meant we were percocious," Greb said.

"That's 'precocious,'" Maerlynn corrected him. "That means you're growing up faster than the average Jantri."

Or else it just meant the Brum-a-dum year was a little longer than the Jantri standard. But Jack wasn't about to bring that up. It would only kick off a new topic of conversation, and he might not get in another word all morning. Getting a Jantri to shut up was like trying to sweep back the tide with a paintbrush. "I'm sure you are," he said instead. "So what do you say we have a party."

Both Jantris blinked in unison. "A *party*?"

"I'm not sure we can do that, Jack," Maerlynn put in warningly. Clearly, she didn't want to get the twins' hopes up and then squash them like an overripe berry. "There isn't any extra food we could use. Or anything we could make special treats from."

"That's okay," Jack said. "A party doesn't need treats. All it needs is fun and entertainment."

"Like what?" Noy asked eagerly.

"Well, you already mentioned games," Jack said. "We might be able to get the Klezmer to come over and play a few tunes."

"Oh," Grib said, sounding a little disappointed. "We get to hear the Klezmer all the time."

"Or," Jack added smoothly, "I could put on a magic show."

Both twins straightened like they'd been poked with sharp sticks. "A magic show?" Grib repeated excitedly.

"A magic show?" Noy echoed, his face glowing. "Can I come, too?"

"Absolutely," Jack told him. "It's for anyone who wants to come and watch."

"Can we do it now?" Greb asked, grabbing Jack's arm. "Can we?"

"Hang on, hang on," Jack said. "I've got a few things I have to do first. My laundry, for one thing—this shirt reeks."

"No, no, no," Grib insisted. "Now, now, now."

"I also have to put together some props," Jack said firmly. He couldn't afford to start the show too early, after all. "How about we do it right after lunch?"

"Okay," Grib said. "Can we tell the others?"

"You can tell everyone," Jack assured him. The bigger and more noticeable the audience, the better. "I've got to go now. See you at lunch."

He had expected there to be a mad crunch at the tiny laundry facility, what with everyone trying to clean their clothes on the same day. But to his surprise, the slaves had the whole operation down to a science. There was a posted list that assigned time at the machines by bed groups, and those in each group seemed to show up exactly on that schedule. Jack's group was next, and with a little coaching by one of the other slaves he got his laundry going.

He should have guessed they would have it organized, of course. These people had been here for years, after all. Some of them, like Greb and Grib, had been here their whole lives.

It took a little more work and ingenuity to assemble the props he needed for his show. He was able to borrow a set of drinking cups and some small vegetables from the kitchen, but the cards and coins he needed for some of his best tricks turned out to be a challenge.

Eventually, he wound up sending Greb and Grib scrounging all around the colony. They returned triumphantly an hour later with five coins and a genuine if slightly ragged deck of cards. The fact that the scroungers were Jantris also meant that the news about the show got out more quickly and effectively than if Jack had sent out engraved invitations.

Which meant that by the time he stood up in front of the berry collection table, practically the whole colony had turned out to watch.

"Good afternoon, everyone," Jack said, picking up three potato-like vegetables he'd borrowed from the kitchen pantry. "Welcome to the first annual Greb and Grib hatch-day celebration. I'd like to start the show with a little bit of juggling."

He tossed one of the potatoes into the air and caught it. "There we go," he said. "Like it?"

"You call that juggling?" someone called scornfully.

"Yeah, we want to see you juggle all of them," Noy added.

"Oh?" Jack asked, acting surprised. "Well . . . sure."

He threw one potato in the air and caught it. Then, shifting it to his other hand, he threw the second into the air and caught it. "Is this what you mean?" he asked as he did the same with the third potato.

"No!" screamed all the children. "All *together!*"

"Oh," Jack said again. He tossed all three potatoes upward, making sure one of them went higher than the others. "Like *this?*"

"No!" they screamed again.

"Well, gee, then." Jack caught the two lowest potatoes as they came down, one in each hand, and sent them back into the air. "In that case—" he caught the third, tossed it up through the center of the pattern "—I don't know—" the two potatoes came down again, and he sent them back up "—what else to do."

He waited until the smattering of applause had faded, then switched to a more standard three-ball rotation. "My uncle taught me that one," he said, shifting this time to a circle pattern. "I had another uncle who was cross-eyed. Let me show you how *he* juggled."

He went through his juggling routine, then switched to some sleight-of-hand tricks. The last time he'd done this, back when he and Draycos had stumbled into a Wistawki bonding ceremony on the Vagran Colony, he'd had the dragon there to help with the performance.

Now, of course, Draycos had to stay out of sight across his back. And much as it hurt to admit it, the act wasn't nearly as good without him.

But the audience didn't care. So starved for entertainment were these people that practically anything he did would have been greeted with the same excitement. He could have spent a whole hour doing cross-eyed juggler jokes, and gotten just as much applause. Even Fleck was watching from the back of the crowd, an odd look on his face.

He went through the card tricks, and the coin tricks, and the pea-under-the-cups tricks that Uncle Virge had taught him all those years ago. The slaves were loving it; but to Jack's increasingly worried annoyance, the audience he'd really hoped for was nowhere in sight. If they didn't show soon, all this would have been for nothing.

Mostly for nothing, anyway. Greb and Grib, at least, would probably never forget it.

He kept the show going for over an hour before privately giving up, and was on his last few lines of patter when he felt the warning touch of dragon claws on the back of his arm. Turning casually back to the table, he spotted what Draycos's sharp K'da ears had already picked up: an approaching car.

And in it were Crampatch and his spoiled daughter. Here to pick up a new toy.

"But as my cousin Fred on my Aunt Louise's side would say, when you need a cross-eyed juggler, there's never one around," he said, revving back up to full speed again. Scooping up the potatoes, he launched into an extra-complex juggling routine he'd saved just for this moment. After that came two more card tricks, one more rope trick, and finally another short juggling routine. Out of the corner of his eye, he could see the two Brummgas watching, as fascinated as everyone else.

Finally, he judged it was time to end the show. If Crampatch and his daughter weren't hooked by now, they never would be. "And that, ladies and gentlemen and honored Jantri guests, completes the afternoon's entertainment," he said, bowing deeply three times. "I hope you enjoyed the show; and I *really* hope someone knows where my laundry is. Thank you again."

The audience exploded into a wild racket of applause, cries, hoots, grunts, whistles, and squawks. Jack bowed again and again, all the time keeping an eye on the two Brummgas. The daughter seemed very insistent about something . . .

Eventually, he stopped bowing, and the audience broke up. Sort of broke up, anyway. While most of the slaves headed back to their other activities, several of them came up to thank Jack personally for the show.

Naturally, Greb, Grib, and Noy were right there in front. The Jantri twins were in the middle of their third round of thank-yous when Fleck bulled his way through the crowd. "Come on," he said, wiggling a finger at Jack. "Crampatch wants you."

"What about?" Jack asked, squeezing Greb and Grib's shoulders one last time as he stepped to Fleck's side.

"Interesting show," the big man said as he led Jack through the milling slaves toward Crampatch and his daughter. "You're not like anyone else we've ever had here. What else can you do?"

"You'd be surprised," Jack assured him. "What does Crampatch want?"

Fleck snorted under his breath. "His daughter wants a new toy," he said sourly. "You're it."

"I'm honored," Jack said.

"Don't be," Fleck warned. "You think they treat us badly here, just wait until they get you to the house."

Jack rubbed his face where the Brummga's slapstick had hit him. "I can hardly wait," he murmured.

"Yeah," Fleck grunted. "Just watch yourself."

CHAPTER 13

They took him through the gap in the hedge and back across the beautifully textured and cared-for Chookoock family grounds. In the daylight, Jack saw, the landscape was even more impressive than it had been at night. He also spotted several clumps of bushes that could easily be concealing guard posts.

At a small side door to the house, Crampatch turned him over to a tall, wiry Wistawk wearing a garish outfit in multiple shades of green and purple. Across his chest he wore the same red sash as Fleck. "Get it ready," Crampatch ordered, jerking a thumb at Jack. "And don't forget to hose it down. It stinks."

"Understood, Your Chanterling," the Wistawk said, bowing low. "Your Thumbleness," he added, bowing to the daughter.

The two Brummgas left. "This way, human," the Wistawk said, gesturing Jack in through the door.

A short corridor led them into the back of a large kitchen. A *very* large kitchen, in fact, far bigger than Jack would have expected even for a mansion this size. It was well equipped, too, with at least four cooking surfaces, six fire ovens, and four microwave ovens nestled in among the various work spaces and countertops. Off in one corner was an even bigger extravagance: a huge radiation oven nearly as big as the hotbox back in the slave colony. Probably for cooking whole animals.

In a pinch, it might also make a good emergency hiding place. Provided, of course, that he remembered to get out before they started cooking something.

Twenty or so slaves were already at work there, no doubt preparing the Chookoock family dinner. Most were hurrying around carrying pots and pans, or were at various work areas mixing or measuring or molding food into odd shapes. Another group was off at the three huge sinks cleaning up pans from previous cooking efforts.

Standing at a small recipe-storage desk, looking rather like the eye in the middle of a hurricane, was another Wistawk wearing a red sash. He was holding up a delicate-looking pastry and speaking into a portable recorder attached to a corner of the desk. Probably preparing the daily report, Jack decided, or possibly adding a new recipe to the collection.

"I am Heetoorieef," his guide identified himself as they exited the far side of the kitchen into a well-stocked pantry. "I am in charge of the household slaves. What are you?"

"I'm Noy," Jack told him. "It's nice to meet you."

"Yes," Heetoorieef murmured, pulling an electronic notepad from behind his sash and scribbling something on it. "Your room is with the rest of the slave quarters downstairs. I warn you it smells of paint—the Dolom who was in there last had been painted quite thoroughly by Her Thumbleness."

" 'Her Thumbleness?' "

"That is how you will address her," Heetoorieef said, a bit

tartly. "You will not be here long at any rate; but addressing any of the Brummgas wrongly will make that stay extremely unpleasant."

He half turned and looked Jack up and down. "I don't believe she's ever chosen a human before. What exactly are you good for?"

"I was doing a magic show when she spotted me," Jack told him, deciding not to take offense at the question. Heetoorieef *was* trying to be civil, he knew. He just didn't do it very well. Probably all that time spent with Brummgas. "I can juggle some, too."

"I see," Heetoorieef said. His tone was still polite, but Jack could tell he really didn't much care one way or the other.

Which wasn't surprising. Heetoorieef's job was to keep the household running smoothly, to make sure the slaves didn't make some mistake that would get them—and him— in trouble with the slavemasters. Having to take time out to teach Her Thumbleness's latest toy how to behave was just one more headache for him to deal with.

"You'll need to take a bath," Heetoorieef went on. "Unless you really would prefer being hosed down?"

Jack grinned. "A bath will do fine," he assured the other. "Can you find me a change of clothes, too?"

"That was next on the list," Heetoorieef said stiffly, as if offended that Jack would think a proper slave overseer would need to be reminded about that. "A magic performer and juggler. Yes, I believe I have just the outfit. I will bring it to your room while you bathe."

"Thank you," Jack said. "What do I do then?"

"When you are dressed report to me in my office," Heetoorieef said. "It is a small room beside the kitchen. You will entertain Her Thumbleness while she eats her dinner."

Jack's room was Nui Trach—Number Eight in the Brummgan numbering system—in the second basement down from the kitchen floor. It contained a wide bed, a two-drawer dresser, a wooden chair, a clock-intercom, and a single overhead light.

The bed's mattress was stiff, the chair was hard, and there was barely enough room for him to turn around without bumping into something else. But after a week and a half in the slave colony sleeping hut, the place felt like the luxury corridor on the *Star of Wonder*.

The slaves' bathroom was at the end of the hall. It was smaller than the wash area back in the slave colony, and not a lot fancier. But it was clean, it had a real bathtub, and it had lots of hot water.

He soaked in the tub as long as he dared—about five minutes—then washed himself thoroughly and returned to his room. Heetoorieef had been there in his absence, and had left him the most ridiculous outfit he'd ever seen. It consisted of a loose tunic, tights, and a floppy hat with bells on it. Everything was done up in the same pattern of huge purple-and-green diamonds.

"An interesting design," Draycos commented as Jack shook out the tunic and held it up. "Is that what is called a harlequin outfit?"

"You got me," Jack said, sitting down on the bed and starting to pull on the tights. They felt prickly and itchy, he noticed. Maybe they would feel better once they were all the way on. "I've never even heard the word before."

"A harlequin was a clown or buffoon in an Old Earth French theater style," Draycos explained. "He typically wore a mask and diamond-patterned clothing."

"Um," Jack grunted, standing up and smoothing out the tights along his legs. Nope; they didn't feel any better this way. He would just have to hope he would get used to the prickling. "Been reading through the *Essenay*'s dictionary, have we?"

"At your suggestion," Draycos said. "That shirt appears too large for you."

"Sure does," Jack agreed, slipping the tunic over his head. Too large, nothing—he could swim a couple laps of backstroke in here. He wondered what sort of alien the outfit had been designed for. "Maybe I can tuck it in somehow."

"If you like, I can help hold it," the dragon offered. "Like this."

Jack felt some weight at the small of his back as Draycos lifted his forepaws out into three-dimensional mode. There was a twitch as the dragon's claws caught the material and pulled it close in against Jack's back.

"Not bad," Jack said, twisting his torso and waving his arms experimentally. "Feels pretty good. On second thought, though, we'd better not. We don't want someone checking out the outfit later and wondering how I was holding it together."

"I understand." Draycos released his claws, and the tunic material billowed out again like a ship's sail looking for a nice westerly breeze. "You expect them to study you more closely, then?"

"They will if we give them enough time," Jack said. "That's why I gave Heetoorieef Noy's name instead of mine."

"You think Gazen will see the list of which slaves are currently in the house."

"I would if *I* were in charge of slaves around here," Jack said, trying to tuck the tunic into the back of the tights. Without a mirror he couldn't see what it looked like, but it felt like it looked stupid. "I figure if he sees my name on Heetoorieef's list, I'll be back on the wrong side of the hedge in nothing flat."

"He may be at dinner tonight."

"In which case, we're probably in trouble," Jack said, giving up and pulling the back of the tunic free again. "Let's hope the Chookoock family doesn't let non-Brummgas eat with them. If we can get through this one meal, we should be in."

"You plan to hit the computers tonight?"

"I'm sure going to give it a try," Jack said. No special shoes had come with the outfit; slipping on his own, he secured them and looked himself up and down. "At least I'm not going out in public in this thing," he said with a sigh. "Let's go entertain Her Thumbleness."

"Yes," Draycos said. "Is 'break a leg' the proper response?"

"That's the one," Jack confirmed.

"Thank you," Draycos said. "Break a leg."

CHAPTER 14

From the information Uncle Virge had pulled up, Jack had known the Chookoocks were a big family, spanning at least six generations and including over a hundred Brummgas.

What he hadn't expected was to find the whole ugly crowd of them dropping in for dinner on this same night.

Maybe they *weren't* all there, gathered around the long tables beneath the hanging flags in the huge banquet hall. Jack never had a chance to actually count them. But if they were missing any of them, they weren't missing very many.

The scene rather reminded Jack of one of those old Medieval costume dramas, the kind Uncle Virgil had always loved. The sort of drama where Robin Hood or someone charged in just before dessert and dropped a deer on the table in front of the king.

Here, of course, the tables were made of long slabs of dark green stone instead of rough-cut wood, and the light came from modern glow domes instead of flaming torches. And given the number of armed guards stationed at the various doors, no one was likely to be showing up with a deer unless it was properly cooked. But aside from that, the effect was much the same.

One of the serving slaves led Jack over to a table off to

one side, where a couple dozen Brummgan children were already seated. Their table, unlike the others, was covered with a brightly colored patchwork tablecloth that hung all the way to the floor. Some of the children were coloring or drawing on it, while others were busy carving slits into it with their table knives.

It wasn't until Jack came closer that a familiar section of the cloth caught his eye: one of the battle flags of the Whinyard's Edge mercenaries.

And then he understood. The tablecloth was composed of mercenary banners and military flags, all sewn together and given to the children to amuse themselves.

And of course, what the children wanted to do most was scribble on or otherwise insult them. Typical Brummgan behavior.

Crampatch's daughter was seated in the hostess's position at the middle of the table. She was wearing a large curly-edged hat, and was beating cheerfully on the kid next to her with a long serving spoon. Stepping in front of her, Jack bowed low. "Your Thumbleness," he said.

She stopped hitting her neighbor and pointed at him with her spoon. *"Brolach-ah mischt heeh,"* she said.

Jack felt his heart catch in his throat. "I'm sorry, Your Thumbleness?" he asked carefully.

"Brolach-ah mischt heeh," she repeated, more insistently this time. *"Brolach-ah mischt heeh simt."*

Jack could feel sweat gathering beneath his collar. He'd spent the journey to Brum-a-dum studying the Brummgan script, but he hadn't counted on having to know their spoken language, too. "I'm sorry, Your Thumbleness—"

The apology didn't make it any further. Without warning

someone grabbed his shoulder and spun him around. He had just enough time to see that he was looking into a large Brummgan face when a hand closed around his throat and lifted him straight up off the ground.

"Do you deaf, human?" the Brummga snarled. His voice was thickly accented and barely understandable. His hot breath, blasting into Jack's face, smelled like barbecued pork mixed with dead seaweed. In his free hand he held a large cup half full of a thick, greasy-looking liquid. Drunk, right up to his eyelids. "Do you deaf?" he repeated. "Or do you stupid?"

Jack clutched at the hand wrapped around his neck, gasping for breath. He tried to say something—to plead, to apologize, to say *anything*. But he couldn't get any words out past that grip. Maybe the Brummga was too drunk to know what he was doing.

He looked around frantically, as least as far around as he could with his head held this way. If someone else was paying attention to what was happening here—if he could just signal that the drunken Brummga was in danger of killing a valuable slave.

They *were* watching. They were watching, and laughing, and cheering their drunken friend on.

And with that the message finally got through. The message that the berry-picking and the slave colony and even the hotbox hadn't been able to teach him.

No one cared about him here. No one cared if he was happy or hungry, or whether he lived or died. He was a slave. He was property. He was a child's toy.

And if he got broken, well, Her Thumbleness would just

go back out through the thorn hedge to the toy store and pick out something else. White spots were beginning to dance in front of Jack's eyes—

And then, suddenly, his vision cleared. The awful pressure on his throat was gone, and he could breathe again.

He blinked with confusion. The pressure was gone, but he was still dangling by his neck in the Brummga's grip, with the Brummga still shouting thickly at him.

No pressure . . . but he was still hanging?

And then he felt a subtle change at his throat; and all at once he understood. He could breathe because the Brummga was no longer holding his neck, at least not directly. Draycos had moved part of himself underneath the alien's hand and risen up from Jack's skin. Not much, but enough to take the pressure of that hand onto himself.

"She tell you perform," the Brummga shouted into his face. "Do you perform *now*."

With a contemptuous shove, he tossed Jack backward. Jack hit the floor, flailing a little for balance as he landed. As he did so he felt Draycos pull away from his neck, retreating back beneath the harlequin tunic. Hopefully, no one had spotted the dragon's gold scales before he'd gotten out of sight.

"Perform, right," he said, turning back to the children's table and scooping up three of the items from the vegetable bowl. They looked like the potato-things he'd juggled for Greb and Grib, only bigger. A higher-quality food than they gave the slaves, no doubt. He tossed one of the potatoes into the air—

A heavy hand slapped against the side of his head, knocking him flat onto the floor. He caught a glimpse of the potato he'd tossed rolling under the table as he dropped the other two beside him. "Do you deaf, human?" the drunken Brummga screamed. "She tell you *perform*. Not eat. Perform."

"I *was* performing," Jack protested, rolling over onto his back and pushing himself up onto his arms into an almost-sitting position. "I needed—"

He saw the foot coming, but there was no time to do anything but get ready for the impact. The kick slammed a glancing blow onto his left shoulder, and he rolled with it, spinning around nearly onto his stomach in the process.

"I *was* performing," he repeated, scrambling back around onto his back again. His leg swiveled around as he did so, his left foot catching the bottom of the tablecloth and sliding underneath it.

And as it did so, he felt a sudden ripping of the tights at his ankle. There was a surge of weight there—

And Draycos was gone.

Jack looked up at the Brummga standing over him, a tangle of conflicting emotions swirling through him. He'd been wrong: there was indeed one person in the room who cared whether he lived or died. Draycos, poet-warrior of the K'da, was loose and ready to protect him from this murderous slab of meat.

But rolling in right behind that thought came the deeper reality of the situation. Draycos couldn't risk his mission and the lives of his people for Jack this way. Even if he took out this one Brummga, there were way too many others in the room for him to handle.

Had he gotten so caught up in these senseless attacks on Jack that he wasn't thinking straight?

And then, even as his racing mind tried to sort out what to

do, he felt something tug at the sole of his shoe. A dragon's claw, digging deftly into the thick rubber there.

Into the secret compartment where Jack's spare comm clip was hidden.

That fact had just enough time to register before the drunken Brummga grabbed his arm and hauled him up onto his feet again. "Now you perform," he repeated, shaking Jack back and forth and then shoving him back against the edge of the table. "Not eat. Not throw. Perform."

"Certainly, sir, at once," Jack promised. "Let me just put the food back first."

Before the Brummga could object, he dropped to his knees. Grabbing the two visible potatoes with his left hand, he stuck his right arm under the tablecloth where the third one had disappeared. He just hoped Draycos hadn't kicked it somewhere else.

He hadn't. The potato was right where he'd expected it to be.

And as his hand closed around the escaped vegetable, he felt the cool metal of the comm clip against his palm. Draycos, anticipating him perfectly, had balanced the device right on top of the potato.

The Brummga behind him was rumbling warningly. "I've got it," Jack assured him quickly as Draycos melted onto his hand and slithered up his sleeve. "See?" he added as he stood up, palming the comm clip and showing the potato to the drunken Brummga. "Let me show you."

He turned back to the table and replaced the vegetables. The children, he noted without surprise, were watching the whole thing with excited glee. They were here to eat, and to play, and to be entertained.

And whether Her Thumbleness's new toy did magic tricks for them, or whether he simply got himself beaten to a pulp in front of them, they would be happy. A show was a show, after all.

"Now, let's see," he said, rubbing his neck where the Brummga had been squeezing. Under cover of the movement, he attached the comm clip to the inside of his harlequin tunic and clicked it on. "*Brolach-ah mischt heeh simt,* was it?"

" 'Do the under-the-cup trick now,' " Uncle Virge's voice murmured in his ear.

Jack grimaced. So that was what she'd wanted. No wonder his attempt to juggle had gone flat. "Right," he said briskly. "One under-the-cup trick, coming right up."

Gathering together three empty glasses, he snagged an acorn-sized nut from a bowl on the table and slipped it under one of the glasses. "Now watch very carefully—"

He did the trick twice, both times to the great and loud amusement of Her Thumbleness and the other Brummgan children. "*Crastni miu simt cumos alekx,*" Her Thumbleness said when he'd finished, banging her spoon on the table.

" 'You may now juggle for me,' " Uncle Virge translated.

Jack sighed to himself. *Now* he could juggle. She could have had the same thing three minutes earlier and saved him a beating in the process. But no. What Her Thumbleness wanted, how she wanted it, when she wanted it, and nothing else.

"Yes, Your Thumbleness," he said, setting aside the glasses and again picking up the three potatoes.

It was going to be a very long night.

CHAPTER 15

The night turned out to be a lot longer than he'd expected.

Earlier, he'd been surprised that the whole Chookoock family seemed to have dropped in for dinner. Now, with Uncle Virge's running translation, he was able to catch enough bits and pieces of conversation to figure out what was actually going on.

It was, it seemed, Her Thumbleness's High Day.

He never did nail down whether it was her birthday, or some other kind of anniversary, or even just the day they all celebrated her favorite color. Whatever it was, though, it was a big deal around the Chookoock household.

And Her Thumbleness was playing it for all it was worth. After dinner came a huge dessert that looked like a sentence of death by chocolate and ground-up tree bark. Apparently, the idea was to make as much of a mess as possible while eating it. Her Thumbleness and her friends did that part very well.

After that came game time, with the chocolate-smeared children and a few of the adults gathering in an underground room about the size of a regulation basketball court. The games generated nearly as much noise as the whole crowd upstairs had been able to produce, with the added feature of bone-crunching thuds and wallops as the kids ran into each other.

They played a number of different games, with a whole range of different types of balls. The nearest Jack got to figuring out the rules to any of them was that whenever one Brummga had a chance to run into another one, he did so.

That, and whenever Her Thumbleness came to the sidelines for a break her new court jester had better have a trick or something ready to amuse her.

Under the circumstances, it was impossible for him to slip away to go computer hunting. Standing at the sidelines, listening to a couple of the adults breathing loudly behind him, he wondered if the party girl was ever going to run out of steam.

He thought that moment had finally come when the children dropped their balls and disks and toss-bladders in the middle of the court and all came jogging back to the sidelines. But no such luck. After the games, apparently, Her Thumbleness had scheduled a sleepover with several of her closer friends.

They headed upstairs again, jabbering away in a dozen different conversations. Jack trudged along behind them, bone-tired but trying hard not to show it. If Her Thumbleness's new toy didn't work the way she wanted it to, she would almost certainly send it back, and he couldn't afford that.

Besides, even a Brummgan kid on a massive sugar high couldn't keep up this pace forever. Eventually, she and her friends would have to give up on the fun and frolic and get some sleep.

Eventually, they did, winding down their chattering and

boardcomp games and collapsing one by one onto the heavy mats that had been set up for them in Her Thumbleness's bedroom suite. But by the time the girl dismissed Jack with a lazy wave of her hand, the sky to the east was starting to glow red. The rest of the slave staff was already hard at work downstairs, cooking breakfast and preparing the house for their masters' day.

And it wasn't just the slaves who were on the move, either. Some of the Brummgas and their staff were stirring, as well. Even as Jack headed along the side of the large entryway toward the stairs to the slave quarters, he caught a glimpse of Gazen going into an office on the far side of the chamber.

Luckily, Gazen didn't see him. But any hopes Jack might still have had of trying to get to the computers ended right there. Wandering slaves he might be willing to risk. A wandering Gazen he wasn't.

"Well, that was fun," he commented tiredly as he closed the door of his tiny room and dropped onto the bed. "Wasn't that fun, everybody?"

"What exactly are you *doing*, lad?" Uncle Virge demanded. "Some kind of marathon magic show?"

"Pretty close," Jack admitted, wincing as he bent his left leg up to get to his shoe. After all those hours on his feet, his knees were as stiff as a customs official's glare.

With a burst of gold scales, Draycos leaped out of his collar and landed on the narrow strip of floor beside the bed. "May I help?" he asked. Without waiting for an answer, he began unfastening Jack's shoes.

"Thanks," Jack said, letting his leg go flat again.

"It is the least I can do," Draycos said, getting the first

shoe off and setting it down on the floor. "I have been of little aid to you so far."

"You certainly have," Jack assured him. "If you hadn't gotten the comm clip out when you did—" He shook his head.

"What do you mean?" Uncle Virge asked suspiciously. "What's been happening?"

"The Brummgas treat their slaves like low-grade costume jewelry," Jack told him. "If the slaves don't understand what they're saying, they treat them like punching bags."

Uncle Virge muttered something nasty under his breath. "Are you all right, lad?"

"I'm fine," Jack assured him, wiggling his toes as Draycos got the other shoe off. "It was really only the one Brummga at the dinner, and he was too drunk to really hit straight. Mostly, I've just been run off my feet."

"And there has been no opportunity yet to locate the computers," Draycos added.

"But I *am* in the house," Jack pointed out. "That's definitely progress." He yawned widely. "I'd better get some sleep while I can, though. Her Thumbleness will probably want me to brush her teeth for her when she wakes up."

Uncle Virge sighed softly. "All right, lad," he said. "Pleasant dreams."

Jack clicked off the comm clip and turned his head to look at Draycos. The dragon was pacing the floor, his back arched and uncomfortable looking. "You coming aboard?" he asked.

"I think I will remain out for awhile," Draycos said.

Jack frowned. Offhand, he couldn't remember ever seeing the dragon quite this twitchy. "What's wrong?"

Draycos paused in his pacing. His long neck twisted toward Jack, then turned away. "I am all right," he muttered.

"Sure you are," Jack said, studying him. "Come on, what's the problem? Her Thumbleness getting to you or something?"

Reluctantly, he thought, Draycos came to a halt. "It is not her," he said. "It is this place. It is all of this place." His tongue slashed out in emphasis. "I am sorry."

"Sorry for what?" Jack asked. "I don't like it much, either."

The dragon twisted his neck oddly. "It is not a matter of liking or disliking," he said, his voice suddenly very quiet. "For a K'da, this is an echo of a time long past. A terrible time."

Jack sat up on the bed, his fatigue suddenly forgotten. Something in the dragon's tone had sent a shiver straight through him. "Sounds serious," he said in his most soothing, tell-me-all-about-it voice.

And was instantly ashamed of himself. Uncle Virgil had taught him that tone for wheedling information out of people they were trying to scam. He shouldn't be using it on a friend. Especially not on a friend who could carve his initials in steel plate. "I mean . . . you want to talk about it?"

For a long moment the dragon was silent. "We were not always with the Shontine," he said at last. "In the beginning we were on another world, with another host race."

"Who?" Jack asked. "I mean, what were their names?"

"We remember them as the Dhghem," Draycos said. "They were strong and cheerful, full of laughter and wisdom. We were both their symbionts and their friends."

"Sounds perfect," Jack said. It sounded *too* perfect, actually, but that was to be expected. Whatever nuggets of real history there might be in this story, they were almost certainly soaked in myth, sprinkled with legend, and served up with a side order of wishful thinking.

Still, he was hardly in a position to point fingers. Uncle Virgil had never talked about Jack's own parents, and he had only vague memories of them himself. But that hadn't stopped him from spending hours wondering what they'd been like, or fantasizing about how his life would have been different if they hadn't died when he was three.

And in every one of those daydreams, his parents had come out taller and kinder and more handsome and more important than any human beings could actually be. Draycos and his half-mythical hosts were probably no different. "So what went wrong?"

Draycos started pacing again. "Our world was attacked by slavers," he said, his voice so low that Jack could hardly hear him. "They came from the stars, with fire and death and supreme arrogance. The Cark, they called themselves. They came seeking lives to steal. They saw us, and decided they wanted us."

"You fought back, of course," Jack murmured.

"With all the power and skill we possessed," Draycos said. "But in the end it was all for nothing. The slavers had strength beyond ours, and weapons far beyond those of the Dhghem. They captured many of us and our hosts and then returned to the sky."

The dragon paused again, his neck arched, his glowing green eyes staring off into the distance. "There are songs about our time of captivity," he said. "One day, perhaps, I will sing one of them for you. For many years, many generations, we served the Cark as slaves. The K'da worked or fought for them, or guarded their slave auctions. Their Dhghem hosts also did some work, but mostly they were held hostage for our good behavior."

"Didn't they try to fight back?" Jack asked.

"Of course," Draycos said. "There are also many songs about those attempts. But in the end all of them failed. The Cark were too strong, and too cunning. Eventually, most of the Dhghem gave up and resigned themselves to their fate."

"Let me guess," Jack said. "The Cark decided they'd beaten you and started getting sloppy."

"You are very perceptive," Draycos said. "But even with relaxed attention, the Cark still watched them closely enough that a rebellion would never have succeeded."

He paused, staring through the wall again. "Well?" Jack prompted.

"Something happened that had never happened before," Draycos said. "Something no one had ever thought *could* happen. Completely by accident, we discovered that a newly collected group of Cark slaves could serve as hosts."

"The Shontine?"

"Exactly," Draycos said. "They were thought to be poor soldiers, so the Cark used them as menial slaves."

He flicked his tongue around again. "Much as you and I have now become for the Brummgas."

"I get it," Jack said, nodding. "Because they were just simple slaves, they gave you the advantage you needed."

"What do you mean?" Draycos asked, turning his eyes on Jack.

"I mean, it's obvious," Jack said, suddenly feeling a little flustered. Even at the most relaxed of times, the dragon's stare was a little disconcerting. "Slaves are treated like dirt, or like animals. But you can turn that to your advantage. As long as the Shontine behaved themselves, the Cark probably hardly even noticed them."

Draycos was still staring, but the tip of his tail was tracing out slow circles. "Interesting," he said. "I do not think I have ever thought of it quite that way."

Jack shrugged. "It's the way I was brought up to think," he pointed out. "No one expects a seven-year-old kid to be able to pull the stunts Uncle Virgil taught me. And you already said they didn't think the Shontine could fight."

"True," Draycos said, still sounding thoughtful. "At any rate, the Shontine were eager to help. Together, we made our plans, and awaited our opportunity."

"Where were the Dhghem in all this?"

"Those who had not yet given up hope of freedom were part of the planning," Draycos said. "The others . . . we could not risk their knowing."

Jack grimaced. "Must have been tough for you."

"We did what we had to do," Draycos said. "Our opportunity came some months later when the Cark landed on a new world to collect fresh slaves. The inhabitants fought back fiercely; and in the battles, some of the best K'da warriors began to slip away."

"Faking their deaths," Jack said, nodding. "And of course, since the Cark were keeping tabs on the Dhghem, they knew that even if the K'da had just run away, they'd be dead within a few hours anyway."

"Correct," Draycos said. "Instead, the warriors slipped onto the bodies of the chosen Shontine, hiding beneath the long clothing they wore. And when the Cark finished their raid and lifted their ships into the sky, we struck."

He stopped, his back crest stiffening with memory. "It was a short battle," he said, his voice quiet again. "We were all aboard one ship, with all our strength gathered, and had the advantage of surprise. But even so we nearly lost the battle."

His tail lashed the air. "Someday I will sing you that song, as well."

"So now you had a ship," Jack said.

"Yes," Draycos said. "But there was no way to return home. We did not know the location, and it had been too long for the ship's records to be of any use. We offered to return the Shontine to their world, but they were afraid other Cark ships would come looking for them and us. So instead we went in search of a new home where we could all live in peace and safety."

"All three groups of you?" Jack asked. "K'da, Shontine, and Dhghem?"

"That was our hope," Draycos murmured. "But for the Dhghem, sadly, the time of peace was all too short. Too many of them were lost in the final battle aboard the Cark ship, and there were no females left among them."

Jack winced. "Oh."

"Those who remained lived out their lives among us in peace and great honor," Draycos went on. "But when they died, it was the end of their line."

Jack felt a tightness in his throat. "So you and the Shontine made yourselves a home," he said. "Only to be driven away from it by the Valahgua."

"Yes," Draycos said. "Still, we had many centuries of peace there. And though we now have been forced to flee, we also found friends and allies during our stay. In balance, we have no cause to complain."

"If you say so," Jack said. " 'Course, that's never stopped anyone else."

Draycos seemed to draw himself up. "Perhaps not," he said firmly. "But a poet-warrior of the K'da must hold himself to higher standards. We must learn from our past, but we must not allow our history to write itself over the present. Our task is to create the future."

"Right," Jack said, deciding to take the dragon's word for whatever it was he'd just said. Did all K'da warriors talk like that, he wondered, or was it just Draycos? "So what part of the future did you want to create tonight?"

"We can only control that part immediately before us," Draycos said. "And our first task to that end is to rest and gather our strength."

"I was hoping you'd say that," Jack said, yawning. "You going to sleep, too, or haven't you finished pacing yet?"

"I have finished," Draycos said. Stepping to Jack's side, he slipped up his sleeve. "Thank you for listening. And thank you, too, for your words of wisdom."

"You're welcome," Jack told him, wondering what words of wisdom the dragon was talking about.

Maybe later he would ask about it. For now, any further conversation would have to be in the form of sleep-talking. "Pleasant dreams," he said, and scooched himself down to lay flat on the bed again.

Draycos might have said something back to him. But Jack was asleep long before he ever could have heard it.

CHAPTER 16

Her Thumbleness woke up five hours later, as preparations for the noon meal were underway in one of the smaller dining rooms. Naturally, she woke up bellowing for her new pet human.

Heetoorieef himself came to fetch Jack, getting a grip on the collar of Jack's harlequin outfit and hauling him up into a sitting position on his cot. He shoved a cup of something hot into his hands, ordered him to drink it, then crouched down and pushed the boy's shoes onto his tired feet.

That task completed, he half pulled, half guided Jack to the stairs. The slave quarters were buzzing with the meal-time preparations, but Heetoorieef managed to move him through the controlled chaos without getting either of them run down.

The stuff in the cup was bizarre, tasting like a mixture of Brussels sprouts, coconut, and apricot jam. It was a combination even Draycos might have turned up his long snout at, and that was saying a lot.

But taster's nightmare or not, the concoction did its job. Even before Heetoorieef got him to the stairs, Jack could feel his brain kicking into gear again. By the time they reached the main floor, and the Wistawk took the cup from him with a muttered "good luck," he was wide awake.

The day started like a rerun of the night before. Her Thumbleness's friends ran around playing loud Brummgan games and activities, mostly ignoring Jack as he stood silently by, against a wall. Every once in a while someone would suddenly notice him, or Her Thumbleness would decide she needed to show off her new toy again, and he would be called on to perform.

But as the afternoon wore on, he could see the signs of fatigue starting to build in his audience. Even Brummgas couldn't keep up this pace forever, and the children had already pushed themselves way too far. The demands on Jack became sharper, and the slaps and shoves more frequent, sometimes even when he'd done exactly as he'd been ordered. A couple of hours more of this, he knew, and Her Thumbleness would collapse into a Brummga-sized heap whether she liked it or not.

The only question was which of them was going to crack first. With only five hours of sleep under his own belt, Jack wasn't exactly at the top of his game, either. Moreover, Her Thumbleness had probably spent the night before her party snoozing lazily in that wide, soft bed she and her playmates had been wrestling on in the early hours of the morning. Jack, in contrast, had spent that night in the hotbox.

But Her Thumbleness was a Brummga, and a child Brummga at that. Jack was human, and fourteen years old. Pride alone insisted that he outlast her.

He did, but just barely. She was halfway through the evening meal when she threw a tantrum over absolutely nothing Jack could figure out. Apparently even her father had had enough of her for one day, and summarily dismissed her back to her room.

Even in his anger, though, Crampatch showed himself to be a tower of jelly as far as his daughter was concerned. When she demanded that she be allowed to take her new toy upstairs with her, he gave in with only a token protest.

Her Thumbleness was still mad when they reached her bedroom. But if her spirit was eager to play punching bag with her slave, her flesh was already halfway to dreamland. She picked on him for a few minutes, demanding a trick and then loudly declaring it wasn't good enough. But she was fading rapidly. She made only a single half-hearted attempt to hit him, and even there the gesture evaporated along the way as she apparently decided it wasn't worth the effort. Ordering him to lie down on the floor at the foot of her bed, she trudged to the small artificial swamp off the sleeping area for her bedtime preparations.

Ten minutes later, the room dark except for a softly glowing starscape set into the domed ceiling, she was snoring peacefully.

Jack listened to the rhythm of her breathing for another half hour before he decided it was safe to talk. "Well," he whispered to Draycos. "Here we are again."

"Yes," the dragon answered. "I am sorry, Jack. I wish there was something I could have done to prevent this."

"Are you kidding?" Jack countered. "This, my gold-plated friend, is as good as it gets."

There was a short silence. "I do not understand."

"Where was I last night?" Jack asked. "Well, this morning, I mean, when I finally got to bed. I was downstairs in the slave quarters, right? Where there are lots of people watching, and probably a few monitors scattered around to make sure the slaves don't wander into places they're not supposed to go."

He smiled tightly in the darkness. "*Now* where are we?"

"We are in the Chookoock family living area," Draycos said, his voice suddenly thoughtful. "Where there may not be any such monitors."

"Exactly," Jack said. "Once everyone goes to bed, we'll have as much freedom of movement as we're ever likely to get."

He eased himself up and looked carefully across the bed. Her Thumbleness was lying half under the blankets like a dropped rag doll, her flat nose waggling in rhythm with her snores. "Which means tonight's the night," he added as he lay back down on the floor. His pulse was pounding in his ears, his whole body tingling with excitement. For the first time in a long time, he felt really psyched up for a job. "Tonight we hit Gazen's computers."

But it was one thing for Jack to be ready for a job. It was something else for the job to be ready for him.

For starters, Her Thumbleness was a kid. That meant that her normal, non–High Day bedtime was earlier than that of the adult Brummgas. And on this particular night, of course, she'd been kicked upstairs early, which gave Jack that much more time to lie around staring at the ceiling.

And then came a twist he hadn't expected. The noise of clumping Brummgas had faded down the hallway; and he was just starting the one-hour countdown he would give them to fall asleep, when he began to hear the soft humming of cleaning machines and the stuttering footsteps of

Wistawki feet. Apparently, only now were the house slaves fanning out through the Brummgan residential areas to do their house-cleaning duties.

It was about as bizarre a setup as Jack had ever heard of. In every other place he'd visited over his lifetime, that kind of cleaning always took place during the day, while the occupants were out working or busy with other activities. Here, it seemed, the Brummgas preferred to have it done practically under their feet as they prepared for bed. Apparently, the Chookoock family didn't want *anyone,* not even their own slaves, poking around when they weren't there.

"Jack?" Draycos's voice said softly in his ear.

Jack jerked silently awake, realizing only then that he'd fallen asleep. The dragon was crouched over him, his green eyes glowing faintly, his red-edged golden scales glittering in the pale light from the ceiling starscape. "What is it?" he whispered back.

"I believe it is clear now," Draycos said. "It is also getting late."

"I'll bet," Jack said, rubbing his knuckles into his eyes. "Any idea what time it is?"

"According to Her Thumbleness's clock, it is just before four in the morning."

Jack winced. By six o'clock, he knew from the previous morning, the breakfast staff would be moving around downstairs. That gave him less than two hours to wring that mercenary data out of Gazen's computers. "Then we'd better get cracking," he said.

The corridor outside Her Thumbleness's room was dark and deserted. Jack eased toward the stairway, keeping near the wall and watching for tripwires or other intruder snares. Given the late-night cleaning activity, he had already decided there probably wouldn't be any. But in this line of work, it didn't pay to take anything for granted.

It was just as well he hadn't. The same person who had wired up the gatekeeper's house had apparently had a few gadgets left over after finishing that job. Jack found a tripwire at the top of the stairway, and a pressure plate four steps down.

Clearly, the Chookoock family was serious about their privacy. Or maybe they just didn't want Her Thumbleness making midnight raids on the kitchen.

But that was all there was, and a few minutes later he was crouched beside Gazen's office door. "There will most likely be security inside," Draycos warned in his ear.

"I know," Jack said, studying the lock carefully. Sturdy enough, but nothing he couldn't handle.

Unless, of course, it held a surprise or two. "How about we take a look?" he suggested, shifting around and pressing his back against the door.

"Certainly." The dragon moved along his skin, and Jack felt him extend his two-dimensional form outward, arching himself "over" the door.

For a minute nothing happened. Jack held position, feeling tiny movements against his skin as Draycos shifted around, studying the door and the office itself. Back when he and Draycos had first met, this little K'da talent hadn't been much more than a curiosity. Draycos had been barely able to speak the language, couldn't read a word of it, and knew absolutely nothing about Orion Arm technology. Sending him to look through locked doors hadn't been much better than giving the job to a trained monkey.

But now, things were different. Draycos was a quick study, and had been eager to learn everything he could about humans and the Orion Arm—

Jack's breath caught suddenly in his throat. For a second there, something about the way Draycos was hanging onto his back had felt different. As if the dragon had somehow been . . .

He frowned. *Slipping* was the word that had come to mind.

But Draycos couldn't slip. Could he? In fact, wouldn't sliding off Jack's skin in his two-dimensional form be fatal?

His mind flashed back to their first meeting, when Draycos had been about to die from being too long without a host. If he'd been alone much longer, he would have gone two-dimensional anyway and drifted off into nothingness.

Could something like that be happening now?

He took a deep breath, careful to keep his back pressed firmly against the door. *Steady,* he ordered himself. After all, Draycos slipped off Jack's body all the time, every time he popped back into his three-dimensional form. It was just a matter of timing, that was all. A matter of the dragon doing the transition right as he came off Jack's skin. No problem.

So why was it suddenly feeling so strange?

"Draycos?" he whispered. "You all right?"

There was no answer. He was opening his mouth to try again when there was a stirring, and the dragon came fully and solidly back onto his skin. "There are no alarms in the door mechanism that I can see," he reported from Jack's right shoulder.

"What about the rest of the room?" Jack asked. "Cameras or motion detectors?"

"There appears to be a single camera in the upper left corner of the room," the dragon said. "It is pointed at the door, but covers most of the office."

"That's it?"

"That was all I could see," Draycos replied. "But I do not claim to be an expert yet at these matters."

"No, but you're probably right," Jack assured him. "Gazen's got that overconfident attitude we professional thieves love to see. Besides, here in the middle of the mansion, what does he need security for?"

"We will hope you are correct," Draycos said. "What about the camera?"

"Were there wires attached?" Jack asked. "Or did it seem to be wireless?"

"There were definitely wires," the dragon said. "I could see them going into the wall.

Jack nodded. Again, as he would have expected. The signal from wireless systems could be tapped into by someone who knew what he was doing, possibly even from outside the house. And if there was one thing Gazen wouldn't want, it would be strangers looking over his shoulder. "We should be able to get to them though the wall," he concluded. "Anything else?"

"Only a device labeled 'Dropskip Sequencer' built into the lock," Draycos said. "It does not appear to be an alarm, but I am certain it has some special purpose."

Jack's brief surge of overconfidence vanished. "Oh, it has a purpose, all right," he said with a sigh. "A sequencer keeps track of how many times the door has been opened. Practically foolproof, and practically undetectable. Except by K'da poet-warriors."

"Can it be disconnected?"

Jack shook his head. "Like I said, foolproof. Even if we were able to take it off, Gazen would know it had been tampered with and figure out someone had been inside. Might as well save ourselves the trouble."

"What is our plan, then?"

Jack chewed at his lip. His time was sliding away, he knew, the seconds vanishing like peanuts at an elephant convention. He had to get in, get the data, and get out. *And* he had to do it without Gazen knowing he'd been there.

Or did he?

He scratched his cheek as a new thought suddenly struck him. Did he really care whether Gazen knew he'd been in here? After all, the minute he got the mercenary data they needed, he and Draycos were going to be out of here. Through the front gate, over or around whatever security the Brummgas had hanging around, back to the *Essenay,* and off this rock.

But to knowingly reveal himself in the middle of a job went against every cubic inch of training Uncle Virgil had hammered into him. Very unprofessional. Also very stupid.

Draycos was still waiting. "All right," Jack said slowly. "Compromise. We'll take out the camera, but we won't worry about the sequencer."

"We do not care if Gazen knows someone has been inside?"

"With luck, we'll be long gone before he finds out," Jack assured him, straightening up.

"Perhaps," Draycos said doubtfully. "It does not seem, though, that this thing you call luck has been with us in any great quantity so far."

"Tell me about it," Jack said dryly, straightening up from his crouch. "But it's got to change sometime. Let's get around the other side of that wall and find those camera wires."

CHAPTER 17

Back aboard the *Star of Wonder,* the wiring for the purser's office security cameras had been hidden inside the walls. Here, in the middle of the Chookoock family stronghold, the designers had apparently decided not to be so fancy. The wires from Gazen's camera ran along the outside of the office wall, snugged up close against the ceiling.

It was a place most intruders wouldn't have a hope of reaching without a ladder, Jack included. Fortunately, he had Draycos instead. By standing on Jack's shoulders, the dragon was just able to reach up to the wires. A delicate puncture with one of his claws, and the camera was out of the game.

The lock on the door itself was only a little trickier. With the help of a flat lockpick Jack had hidden in his other shoe, he had it open in under two minutes.

And with less than fifteen minutes gone since they'd sneaked out of Her Thumbleness's room, they were inside Gazen's office.

"Okay," Jack breathed, standing with his back to the door and giving the room a quick once-over of his own. It looked clean, all right. Gazen definitely liked his privacy. "It should be downhill from here."

"Pardon?"

"It should be easy," Jack translated, crossing the room and sitting down in Gazen's chair. It was a very comfortable chair, soft and smooth and luxurious, and he found himself feeling a twinge of discomfort as he settled against the smooth material. He shouldn't be even touching something this nice, let alone be sitting in it.

He blinked, an ugly shock running through him. *I shouldn't even be touching something this nice?* What in space was *that* supposed to mean?

Because he'd certainly touched fancier stuff than this. Way fancier. He could remember standing on a carpet once that would have cost Gazen's entire year's salary, in the middle of a room decorated with original da Vincis and Michelangelos and ancient Chinese urns. What was this nonsense about not being good enough to sit in Gazen's lousy chair?

Because he was a slave, that was why. And even in the short time he'd been playing that role, the whole slave mind-set had wiggled its way into him. Quietly, subtly, and a lot deeper than he'd realized.

Until now.

Back in the slave compound, he'd often wondered why none of the others seemed interested in escaping from such a horrible place. Greb and Grib he could understand— they'd grown up there. But that didn't explain the others.

Now, he was finally beginning to understand. Once a person got used to something, it became normal. Normal, and familiar, and in a weird way even sort of comforting.

You knew what the boundaries were. You knew what you could do, and you knew what everyone else could do. You didn't have to think, or plan, or take any real responsibility for your life. In spite of all the work, and all the drabness, in some ways being a slave was easy.

And apparently for most of those back in the compound, that was what mattered.

Deliberately, defiantly, he ran his hands along the arm of the chair, pressing his fingers hard into the material. He was not a slave, and he would *not* think like one.

"Your language seems overfilled with these odd figures of speech," Draycos murmured. "I sometimes wonder that you can find any rules in it at all."

"We didn't exactly sit down and map the thing out ahead of time," Jack reminded him, forcing his mind back on track. Giving the arm of the chair one last squeeze, he leaned forward and switched on Gazen's computer. "The next time we invent a language, we'll take better notes."

"Thank you."

"Don't mention it," Jack said, watching as the computer ran through its startup procedure. Still, to be honest, were the slaves back there doing anything worse than what he himself had done?

Because he'd stolen and conned and cheated people knowing full well that it was wrong. He'd taken the easy route himself, sitting back and letting Uncle Virgil tell him what to do.

So he had no business feeling superior to Lisssa and Maerlynn and the others. In a lot of ways, he'd been a slave, too.

And *he'd* only had Uncle Virgil to keep him there. Not a laser-equipped wall and a few acres of armed Brummgas.

"You will be using your sewer-rat program, I presume," Draycos commented. "Someday I must meet the creature it is named after."

Jack frowned down at what he could see of the dragon's head beneath his shirt. That was the second time in as many minutes that Draycos had cut through some unpleasant thoughts with an odd and vaguely humorous comment. Was he getting nervous?

Or could he somehow be sensing Jack's dark mood and trying to nudge him out of it? "I'm sure you'd both be charmed," he said, hitching his chair closer to the keyboard. "And yes, that's what we're going to use. Unless you want to try slicing open the computer and seeing if you can sift all the right zeros and ones out of it."

"No, thank you," Draycos assured him.

The display finished its sequence and cleared to an impressive image of the Chookoock family mansion with the rising sun shooting rays of light across the sky behind it. "They don't think much of themselves, do they?" Jack muttered, peering down at the keyboard. It was all done up in Brummgan letters, naturally. Carefully, making sure he got it right, he keyed in the first part of the sewer-rat sequence.

Nothing happened.

Draycos's head rose slightly from his shoulder. "When will something happen?" he asked.

"In theory, about three seconds ago," Jack said. He tried the sequence again, double-checking it as he did. Still nothing. "We got trouble," he told the dragon, calling up the computer's spec page. A triple column of Brummgan words scrolled down on top of the picture of the mansion.

Even with the alien words, one glance was all it took. "Great," he growled. "This piece of junk isn't using a human operating system. It's running something Brummgan. Pretty old-fashioned, too, from the looks of it."

The dragon's head lifted higher, pushing the collar against the side of Jack's neck. "The sewer-rat trick works only with human-designed systems?"

Jack let his hands fall uselessly back into his lap. "You got it."

"Did you not consider this possibility? This *is* a Brumm-gan facility, after all."

"Sure, but Gazen is a human." Pushing back from the desk, Jack crossed his foot across his knee. A brief stab of pain ran through the thigh as he did so, a souvenir of one of Her Thumbleness's casual kicks. "Besides, who doesn't use human operating systems these days?"

The dragon's tongue flicked out toward the computer. "The Chookoock family, apparently," he said.

"Yeah," Jack agreed. Pulling out the hidden comm clip, he clicked it on. "Uncle Virge?"

"I'm here," the computer voice came back. "Are you all right, lad?"

"I'm alive," Jack said sourly. "For a slave, that's doing pretty good. Where are you?"

"Still at the Ponocce Spaceport," Uncle Virge said. "I've been putting Gazen's credit line to use fixing some of the damage and deterioration we've collected over the past few months."

"I hope you aren't letting them take apart anything vital," Jack warned. "We may need to get out of here on a minute's notice."

"Don't worry, I'm not," Uncle Virge said. "I hope that means that this call is good news."

"Actually, it's kind of mixed," Jack said. "The good news is that I'm in Gazen's office. The bad news is that the

Chookoock family's using an old Brummgan operating system."

"How old?"

"Uh—" Jack peered at the complicated script, trying to find the registration date.

"There," Draycos said. A foreleg rose from the back of Jack's right hand, an extended claw pointing to the lower left part of the display. "If I read correctly, that would be . . . forty years ago."

Uncle Virge whistled softly. "Forty *years*? I'm sorry, lad, but all the tricks I know are for modern computers with modern operating systems. Not for something that came off the Ark."

Jack sighed. "I was afraid of that."

"What about other information sources?" Draycos asked. "Surely someone has broken into such systems in the past."

"Yeah, what about that?" Jack asked. "Any of Uncle Virgil's old friends ever work on Brum-a-dum? Or could someone have a file in a thieves' database somewhere?"

"I can look," Uncle Virge said, his voice tight. "But unless we're very lucky, I don't think we'll have enough time to find anything."

An uncomfortable shiver ran up Jack's back. "Why not?"

"Gazen has set up a special slave auction for five days from now," Uncle Virge said. "The prize item up for sale is you."

CHAPTER 18

"Okay," Jack said, trying to keep his voice calm and casual. "That's not so bad. Matter of fact, that might be the best way to get me out of here. Let them sell me, then I'll duck out on the buyer once we're off-planet."

"I wouldn't count on that if I were you," Uncle Virge warned. "Or don't you think the Chookoock family has dealt with unwilling slaves before?"

Jack felt his throat tighten. "You mean not just handcuffs or those control collar things they used on us on Sunright?"

Uncle Virge snorted gently. "Amateur stuff, used by people in a hurry. No, I expect the Chookoock family will be more thorough. A *lot* more thorough."

"So you're telling me I'm in trouble?"

"I'm telling you this whole plan was insane to begin with," Uncle Virge said flatly. "I'm telling you it's time to give up, pull the plug, and get out while you still can."

Jack stared at the picture on the display, his eyes tracing along the patterns of the stone making up the mansion walls. Big stones. Hard stones. As hard and cold and unfeeling as the people who lived within them. Even the mercenaries he'd dealt with had cared more about people than Gazen and the Chookoock family did.

What in space was he doing here, anyway?

"Jack?" Uncle Virge prompted. "Come on, lad, it's over. Cut your losses and let's blow this pop stand."

"And what will we do then?" Draycos asked. "Where will we go for the information we need?"

"Where we should have started in the first place," Uncle Virge said. "We dump this in StarForce's lap and let the professionals handle it."

"We've been through this, Uncle Virge," Jack said. "We can't let anyone else know about Draycos."

"Maybe we don't have to," Uncle Virge said. "Correct me if I'm wrong, but all we want is to keep Draycos safe from whoever the Valahgua have teamed up with. Right?"

Jack frowned. He knew that tone of voice. There was some trick here. "All right," he said cautiously. "So?"

"So we go to StarForce," Uncle Virge said. "But we go anonymously."

"Pardon?" Draycos asked.

"Anonymously," Uncle Virge repeated. "We don't let them know who we are."

"I understand the word," Draycos said. "I do not understand the logic. How can we convince them of the truth without revealing my existence?"

"Ah, but we don't have to convince them of anything," Uncle Virge said. "That's the beauty of it. All we have to do is drop them an anonymous tip that some mercenary group is using Djinn-90s to smuggle contraband. They get all hot and huffy and rush off to investigate."

"Assuming they believe us," Jack said. "They must get a million anonymous tips a day."

"Even if they do believe, how does that help us?" Draycos added.

"Easy," Uncle Virge said. "We just watch over their shoulders while they investigate. They find our mercenary group, and there we are."

Jack rubbed his cheek. On the surface, it sounded reasonable enough. Best of all, he could do it from the comfort of the *Essenay* instead of from a dirty slave colony.

"What if they are delayed, or are too slow?" Draycos asked. "What if they give up their investigation and we do not know about it?"

"Nonsense," Uncle Virge scoffed. "We'll be on them like white on rice. We'll know everything they do, practically before they do it."

"And if we miss something important?" Draycos persisted. "We have less than three and one-half months before the full refugee fleet arrives. We cannot afford to waste any of that time."

"It wouldn't be a waste," Uncle Virge insisted. "StarForce knows what they're doing."

"No, he's right, Uncle Virge," Jack said. "We can't afford to take ourselves out of the game."

"But we wouldn't be," Uncle Virge said, almost pleading now. "And we could still poke around on our own if you wanted to. We could check with people who watch merc groups, or even go back to sorting through Djinn-90 sales records."

Jack shook his head. "No," he said firmly. Firmly, but with a wispy smoke ring of regret floating about the words. He hadn't realized just how much he wanted out of this until

Uncle Virge dangled the possibility in front of him. "The timing's too tight to play games."

Uncle Virge sniffed loudly. "And exactly how much time have you wasted playing this slave game?"

"That's different," Jack said, glaring at the computer display. "It's *here,* right in front of me. I just have to figure out how to get at it."

"And then what?" Uncle Virge asked. "What if you *do* find the group involved? Are you and Draycos going to take them on all by yourselves? Them, and however many of the Valahgua have moved into the Orion Arm?"

Jack glanced down at Draycos's head. "We'll figure out that part when we get there."

"Of course," Uncle Virge said, his voice dripping with sarcasm. "Forgive me if I'm being difficult, but don't most professional assault teams do just a *little* more planning before hitting the beaches?"

"Uncle Virge, look—"

"No, *you* look, Jack lad," Uncle Virge interrupted. "Point one: you two can't stop the Valahgua alone. Not a chance. Point two: you probably can't even find the Valahgua and their allies alone. Tell me I'm wrong."

"Uncle Virge—"

"And point three," Uncle Virge went on quietly. "It seems to me that you've more than paid back your obligation to Draycos and his people. It's time for you to point him to the proper authorities, give him a hearty handshake—"

"Hold on a second," Jack cut him off. "I agreed to help Draycos save his people, remember? His part was to get me out of that jam with Braxton Universis, and he did. This is my half of the deal."

"Yes, I remember," Uncle Virge said. "I also remember that he spent maybe three weeks on your problem, while you've already put in a month and a half on his. With no end in sight, I might point out. Doesn't seem very fair to me."

It *didn't* seem very fair, Jack had to admit. Especially since Draycos's part of the deal hadn't involved anything nearly as unpleasant as what Jack had had to go through, first as a junior mercenary soldier, and now as a slave.

And the dragon wasn't even arguing the point, he realized suddenly. He was just lying there quietly against Jack's skin, waiting for the discussion to be over.

Waiting for Jack to make a decision.

Jack felt his lip twist. Yes, he hated this. He really did. And Uncle Virge was right on all the other points, too. Even if he *did* manage to shake loose the data they were looking for, did any of them honestly think they could take on the bad guys all by themselves?

Uncle Virge was arguing for fairness. Draycos, Jack knew, would argue on the basis of right and wrong. That keeping a promise was the right thing to do, whether it seemed like a good deal or not.

But at the moment, neither argument mattered a rat's nest to Jack. What mattered was that he'd suffered through two weeks of slavery; and he was *not* going to let those two weeks go to waste. Come hell or high water or interstellar tax audits, he was going to get what he'd come here for.

Fairness could go jump. The noble K'da warrior ethic could go pole vault. It was Jack's professional pride that was on the line here.

"Yeah, well, life never claimed to be fair in the first place," he told Uncle Virge. "And I've still got a couple of ideas to try."

"Jack, lad—"

"In the meantime, how about making yourself useful?" Jack said. "See what you can dig up about forty-year-old Brummgan computer systems."

Uncle Virge gave a sigh. "If you like," he said. "But I would strongly—*strongly*—suggest that you reconsider. The minute they start getting you ready for the sale, our chances of getting you out go way down."

"I'm not worried," Jack said, wishing that was actually true. "Look, I've got to go. I'll talk to you later."

He turned off the comm clip and returned it to its hiding place. "That was our bi-monthly argument with Uncle Virge about chucking this whole thing," he commented as he smoothed the sole back in place. "I don't know why we have to keep going over the same territory this way."

"Decisions of ethics and behavior are not one-time events," Draycos told him. "A person must renew such decisions each day. Sometimes several times in the same day."

"I suppose," Jack said. "Seems like an awful waste of effort, though."

"Not really," Draycos said. "Each time you make such a decision, you grow stronger and more resolved. You become able to face even more difficult challenges."

"Great," Jack growled. "Make the tough choices, and they get tougher."

For a moment Draycos was silent. " 'A tree within a quiet glade will break in gentle rains,' " he murmured. " 'But one upon a windy coast can face the hurricanes.' "

Jack rolled his eyes. "Don't try to tell me *that* one comes from an old K'da warrior poem."

"Not a warrior poem, no," the dragon said. "But I spent

some time on the seashore once, and what I observed there—"

"Never mind," Jack interrupted. "I'm sorry I asked."

"As you usually are with such things," Draycos said, a hint of humor peeking through. "What do we do now?"

"Good question," Jack confessed. "Let me think." For a long minute he stared at the stubborn computer, shifting plans and ideas around in his mind like pieces of a jigsaw puzzle.

He couldn't get into the system. Therefore, he had to sneak in when the system was already up and running. That would be pretty tricky. Alternatively, he could be here when Gazen first started up the computer in the morning and read the codes as they were fed in. That would be even trickier.

But then, as Uncle Virgil had been fond of saying, tricky was the Morgan family middle name. "Okay," he said, shutting off the computer. "Time to switch to Plan B."

"Which is?"

"You'll see," Jack said, standing up and glancing over Gazen's desk. A small but distinctive paperweight caught his eye. Easy to carry, and something Gazen would definitely miss. Perfect. Picking it up, he dropped it into his pocket.

"What is that for?" Draycos asked as Jack started for the door.

"A souvenir of our visit," Jack said. "Come on, we've got work to do."

"Where are we going?" Draycos asked as Jack eased the door open a crack.

"To the kitchen," Jack told him, looking carefully outside. No one was in sight. "I just hope they haven't gotten started on breakfast yet."

"The kitchen?" Draycos asked, sounding confused. "Why?"

Jack smiled tightly. "I'm hungry."

CHAPTER 19

The kitchen was deserted when Jack and Draycos arrived. Deserted and dark both, with only a handful of small night-lights showing.

"The food supplies will be back in the pantry," Draycos pointed out as Jack wove his way carefully through the maze of shadows.

"I was kidding about being hungry," Jack told him. His stomach growled. "Mostly, anyway."

He stopped beside the recipe desk, and the corner-mounted recorder he'd seen on his first trip through the place. "This is why we're here," he said, pulling the recorder from its attachment.

"What is it?" Draycos asked.

"A recorder," Jack said, turning it toward one of the lights for a better look. "Video and audio both. I figure there's no reason to let that camera in Gazen's office go to waste."

He glanced around, looking for tools. A butter knife and seafood fork would probably do, he decided. "Watch the door," he ordered Draycos, heading for a stack of silverware drawers. "Let me know if you hear any movement over by the slave stairs."

There was a surge of weight on his shoulders as the

dragon leaped out from the back of his shirt collar. Silently, he padded off toward the door.

The recorder was a simple, off-the-shelf model, with few complications and not a single shred of security. It took Jack only a minute to take off the outer casing, strip the guts out of the gadget, and put the casing back together. Reattaching the empty shell to the desk, he put the recorder equipment into his pocket and headed for the exit. "Finished," he called softly. "Draycos?"

He rounded a preparation island and stopped. There was the door straight ahead, a wide, dark shadow against the pale white kitchen walls. The dragon was nowhere to be seen. "Draycos?"

"Here," the other called from somewhere to Jack's left. "Come and see."

Frowning, Jack followed the voice. Behind a large food warmer, he found Draycos standing against the wall. Above his head was a wide, flat gray box set into the wall at Brummgan eye-level. "Trouble?" Jack asked.

"Just the opposite," Draycos said. "I was scouting and found the box you see above me. Do the words on it say what I believe they say?"

Jack stepped close and squinted at the box. In the dim light the lettering was hard to make out. "Spare . . . spare something," he said. "Spare . . . ?"

"Spare keys?" Draycos suggested.

Jack felt his heartbeat pick up slightly. Spare *keys*? "This is definitely worth a look," he agreed. Pressing his back against the box, he held a hand out to Draycos. The dragon put a forepaw on it and melted up his sleeve. There was the usual shifting on his skin as he leaned out over the box door.

And there was it was again: the same odd sensation Jack

had felt outside Gazen's office. As if the dragon were some-how slipping . . .

Another wiggle, and he was back. "There are six rows of hooks inside, with five in each row," he reported. "Each hook is labeled, and holds one to three keys."

"Any alarms?"

"None that I could see," Draycos told him.

Jack looked at the side of the box, noted the simple-looking lock that held the lid in place. This seemed way too good to be true. "I guess they figured hiding it back here was enough," he said. "Could you see the labels?"

"Not well enough to read," Draycos said.

"Well, keys are always worth checking out," Jack said, pulling out his lockpick. "Let's get this thing open."

He had the lock popped in ten seconds flat. Even with the out-of-the-way location, he thought dryly, whoever had been in charge of extra keys must not have read the Chookoock family security manual. Taking half a step back, he swung back the door.

And was slammed suddenly and violently backward as Draycos leaped out between him and the box.

He flailed for balance, but the shove had been too hard. Gurgling helplessly in his throat, he fell back onto the tile floor. "Draycos!"

"Stay down," the dragon said sharply. He was crouched beneath the box, his long neck twisted as he peered cau-tiously up at it. "I heard a spring twitch as you opened the door, and then a click. A trap may have been activated."

"Oh, great," Jack muttered. Keeping low to the floor, he skittled around to the wall beside the box. Then, gingerly, he eased himself upward.

One look was all it took. "There was a trap, all right," he said. "But it's already been sprung. Have a look."

Carefully, Draycos straightened up. "There," he said, his tongue flicking out to point at the hinge side of the box lid. "There is the spring I heard."

"That's the trigger," Jack agreed. "And there's the trap, that little hole between the first and second row of keys. See it?"

"Yes," Draycos said. "I assumed it was merely a defect in the material."

"It's supposed to look that way," Jack said. "It's the lens of a security camera, set to go off as the door is opened. One of us just got his picture taken."

Draycos muttered something evil-sounding under his breath. "My fault."

"Don't blame yourself," Jack told him, peering at the disguised lens. Probably a remote camera, with a light-pipe system carrying the image through the wall to somewhere else. "That kind of trigger is hard to detect. Especially when you're looking at it with the box closed the way you K'da do."

"It is still a disaster," Draycos said in a low, pain-filled voice. "I have failed."

"Let's not panic yet, okay?" Jack said. "You said you heard the click when the camera went off. When was that, exactly?"

"It closely followed the sound of the spring," Draycos said slowly. "I believe I had already gone back to my three-dimensional form, hoping to protect you from any deadly weapon."

And to take the full impact of that weapon on himself? Probably. Typical K'da warrior thinking. "So you think you'd already come out when the camera fired?"

"Yes, I am certain," the dragon answered. "I was between you and the box at the time."

Wedged in rather tightly between Jack and the box, too, as Jack remembered it, "So you were pressed up against the box," he said. "Blocking most of the light. And with, what, your back to the camera?"

"Most likely my right shoulder," Draycos said. "I was twisting that direction, but did not yet have my back to the box."

"So in other words, they haven't got a picture of Jack Morgan with his fingers in the candy dish," Jack concluded. "All they've got is a close-up of a K'da scale pattern."

"But surely they will not be able to identify it," Draycos said hopefully. "No one here has ever seen a K'da."

"We're assuming that, yeah," Jack said grimly. "Problem is, we don't know for sure. We *do* know that these guys supply Brummgan mercenaries to whoever the Valahgua are working with. What if they're not just suppliers, but also partners?"

"If so, they may show the picture to the Valahgua," Draycos said. "You are right. We must destroy that picture."

"If we can," Jack said, glancing over his shoulder at the kitchen clock. They were running dangerously low on time. "First things first. As long as we're here, let's take a look at these keys."

The labels had, of course, been printed in Brummgan script. But someone had thoughtfully added hand-written translations in English and Dynsci, probably for the benefit of slaves for whom one of the Orion Arm's major trade languages was more familiar.

And as Jack ran his eyes over the labels, he realized that the lack of security here wasn't nearly as big a mistake as he'd hoped. Most of the keys were to meat lockers, or pastry storage areas, or even one to a freezer temperature control. If they'd tipped off the Valahgua for this, they'd paid a pretty high price for pretty cheap goods.

Then he spotted a single small and oddly-shaped key on one of the hooks in the bottom row, looking almost like an afterthought. Leaning down, he squinted at the label.

And smiled tightly. As Uncle Virgil used to say, at least until he had decided it was safe to swear in Jack's presence— "Bingo," he murmured.

"What?" Draycos asked.

"A key to the slave hotboxes," Jack told him, taking the key and dropping it into his pocket. "And since it says hot-*boxes,* plural, I'm guessing it opens all of them. *That* could be extremely useful."

"They will notice the loss," Draycos warned.

"Only if they look really closely," Jack said, shifting one of the spare keys onto the now-empty hook. "This ought to make it less obvious."

"What about the camera?"

"We'd have to take the whole box off the wall to see where the optic line goes," Jack said, closing the door and relocking it. "And then we'd have to trace it to the camera itself. We'll just have to hope no one bothers to check the pictures every day."

"But if they do—"

"Then we may be in trouble," Jack cut him off harshly. He didn't like this any more than Draycos did. But there wasn't a knitted, purled, or darned thing either of them could do about it. At least, not right now. "Or not. I doubt there are any Valahgua here in the house—you'd probably have smelled them if there were. And a close-up view of K'da scales isn't going to be very helpful to anyone else."

"Perhaps," Draycos said reluctantly. "What now?"

"We go back to Gazen's office," he told Draycos, heading for the door again. "And hope he's not getting up extra early this morning."

Getting the recorder set up took longer than Jack had expected. The cable feed from the security camera vanished back into the wall a short distance from Gazen's office, and it took him and Draycos several precious minutes to track it into the conference room next door.

Once there, though, things went quicker. From the inside of a handy ventilation grille, Draycos dug a short tunnel into the soft material to the point where the cable ran through the wall. Wiring the recorder into the circuit, Jack stashed the device out of the way and resealed the grille.

"You realize, of course, that this communication cable is one of the wires we punctured earlier," Draycos pointed out.

"That's okay," Jack assured him, brushing the last bits of tell-tale dust from beneath the grille, trying to spread it evenly across the floor. "They'll fix it as soon as they realize they're not getting a picture. Probably have it back up in an hour."

"And then?"

"That camera has a perfect view of Gazen's keyboard," Jack said. "We come back tomorrow and retrieve the recorder, and we ought to have a complete record of what it takes to get into the Chookoock family computer system."

He felt a ripple across his skin as the dragon shook his head. "Sometimes you amaze me, Jack."

"With my creativity?"

"With your sheer nerve," Draycos corrected. "Who else would use an enemy's own security system against him?"

"Oh, pretty much any thief worth his bail money," Jack said with a tight smile. "That's how we do our job."

"How you *did* your job," Draycos corrected. "You are re-formed now."

"Right," Jack muttered. "Sure couldn't prove it by me."

He stood up, brushing the remaining dust off his hands as he surveyed the area. Not perfect, but good enough. Stepping to the door, he opened it a crack and peered out.

He'd pushed his timing just a little too far. Across the big entry chamber, he could see muted lights and hear a quiet commotion coming from the kitchen. The breakfast crew, apparently, had started work.

"The way to the stairway is still clear, if we hurry," Draycos murmured in his ear.

Jack swallowed. "Let's go."

Luck, or K'da warrior fortune, was with them. The slave activity was confined to the kitchen, and most of the residential area was still asleep. They ran across only one Brummga already on the move, and Draycos's ears caught his footsteps in time for Jack to duck out of sight behind a large decorative planter. Two minutes later, they were back in Her Thumbleness's room.

"And now?" Draycos asked as Jack lay back down at the foot of the snoring Brummga's bed.

"We try to get some sleep," Jack said, stretching out on the hard floor and closing his eyes. "I've got a feeling this is the most comfortable we're going to be for a while."

CHAPTER 20

Jack had hoped to get in at least a couple of hours of sleep before the roof fell in on him. But he'd been asleep no more than half an hour when he was jolted awake by the slamming of the door against the wall. He'd barely pried his eyes open when rough Brummgan hands grabbed him under the armpits and hauled him to his feet.

"Hey," he protested, blinking his eyes against the glare of light spilling in from the hallway. "What's going—?"

One of the Brummgas cut off the question with a slap to the side of his head. "Quiet, slave," he growled, slapping Jack again to emphasize the point. "Come."

With a Brummga gripping each arm, he was carried through the door and out into the hall, the sound of Her Thumbleness's snoring fading away behind him. Down the hall they went, then down the stairs, with Jack's feet only occasionally touching the floor. It was, he thought once, what it must feel like to get caught in a river flash flood.

Gazen was waiting in his office, seated in the comfy chair Jack had so recently had the chance to try out. "Thank you," he said to the Brummgas as they deposited Jack on the floor in front of him. "Leave us."

Silently, the Brummgas went out, closing the door behind

them. For a long minute Gazen just stared at Jack, his face a smooth mask, his dark brown eyes impossible to read. "Well," he said at last, his voice as unnaturally calm as his expression. "Here we are again."

Jack shrugged slightly. "I guess so," he said.

An instant later he was on his knees, a knife-edge of pain ripping through his shoulder. "Some respect, if you please," Gazen said, his voice still calm. Waving idly in his hand like a stalk of wheat in a gentle breeze was a long, thin slapstick Jack hadn't even seen him holding.

"Yes, sir," Jack managed.

An instant later he'd gone from knees to stomach, a new focus of agony deep within his left thigh. " 'Sir'?" Gazen's voice came through the haze. " '*Sir*'? That's not my title, slave."

Jack clenched his teeth against the pain, trying desperately to remember what the Brummgas had called him when he'd first been brought inside the white wall. Pancake? Pan-rig? Panjam?

Panjan. That was it: *Panjan*. "I'm sorry, *Panjan* Gazen," he said.

And bit back a scream as a third slapstick blow caught him across his back. "*Panjan* is a Brummgan title," Gazen said, his voice almost too quiet to hear over Jack's own gasping. "Not proper for a human to use. Try again."

Jack shook his head, the movement sending fresh waves of pain through him. "I don't know . . . what you want," he panted. "I don't know . . . what to say."

He braced himself for another blow. But it didn't come. "That's better," Gazen said. "You're starting to understand."

Suddenly, there was a shoe filling Jack's field of view. He winced back, fully expecting that the next thing he felt would be that shoe connecting hard with his cheek.

But again, the expected didn't happen. "Get up," Gazen said.

Jack tried to obey. He really did. But his muscles were still shaking too badly from the slapstick's sting. "I—"

He twitched violently back as the tip of the slapstick swept past his eyes. The movement sent fresh waves of pain washing over him, almost as bad as if Gazen had actually hit him. "I said get up."

Setting his teeth together, Jack forced his hands under his chest. Slowly, inch by inch, he got himself pushed up off the floor. Rolling over onto his side, he looked up at Gazen.

The man was back in his chair. Still fingering his slapstick, he was watching Jack with the same vaguely interested expression someone might give a slug working its way through the grass.

And that really was all he was to Gazen, Jack realized dully. A slug, living under his feet with a bunch of other slugs. All of them alive only because they weren't quite worth the trouble of killing.

Clenching his teeth some more, he got back to the task of getting up.

It seemed to take forever. But finally, his shirt soaked with sweat, his body feeling like he had a three-alarm sunburn, he pulled himself more or less upright.

"Impressive," Gazen said. "You're tougher than you look, McCoy. I'll have to remember to use a stronger setting next time."

He waved the slapstick for emphasis. Instinctively, Jack flinched back, the movement nearly throwing him off balance again.

That one earned him a cold half-smile. "And you're a quick learner on top of it," Gazen added. "Good. I trust we won't have to repeat this lesson."

Jack shook his head, not daring to try to speak. "Good," Gazen said. That seemed to be his favorite word this morning. "There's a chair behind you. Sit."

It hurt almost as much to sit down, Jack discovered, as it had to drag himself to his feet in the first place. But at least now he didn't have to worry about his knees giving way. "Now," Gazen said briskly, laying the slapstick on the desk beside his computer. "You were in here tonight. Why?"

Jack took a deep breath. Originally, his plan had been to deny everything, in the hope of maneuvering Gazen into telling him exactly what he knew about Jack's nighttime activities. But the slapstick beating had demolished any interest in playing psychological games with this man. "I was tired of picking berries and playing punching bag for Her Thumbleness," he muttered between slightly numb lips. "I thought this would be a way to remind you that I was more valuable than that."

"And exactly how valuable do you think you are?"

Jack started to shrug, remembered what had happened the last time he did that. "I disabled your security system and got into your office," he said. "I took this to prove it."

He pulled the paperweight from his pocket and set it on the nearest corner of Gazen's desk. "Not just anyone could do something like that and get away with it."

Gazen's eyebrows lifted slightly. "Do you really think you got away with it?"

Jack winced. "No, not really."

"Good," Gazen said. "Then all we have to do is decide what exactly I'm going to do with you."

Jack's pulse was pounding unpleasantly hard in his neck. The basic assumption here had always been that he was worth too much money to kill out of hand. Now, looking into Gazen's dead eyes, he wasn't at all sure about that anymore. "I'm a professional thief," he said carefully. "A good one, too. I could do those kinds of jobs for you."

"I've got my own thieves," Gazen said. "What do I need you for?"

Jack's pulse picked up a little more speed. Had Gazen given up on the auction Uncle Virge had mentioned? Or was this a psychological game of his own? "People don't expect a kid like me to be a thief," he said.

"Especially when that thief goes under another name?" Gazen suggested. "Or did Heetoorieef merely get your name wrong when you checked in with him?"

"No, I gave him the wrong one," Jack admitted.

"Why?"

That was a darn good question, Jack decided. It deserved a good answer, too.

Problem was, he didn't have one to give. "It was mostly because—"

He broke off as a knock came at the door. "Enter," Gazen called.

The door opened, and an extra-wide Brummga lumbered in. "Morning slave report, *Panjan* Gazen," he announced, handing Gazen a data tube.

"Thank you," Gazen said, plugging the tube into his computer. He flipped a few pages, his eyes skimming across the display. "Still sick, I see."

He looked back at Jack. "The next time you borrow a name, try to pick someone who isn't already showing up on the sick reports," he said. "Or did you think Brummgan computer systems would be too stupid to notice something like that?"

Jack felt his throat tighten. The day of the magic show, he remembered, Noy had been coughing a lot. "I didn't know he was sick," he said.

"And didn't care either, I suppose." Gazen shifted his eyes back to the computer display. "Put him in an isolation hut," he told the Brummga. "We don't want this spreading to the rest of them."

"Treatment?" the Brummga asked.

"None," Gazen said darkly. "I'm tired of this. The boy's always been more trouble than he's worth."

"Like his parents," the Brummga said.

"Exactly like his parents," Gazen agreed, an edge of contempt in his voice. "Put him in a hut and leave him there. If he gets well, fine. We'll get a little more work out of him." He pulled the tube out of the computer and handed it back. "If he doesn't, make sure you decontaminate the body before you get rid of it."

The Brummga nodded as he took the tube. "I obey, *Panjan* Gazen." He lumbered back out, closing the door behind him.

"Now," Gazen said, leaning back in his seat and crossing his legs. "Where were we?"

Jack took a careful breath— "Oh, that's right," Gazen said before he could speak. "You were going to spin me some lie as to why you used a false name when you were brought in here."

He picked up the slapstick and began waving it gently around again. "Would you like me to tell you what *I* think?" he asked.

Jack was still trying to decide whether he was supposed to answer when Gazen flicked the slapstick toward him—

And a fresh slash of pain burst across on his shoulder like a bolt of lightning.

He gasped, jerking back in shock and pain. And only then did his squinting eyes register what had just happened.

Gazen's weapon wasn't an ordinary slapstick, he realized now. Instead, it was composed of a slightly flexible cylindrical spiral that could extend several feet outward at the flick of a wrist. Even as Jack clutched at his shoulder, Gazen lifted the slapstick back toward the ceiling, letting the extended sections slide smoothly back into the outer sheath. "When I ask a question, I expect an answer," he said. "Shall I repeat it for you?"

Jack shook his head. "Yes, I'd like you to tell me what you think," he managed.

"Better," Gazen said approvingly, waving the slapstick idly in his hand again. "I think this whole thing about your partner selling you to us was never more than a complete scam. I think he's sitting in your ship right now, monitoring your activities and waiting for you to reach your objective."

He lifted his eyebrows. "Go ahead. Tell me I'm wrong."

CHAPTER 21

Jack thought his heart had been trotting along at a pretty good clip before. Now, as he stared into Gazen's face, he could feel it going into sprint mode. "I don't understand," he said. "What do you mean, selling me to you?"

Gazen gave him a smile as thin as a con man's promise. "Oh, of course," he said. "I forgot. You knew nothing about that, did you?"

"I still don't—I mean—"

"You see, we have a problem here," Gazen went on. "The problem is that he's still sitting out there at the spaceport. If he'd really sold you as he claimed, don't you think he'd have taken off for parts unknown the minute he had his money?"

Except that Gazen's payment hadn't been made in cash, Jack knew. It had been in the form of credit, good only at the Ponocce Spaceport. Uncle Virge *couldn't* go anywhere else, at least not if he wanted to spend that money. He opened his mouth to point that out—

And strangled back the words just in time. He wasn't supposed to know anything about the deal, after all, including how the payment had been made. Mentioning the credit line would be a dead giveaway that he was still in contact with the partner who'd supposedly sold him into slavery.

And from the look in Gazen's eyes, he realized with a creepy sensation, that was exactly what the slavemaster had been fishing for. Proof that Jack wasn't what he claimed to be.

Jack's mouth was still open, waiting for words to come out. "He's probably trying to get me out," he improvised. He could hear a quaver in his voice, one that had nothing to do with his acting skills. "Maybe trying to work a deal with the authorities about that burglary charge."

"Very good," Gazen said softly. Either Jack's act hadn't fooled him, or else he wasn't ready to abandon the bluff just yet. "Stubborn loyalty, naïve unthinking trust. Honor among thieves. Is that it?"

"I don't know about honor," Jack said. "But he *is* my partner. We've been together a long time."

"Of course," Gazen said. "Tell me something. Just for my own curiosity, you understand. Are you an actual member of the Daughters of Harriet Tubman? Or are you simply a stupid young fool they talked into doing this job for them?"

Jack blinked. "A member of *what?*"

"Don't insult my intelligence, McCoy," Gazen said, his voice abruptly as cold as Neptune's north pole. "*If* that's even your real name. I was watching just now as we discussed that useless Noy kid. You reacted far too strongly for a simple professional thief. I know the type, and none of them cares about anything but the continued safety of his or her own skin."

"I don't care about Noy," Jack protested. Even to his own ears the words sounded lame. "I don't care about any of them."

"Of course not," Gazen said, clearly not believing a word of it. "Did the people who hired you happen to mention that they've been a splinter up my fingernail for longer than you've been alive? Or that I hate everything and anyone associated with them? Hmm? Did they?"

And then, suddenly, the name clicked. *The Daughters of Harriet Tubman:* the building Draycos had spotted across from the gatekeeper's house. "I don't know what you mean," he insisted. "I never even heard of them before."

"Still, I have to admit they've come up with something new this time," Gazen went on. "Usually they try official protests or attempts to interfere with Chookoock family business. Sending in a thief to steal our records is beyond even their usual level of insolence."

He tilted his head toward his computer. "I trust you had no trouble with my files?"

"I didn't touch your computer," Jack said. "I told you, I only came in—"

"Of course, as they say, it doesn't always take a genius to create a clever plan," Gazen cut him off. "Sometimes an idiot can fall over one by accident."

He smiled faintly. "But as they also say, you can't make lox without smoking a few fish. In this case, you're that fish."

Again, he flicked out the slapstick. Jack flinched away, the movement sending another splash of pain through him. But the tip of the weapon passed harmlessly past his left shoulder. Gazen was just playing with him. "What that means is that you're going to disappear," the slavemaster continued, his voice as calm as if he were ordering dinner. "You will be prepared for service; and then you will be quietly smuggled off-planet and delivered to your new owners."

He waved the slapstick idly. "Leaving your friends at Tubman to sit around their meeting rooms, sipping their tea and eating their scones. Wondering occasionally whatever happened to you."

A heavy silence filled the room. Jack tried to swallow, but his mouth and throat were as dry as a summer's day in the Gobi. Certainly he'd been in tighter situations than this one, facing ruthless people like Snake Voice and the enemy mercenary he'd dubbed Lieutenant Cue Ball.

But all the others had at least seen him as a person, someone to be manipulated or squeezed or maybe bargained with. Gazen saw him as nothing more than an old hat he might sell for a little pocket change.

And somehow that fact was more chilling than any of the man's veiled threats. Death he could face, and maybe talk or wiggle or con his way out of. A lifetime of slavery stretching out in front of him was a more horrible thought.

And for perhaps the first time, he truly understood why it was that Draycos hated slavery so much.

Draycos.

And suddenly the spiderweb of fear and pain Gazen had spun with his words and slapstick collapsed into the proper perspective. Jack wasn't alone here, after all. Not by a long shot.

And humming away almost within arm's reach was Gazen's computer. Already up and running, with all the passwords already entered.

Exactly the situation he'd been looking for.

A kaleidoscope of possibilities flashed across his mind like the lights of a broken status board. He could do it; right here, right now. A simple order to attack, and he would get to see the expression of horror on Gazen's face as he saw a poet-warrior of the K'da come boiling out of Jack's shirt collar.

Not that the expression—or the face—was likely to last very long. Slapstick or no slapstick, the dragon would make hamburger out of him in nothing flat. Jack could dig out the mercenary data, they could cut their way through however many Brummgan guards were loitering around outside, and head for the main gate. It was almost too easy.

And then he took another look at Gazen's face. He was watching Jack closely, like some interesting specimen squirming under a microscope.

No, not like a specimen under a microscope. Like an approaching spaceship that seemed way too harmless to be real. A ship that somehow, somewhere, had hidden weapons that had to be located and identified.

The setup wasn't *almost* too easy. It *was* too easy.

This was a test. The whole thing; from the humming computer, to the deliberate mention of Noy's sickness, to even being in here alone with Gazen.

The slavemaster was trying to goad him into some kind of reaction. Feeding him rope and waiting for him to take it, obligingly tie a noose, and hang himself.

Which meant Gazen's apparent helplessness was an illusion. The first move Jack made in that direction, and it would be as if somebody had dumped a bucket of Brummgas over his head.

He took a careful breath, quieting his emotions. No, Gazen was still motivated by money, and Jack was worth a lot of it. According to Uncle Virge's eavesdropped timetable, there were still a few days before they would be ready to ship him off the planet. He would continue to play innocent—or at least as innocent as he could under the circumstances—and wait for the right opportunity.

An opportunity, and a timing, of *his* choosing. Not Gazen's.

"You're taking this remarkably well, I must say," Gazen murmured into Jack's thoughts. "Perhaps you're expecting to be rescued? If so, I'd advise you to lay that hope to rest. It won't happen. Guaranteed."

He slid his slapstick back into the holster at his waist. "Or perhaps it's just that you're too stupid to comprehend the fate that awaits you," he added in a nastier tone. "Perhaps a small taste will help spur your imagination. Guards!"

The door slammed open, and three Brummgas bounded into the room. Their headlong rush seemed to falter, the rear one almost stumbling over the other two, as they caught sight of Jack still sitting quietly in his chair. "Yes, *Panjan* Gazen?" one of them said, looking uncertainly between Gazen and Jack.

"He needs more of a lesson than the regular hotboxes can provide," Gazen said.

His dark eyes focused one final time on Jack's face. Then, as if in complete dismissal of Jack as both puzzle and person, he turned back to his computer. "Take him away," he said over his shoulder, "and put him in the frying pan."

CHAPTER 22

Jack cleared his throat as the Brummgas surrounded his chair. "Aren't you forgetting one small thing?" he asked.

Reluctantly, it seemed, Gazen turned back around to face him. "And that is . . . ?"

"Her Thumbleness will be expecting me to play with her today," Jack said. "She's likely to be upset if I don't turn up."

Gazen's eyes flicked to the Brummgas. "Her Thumbleness needs to learn she can't have everything she wants."

"Absolutely," Jack agreed. "But I wouldn't want to be the one who has to teach her that."

Gazen smiled thinly. "Don't worry about it," he said. "I can handle Her Thumbleness."

His eyes flicked to the Brummgas again. "The frying pan," he ordered again. "Make it the full treatment."

The frying pan turned out to be a small metal shed tucked out of sight in a clump of bushes about fifty yards from the mansion's kitchen entrance. Probably hidden, Jack thought cynically, so as not to disturb the more delicate members of the Chookoock family. Other than that, it looked pretty much like the regular hotboxes he'd become acquainted with over the past couple of weeks.

Uneasily, he wondered what extras Gazen had added to give it such an ominous name.

The answer came as the lead Brummga led the way around to the far side of the frying pan and levered up the door. The other hotboxes had been plain tin structures, with plain tin insides. This one, in contrast, was lined with a bright copper mesh, with horizontal and vertical wires carefully separated by thin black rubbery spacers.

The Brummgas shoved him inside and swung the door closed again. The lock clicked, and with a muttering of deep voices the aliens clumped their way back toward the main house. "I had wondered what was meant by the name 'frying pan'," Draycos murmured when the footsteps had faded away. "These wires are electrical, correct?"

"Afraid so," Jack agreed grimly, searching the walls and ceiling for evidence of listening devices. There hadn't been any in the other hotboxes, but one so close to the main house might run under different rules.

An instant later he jerked violently as a jolt of current burned through him. "Ow!"

"Are you injured?" Draycos asked anxiously.

"No, I'm just fine," Jack gritted out, his teeth clenched against the fresh waves of pain rolling through his body. The shock itself hadn't been all that painful, but it had reawakened all the nerve endings already scrubbed raw by Gazen's slapstick.

He wondered if Gazen had thought about that part before throwing him in here. Odds were, he had.

"Jack—"

"No, it's okay," Jack reassured the dragon. "Really. If they wanted to kill me, there are easier ways."

"Nevertheless, it is clearly painful," Draycos said. "Move as far as you can to the side."

"You must be kidding," Jack said, looking around. Like the regular hotboxes, there wasn't enough spare room in here for a decent hamster cage. "Move to what side where?"

"Press your body against the right-hand wall," Draycos ordered, sliding around on Jack's back. "And raise the lower part of your shirt."

Another jolt sparked through the mesh. This time, Jack's spasming legs drove the back of his head against the ceiling. "Now; move quickly," Draycos said as the current shut off and Jack sagged back down. "Before it happens again."

"Sure," Jack muttered, tasting blood where his clenching teeth had caught the side of his tongue. Rolling partway onto his side, he pressed his chest against the wires and raised the back of his shirt.

Draycos lifted up from his lower back, squeezing himself into the remaining space. The sudden change in the number of occupants shoved Jack hard against the wall, forcing the side of his face up against the cold metal as well.

He closed his eyes, muscles tightening in anticipation and dread. If another shock came now, there would be nowhere for him to even twitch away to. Draycos's own body would hold him against the mesh until the current knocked him unconscious.

Or else seriously burned him. Maybe even killed him.

Gazen would be very unhappy if that happened. Slaves of the Chookoock family were not supposed to do anything, not even die, without official permission.

The kind of permission Noy had been given this morning.

Abruptly, Draycos melted back onto Jack's skin. "What?"

Jack demanded as the unexpected loss of pressure sent him rolling over onto his back.

"I have altered the wiring," the dragon said, a grim satisfaction in his voice. "It will no longer send current through the mesh."

"Great," Jack growled. "At least, not until someone notices and sends out a repairman. Then they'll see what you've done, and wonder where I got any tools—"

"No one will come," Draycos interrupted him. "No one will notice. I have not simply connected the outer wires together, but have run them through a small piece of wood. If I have calculated correctly, the wood will indicate a similar level of electrical resistance as a human body."

Jack shook his head. "I have no idea what any of that means."

From below him came a sudden crackle of electricity. He tensed, but no shock stabbed into his skin. "It means," Draycos said as the crackling stopped, "that any instruments they have attached to the system will show that it is still hurting you."

"Oh," Jack said. "Well . . . okay. Thanks."

"You are welcome."

For a minute neither of them spoke. Jack shifted around, trying to get comfortable. It was a futile task, as every move brought fresh agony to his muscles. But oddly enough, and rather to his own surprise, his thoughts weren't on his own aches and pains.

Instead, they were with Noy. He could practically see the younger boy's face floating in front of his eyes there in the gloom of the frying pan. He could hear his voice, too, cheerful but with a hidden defiance lurking beneath it. Unlike Greb and

Grib, Noy hadn't simply accepted his slavery as if it were just the way things had to be, even though he'd been born into it.

But then, Maerlynn had said something about his parents trying to escape once. Maybe they'd managed to teach him about freedom before they'd died.

And now Noy was sick, stuck away somewhere in the isolation hut Gazen had ordered him tossed into. Sick, and weak, and hungry. Maybe dying.

All alone.

Another crackle came and went. "You are very quiet," Draycos said softly. "Are you in pain?"

Jack's first impulse was to lie about it. Compassion had not exactly been at the top of Uncle Virgil's list of prized qualities. He'd considered it a sign of weakness, in fact, and had done his best to hammer that same way of thinking into Jack's skull. Since his death, it had been a task Uncle Virge had done his best to continue.

But Jack was getting tired of that kind of life. He was also getting tired of lying. "I was thinking about Noy," he told Draycos. "Wondering how he was doing."

For a moment the dragon was silent. Automatically, Jack braced himself for the scorn and ridicule that would have come instantly from either version of his uncle. "His situation did not sound good," Draycos agreed. "Do you think there is anything we can do for him?"

"It could be dangerous," Jack warned. "You game to give it a try?"

"Absolutely," Draycos said, sounding vaguely insulted. "Did you have any doubt?"

Jack smiled. The K'da warrior ethic. "No, not really," he said.

"Good," Draycos said firmly. "What is your plan?"

"Come on, give me a break," Jack protested. "I just started thinking about this. You expect me to have a plan already?"

"Of course not," the dragon murmured. "Forgive me."

"But I'm working on it," Jack assured him, wincing as he shifted aching shoulders again. "Gazen sure is a fun person to have around, isn't he?"

"In my opinion, he is mentally unstable," Draycos said firmly. "But one thing still bothers me."

"Only one?"

"The Daughters of Harriet Tubman," Draycos went on, ignoring the comment. "If Gazen dislikes them so much, why does he tolerate their presence near Chookoock family property?"

"Mainly, because he hasn't got a choice," Jack said. "Remember the rest of the sign? 'Internos Consular Adjunct.' The *consular* part means the place is part of the Internos diplomatic system. I don't know how the Tubman Group managed that one."

"And the Internos would be upset if the Brummgas threw them out?"

Jack shook his head. "You don't get it. Foreign embassies are considered the property of that particular nation or government. By being a consular station, the Tubman house is basically a small chunk of Internos territory on Brum-a-dum. Internos law applies there, not the Brummgan versions."

"Interesting," Draycos said thoughtfully. "How is it you know all this? Is it common knowledge?"

"It's common enough," Jack said. "I know it mostly because Uncle Virgil once did a scam that depended on how diplomatic privilege works."

"So you are saying that an attempt to move the Tubman Group out could be considered the same as an invasion?"

"The diplomats would probably find nicer-sounding words," Jack said. "But, yeah, that's what it boils down to. Gazen can hate it all he wants, but there's not a grease-stained thing he can do about it."

"An interesting system," Draycos said. "And this applies to government and diplomatic stations throughout the Orion Arm?"

"Pretty much," Jack said. "It's at least as old as pre-space Earth politics. The idea is that everyone wants their diplomats to be as secure as possible. Sometimes they're the only ones who can keep two sides from stumbling into a war."

"But only when neither side actually desires that war," Draycos said grimly. "The Valahgua—" He broke off. "Someone is coming."

Jack tensed. Maybe Draycos's little rewiring job hadn't been quite as undetectable as he'd thought. He could feel the ground shaking beneath Brummgan feet . . .

There was the click of a key in the lock, and abruptly the door was thrown open. "You," a Brummgan voice said. "Out."

"What?" Jack asked, squinting against the blaze of sunlight and blue sky behind the broad shoulders.

"I said out," the Brummga grunted, reaching in and grabbing the front of Jack's harlequin shirt. "Her Thumbleness wants you."

The Brummga wasn't particularly gentle, and in the process of getting Jack out of the frying pan he managed to restart at least a dozen of his collection of aches. Even so, Jack found himself grinning inside as he was marched back across the lawn toward the kitchen door.

So he'd been right. Her Thumbleness had found him missing, had thrown the predictable tantrum, and Gazen had been forced to give him back to her.

So much for the slavemaster and his threats.

The feeling of satisfaction lasted all the way up to Her Thumbleness's room. It was there as she loftily ordered the guards out and then told Jack to juggle for her. It even lasted until he picked up the small fruits he'd been using to juggle with.

It wasn't until the first one slipped from numbed fingers that his inner smile vanished.

"Shaak ri'hin mree ka'chu," Her Thumbleness growled.

Jack's comm clip was still hidden in his shoe, which meant no instant translation from Uncle Virge. But it didn't take a genius to tell that she was annoyed. "Yes, ma'am," he said, hastily stooping down and retrieving the fruit. Again, he got them set up to juggle.

And again his fingers refused to cooperate. The repeated hits with Gazen's slapstick, plus the additional shocks from the frying pan, had left his muscles too drained and twitchy to handle delicate maneuvers.

And with a sinking feeling, he realized Gazen had known exactly what he was doing. Including how to handle Her Thumbleness and her tantrums.

This second failure earned him an impatient kick that sent him sprawling across the room. "Maybe we could try a trick instead?" Jack suggested, stifling a groan as he picked himself up off the floor.

He wasn't even quite vertical yet when a slap against his shoulder knocked him over again. "Wait!" he pleaded, blinking back stars as the back of his head hit the floor. "Please. Just give me a minute."

He might as well have asked storm clouds to stop raining. Her Thumbleness wasn't interested in waiting. She wasn't interested in anything but getting what she wanted, when she wanted it, and exactly the way she wanted it.

And in the age-old manner of careless and spoiled children everywhere, she was going to fix her broken toy by beating it until it started working again.

Howling in frustration, she charged.

Jack did his best to fend off the flailing hands and feet. But Her Thumbleness was too enraged, and too big. Another kick got through, this one landing in his lower rib cage. He gasped for air, spinning helplessly as two more slaps bounced off his shoulders.

And then, suddenly, he caught a glimpse of a huge hand sweeping toward the side of his head. He tried to get his arm up in time to block it, or to at least absorb some of its impact.

But he didn't make it. An instant later, the world went dark.

CHAPTER 23

He woke up in stages, passing from simple darkness to not-so-simple confusion, and finally to the realization that he was not at all comfortable.

"Are you awake?" Draycos's voice asked quietly in his right ear.

"I think so," Jack said, prying his eyes open.

The darkness didn't change. "Or maybe not," he amended, blinking a couple of times. He still couldn't see anything. "Where are we?"

"Back in the frying pan," Draycos told him. "You cannot see anything because it is night."

"Night?" Jack echoed, frowning. The last thing he remembered was Her Thumbleness trying her best to make a rag doll out of him. "How long was she beating on me, anyway?"

"Not long," Draycos said. "The guards came in only a few seconds after you lost consciousness. They took you away from her."

"Did anyone see you?"

"No," the dragon assured him. "I was not required to assist you in combat."

"Oh," Jack said, feeling vaguely disappointed. He'd always assumed that if things ever got seriously dangerous, his private K'da poet-warrior would be out of his collar in an instant to protect him.

"Gazen ordered you returned here after the guards rescued you," Draycos went on. "At that point I decided there was no reason to wake you. You have had very little sleep the past few days and needed the rest. In addition, I did not think there was much we could do until nightfall."

"Right on all counts," Jack said. He did feel better, actually.

Though that feeling was likely to change the minute he started moving around and found out what kind of new injuries Her Thumbleness had thoughtfully provided. Carefully, gingerly, he probed at the ribs where the spoiled little brat had kicked him.

And got his second major surprise of the evening. The skin was definitely tender, but there was no sign of muscle or bone damage.

But that was impossible. That kick had sent him flying halfway across the room . . .

Frowning, he moved his fingers to his legs, and then to his shoulders. Again, there was nothing more serious than a few bruises.

"I did not fight, but I did what I could to protect you from harm," Draycos said. "When I could see where the blows would be striking, I raised my body slightly from your skin to take some of the impact on myself."

"You're kidding," Jack said, blinking in the darkness. "I didn't know you could do that."

"The ability is not common," Draycos said. "I was only rarely able to do such things with my last Shontine host, Polphir. I was never able to do so with any of my previous hosts."

"I guess K'da skills improve with age," Jack said. "You're more like wine than dogs."

"Pardon?"

"Wine improves with age," Jack explained. "And we have a saying that you can't teach an old dog new tricks."

"Can you not?"

"Can you not what?"

"Teach an old dog new tricks."

"I don't know," Jack said. "I've never owned a dog. Any idea what time it is?"

"It is likely after midnight," Draycos told him. "The noises from the house have been largely silenced."

Which meant the Chookoock family had largely gone to bed. "That's all I needed to know," Jack said, wincing as he sat up straight and pressed his back against the copper mesh. "Better check and see if the coast is clear."

He had wondered if having the mesh between his back and the metal wall would make the gap too wide for Draycos to see over. But apparently not. "There is no one currently visible," Draycos reported as he shifted around on Jack's back. "However, from the sounds of footsteps I have heard, I believe there is a regular guard route that passes between us and the house."

That could be trouble. "How often do they come by, and how soon until the next one?"

"I do not know precisely," Draycos said. "But from counting your heartbeats as you slept, I estimate they come past four times per hour. The last one was just before you woke, so we should have at least ten more minutes."

"Good enough," Jack grunted, moving carefully in the cramped space. "Okay, here's the plan. I pick the kitchen door. We raid the slaves' storage locker for food packages and as many juice bottles as we can handle."

"You are hungry?"

"It isn't for me," Jack said, his fingers probing the edge of the copper mesh where the door met the floor. There had to be a break there somewhere, where the door swung upward.

"For Noy, then?"

"Bingo," Jack said. "I'm not going to just sit back and let him die out there. At least, not if there's anything I can do."

"I am pleased," Draycos said softly.

Jack grimaced. "Yeah, well, don't start handing out the warm fuzzies just yet," he warned. "I'm not doing this for any noble K'da warrior ethic reasons. I just remember being sick once when Uncle Virgil had to go off on a job, that's all."

"How old were you?"

"About Noy's age," Jack said. "I was already pretty good at taking care of myself, so it shouldn't have been a problem. Only the sickness made me so weak I couldn't go make myself any food. By the time the fever was gone, I was too dehydrated to get more than a few steps from my bed without getting dizzy. I was scared I was going to starve to death."

"What happened?"

"I died, of course."

Draycos's head rose up from his shoulder. "What?"

"Well, obviously, Uncle Virgil got back in time," Jack said with a snort. There it was: the gap in the mesh. He wiggled his fingers through it and felt around for the similar opening under the door that he'd used in the slave hotbox to let Draycos out. "But I still remember how scared I was lying there all alone. I don't want Noy to . . ."

He trailed off. "What is it?" Draycos asked.

It took Jack two tries to get the words out. "There's no gap under the door," he said quietly. "At least, not one big enough for me to get my fingers under."

Draycos slid around onto Jack's right arm. "Let me see."

Jack kept his hand steady as a clawed digit lifted from his hand and probed the area. "There is an extra level of material beneath the door," the dragon said.

"Like an extra chunk of door sill," Jack agreed. "Leaves only about a quarter of an inch to spare, just enough to let some air in."

"Yes," Draycos said, the claw scratching gently at it. "Still, it is only wood. I would have no trouble cutting through it."

"Yeah, but the guards would be bound to notice," Jack said, shaking his head. "They'd wonder how I did that. Don't forget, so far Gazen hasn't bothered to do a real search of me and my clothes."

"Or your shoes," Draycos conceded. "A good point. We certainly do not want him to find the comm clip now."

"Not to mention the hotbox key we borrowed," Jack said. "*Or* you."

"No," Draycos murmured. "But perhaps there is another place where I could create an opening that would not be noticed."

"I don't know where," Jack said, turning with some difficulty and pressing his back against the side wall. "But you're more than welcome to look."

The dragon rearranged himself, and Jack felt the familiar sensation as he leaned out over the wall again. It was an awfully handy trick, that, as Jack had learned many times already. Too bad the dragon couldn't carry anything over the wall with him. If he could lean far enough outside to unlock the door, they'd be out of here in nothing flat.

But no. The dragon couldn't actually reach outside. All he could do was stretch far enough to look around.

He was certainly doing a lot of that right now. Jack could feel the sensation on his back shifting back and forth as the dragon hunted for a good spot to put their mousehole. He could feel Draycos stretching to the limit—

And then, suddenly, the dragon was gone.

Not shifted. Not moved somewhere else on Jack's skin. Gone. Lost somewhere in the fourth dimension.

Dead.

A breath caught like broken glass in Jack's throat. "Draycos!" he gasped.

And then, to his astonishment and relief, the dragon's voice came faintly through the wall. "It is all right," he said. "I am here."

Jack let his breath out in a huff. "Don't *do* that to me," he snapped. "Where are you?"

"I am outside," Draycos said. "I apologize for frightening you."

"You'd *better* apologize," Jack growled. "Why didn't you tell me you could do that?"

There was a slight pause. "Because I did not know I could," Draycos said. "In fact, I did not even know that it was possible."

Jack opened his mouth. Closed it again. "What do you mean, you didn't know it was possible?"

"To the best of my knowledge, no K'da has ever done such a thing," Draycos said. "I believe we have made history tonight, Jack."

A bad taste was starting to collect at the back of Jack's throat. "I don't like this, Draycos," he said. "You can call it making history if you want. *I* call it something going wrong."

"In what way?"

"I don't know," Jack told him. "But the last couple of times you looked over walls you felt sort of loose. Like you were getting ready to slide off or something."

"Which is precisely what has just happened."

"Yes, I understand that," Jack said. "What I'm wondering is if my body is rejecting you or something. Like sometimes a person rejects an organ transplant."

There was another silence from outside. "That has also never happened in the history of my people," Draycos said. "If a species can serve as host, that ability does not change."

"Only you've never tried humans as hosts before," Jack pointed out darkly. "Who knows what quirks we might have?"

"True," Draycos admitted reluctantly. "Still, there is little we can do about it."

"Except maybe think about where we can find another host to have waiting on standby," Jack said. "If it ever happens that you can't attach to me, you've only got six hours before you die."

"I remember, thank you," Draycos said. "But for now, we still have a mission to accomplish. Can you pass the key under the door?"

"Sure," Jack said, pulling open his shoe flap and digging it out. "Do you feel sick or injured or anything?"

"I appear to be unharmed," Draycos said. "It felt very strange at the time, though."

"I'll bet," Jack grunted, sliding the key out through the narrow gap. "Here."

"I have it."

Jack hunched his shoulders to stretch them. Only now, as he waited, did it suddenly occur to him that all their work and cleverness might be for nothing. The key he'd stolen had been to the slave hotboxes; but there was no guarantee that the frying pan didn't have a different lock entirely.

And then there came a click, and the door swung open, letting in a rush of fresh air.

Jack let out a breath. "Okay," he said, trying to sound casual. "Well. Let's get to work."

CHAPTER 24

The first job was to see if they could fix the door so that Draycos could get in and out the usual way. Or at least, the usual way for poet-warriors of the K'da.

Fortunately, it turned out to be easier than Jack had feared. The extra slab of wood that had kept him from sliding his hand outside turned out to be a simple add-on, attached to the bottom of the door frame with three nails.

With the door closed above it, the nails were impossible to reach. With the door open, though, it was simple. At Jack's direction, Draycos used his claws to pry up the slab. The three nails came up with it, and Jack had him slice them off so that they were even with the wood.

Now, when the slab was back in position, it looked as solidly in place as if it were still nailed there. It even fit tightly enough against the frame on both sides that a slight bump wouldn't knock it loose. But with a little pressure, Jack could push it out to drop onto the ground outside.

"Or I can take it in with me and slide it back into position from inside," he explained to Draycos as he tested the fit. "Either way, the Brummgas will never have a clue."

"Unless they try pushing on the slab themselves," Draycos pointed out thoughtfully. "Tell me, where are the ends of the nails I cut off?"

"Uh . . ." Jack glanced around. "Here they are," he said, picking the three pointy ends off the ground. "I was going to toss them into the bushes."

"Give them to me," Draycos said. "Then lift the slab out of the way."

Jack did so. Draycos delicately shoved the nail points back into the holes where they'd originally been, pressing them into place with his claws. "There," he said. "Now if anyone examines them, they will conclude the nails simply rusted through and broke."

"Maybe," Jack said doubtfully. "They don't look all that rusted to me."

"It will take a close examination to show the truth," Draycos said. "They are not likely to have the time—"

He broke off, his ears twitching around toward the house. "Someone is coming," he said quietly. "Not a Brummga."

Carefully, Jack peeked around the side of the frying pan. There was a figure coming toward them, all right, silhouetted against a crack of light from the open kitchen door. Definitely too small for a full-sized Brummga.

Her Thumbleness?

"Inside," Jack hissed, ducking back around the front. Draycos was holding the door open; scooping up the wooden slab, Jack scrambled inside. The dragon eased the door closed, and as Jack poked his hand through the opening he heard a soft click as Draycos locked the door. A second later the key came sliding through the gap, followed by a brief weight on Jack's outstretched hand as the dragon came aboard.

There wasn't enough time to hide the key in his shoe. Instead, he shoved it out of sight beneath the copper mesh behind him. Even if Her Thumbleness had come to drag him back to one of her games, Gazen would probably toss him back in here as soon as she got tired of him again. He could hear the footsteps approaching.

"Jack?" a familiar voice called. "Are you in there?"

He felt Draycos twitch. So the dragon was surprised, too. "Yes, I'm here, Lisssa," Jack called back. "What are you doing here?"

"What do you think I'm doing?" Lisssa countered disgustedly. "I'm Her Thumbleness's newest art project."

Jack winced. "I'm sorry," he said, and meant it. Bad enough to be dressed up in a clown suit and made to perform magic tricks. Having to stand there while Her Thumbleness gleefully ran a paintbrush over your body would be ten times worse. "When did you get here?"

"They came and got me this morning," Lisssa said. "That Wistawk—Heetoorieef—told me they'd put you in here."

"They did it twice, actually," Jack said, rubbing at the bruises on his ribs. "You'd better get back before she misses you."

"Not a problem," Lisssa said. "Her Thumbleness is having a long bath in that swamp off her room. Are you hungry or anything?"

Actually, he was starving, now that she mentioned it. "I'm okay," he said.

"Yeah, right," she said. "Here, I brought you this."

There was the sound of something scraping against the

wood beneath the door. Jack tensed; but before he could move, Draycos's rear legs bulged out from his ankle to press against the wooden slab and hold it firmly in place. "I swiped a few of these from the kitchen," Lisssa added as something round and thin slid faintly into sight. "They're cold, and they didn't taste all that good hot. But they're probably better than what you've got."

"Grilled sand would be better than what *I've* got," Jack grunted, prying up the copper mesh and pulling the round thing all the way in. It was some kind of pancake, he decided as he lifted it to his nose. It smelled odd, but no worse than some of the things he'd eaten in his travels around the Orion Arm. "Thanks."

"Hang on, I've got three more," Lisssa said. "Catch." She passed the rest of the pancakes through the narrow gap. "Hope that'll tide you over," she said as Jack pulled the last one in. "It's getting chilly out here. You going to need a blanket or anything?"

"I'm fine," Jack said. "I don't want to sound ungrateful, but you'd better get out of here before one of the patrols sees you. I don't want your beating on my conscience."

"Oh, that's right," she said with an audible sniff. "You still have a conscience. I forgot."

"So humor it already," Jack said. "Thanks for the food. Now get lost."

"What about that blanket?" she persisted. "I've been in hotboxes before. They're pretty miserable at night. And you don't even have scales to keep you warm."

"I'll be okay," Jack insisted. "Besides, you'll never get a blanket in through that gap."

"I suppose," she agreed reluctantly. "Look, I'll see what I can do. Don't go anywhere, okay?"

Jack grunted. "Funny."

"I try. See you later."

The footsteps moved off. "To the wall," Draycos whispered.

Jack pressed his back against the wall behind him. Draycos shifted, paused for a minute, then shifted again. "She has returned inside," he reported. "I saw no patrols that might have noticed her."

"Good," Jack said. The last thing he wanted right now was to draw curious Brummgan eyes in this direction. "Well, *that* was different."

"What do you mean?"

"Lisssa sticking her neck out for me," Jack said. "Or for anyone, for that matter."

"Yes," Draycos said thoughtfully. "Perhaps the experience of being one of Her Thumbleness's playthings has given her a new view of life."

"I think that only works with K'da," Jack said dryly. "But we can ask her about it later. Right now, we need to get moving."

"That may not be easy," Draycos warned. "She implied she would return with a blanket."

Jack hissed between his teeth. He was right, blast it. "And if she strolls by when we're not here . . . ?"

"Then we shall be burned cinnamon bagels," Draycos said solemnly.

Jack grimaced. "Toast, Draycos," he corrected. "We'll be burned cinnamon *toast*."

"My error," Draycos said. "Still, the point remains. What do you suggest we do?"

"You got me, buddy," Jack said. Blast it, and blast Lisssa, too. "I guess we wait."

"And if she does not return, or does not return soon?" Draycos asked. "What, then, about Noy?"

"We don't have a choice," Jack bit out irritably. "I don't like it any better than you do. But if she comes and tries to stuff a blanket under the door, she's going to push that slab inside. She wouldn't be able to get it back out, even if she wanted to. And the first Brummga who saw it . . ." He shook his head. "Burned cinnamon toast, all right. Butter side down."

There was a moment of silence. "There is one alternative," Draycos said. "You could stay here while I tend to Noy."

"Right," Jack said with a snort. "He's lying in bed when a gold dragon pops in to have tea and scones with him. Nothing strange about that. Definitely nothing he'd think to mention to anyone else."

"He will not see me," Draycos promised. "I can deliver the food and juices without him noticing."

"No," Jack said firmly. "We can't risk it."

The dragon seemed to sigh. "Then Noy will have no help. From anyone."

Jack bit down hard on his lip in frustration. But Draycos was right. "Fine," he growled. "So go. Just be careful."

"I will," Draycos said. He lengthened his stretch off of Jack's ankle, pushing the wooden slab outside.

Jack stuck his hand through the gap; and with a surge of weight, Draycos was out. "I will be back soon," the dragon promised softly through the door as he pushed the slab back into place. "Do not go anywhere."

Jack rolled his eyes. "Everybody's a comedian," he muttered under his breath.

But Draycos was already gone. Settling himself as comfortably as he could in the cramped space, Jack began nibbling on the cold pancakes Lisssa had brought. And tried hard not to think about the danger out there. To Draycos, and to Noy.

It was going to be a very long night.

CHAPTER 25

Draycos didn't see, hear, or smell anyone as he made his way across the starlit ground toward the kitchen door Lisssa had used a few minutes earlier. From the way she had made sure to leave it open when she left the building, he suspected he would find it locked. It was.

Jack, of course, would have simply picked the lock. A highly useful skill, and one that Draycos had practiced hard during their travels between planets aboard the *Essenay*. But his paws were not as nimble as Jack's, and he was not yet good enough to manage such a feat. Certainly not in the dark. Certainly not with a Brummgan patrol due to appear around the corner at any moment.

Fortunately, there were other ways. The Chookoock family had built their mansion with broken-edged stonework all across the outer walls. Very decorative. Also very easy to climb.

He had reached the third floor when he heard the sounds of the approaching Brummgan patrol on the ground below. By the time they actually appeared, he was crouched motionless in the shadow of a stubby smoke vent. They passed by without so much as breaking stride and disappeared around the corner of the building. Shifting his grip on the stones, Draycos continued on his way.

In warfare, he had long ago learned, it was usually impractical to make detailed preparations before a battle. Either the enemy came from the wrong direction, or they came with the wrong number of troops, or they used a completely unexpected strategy. Sometimes they were inconsiderate enough not to show up at all.

But a good warrior still did what he could to prepare first, second, and even third plans ahead of time. On occasion, such plans even proved to be useful.

As it happened, this was one of those occasions.

The windows of Her Thumbleness's room were protected by alarms like the one Jack had found at the gatekeeper's house the night this mission first started. Unfortunately for the Brummgas, they had no idea that an enemy had already been inside their fortress.

Not only inside, but with the time and freedom to study the windows at his leisure. Last night, as both Jack and Her Thumbleness slept, Draycos had examined both the alarm and the window lock itself, and had disabled both.

At least, he hoped he had disabled them. Easing a claw through the gap between window panes, he gently pried the panel open.

No alarms went off, nor did the sound of breathing from inside change. Opening the window just enough to allow him to slip inside, he dropped silently to the floor beneath it.

There he paused, senses alert. He had already noted how soundly Her Thumbleness slept, and there was little danger of her awakening even if an entire field army of K'da tromped through her bedroom. Possibly not even if they'd brought a section of percussion masters and concert drums along.

Lisssa, however, was another matter. Draycos still remembered her moving about in her bed as he returned to Jack that first night. If she was here, he would need to be especially careful.

But there was no hint of her Dolom scent anywhere in the room. Apparently, she was down in Jack's old bed in the underground slave quarters.

He closed the window and made his way across the room. All was quiet out in the corridor. Opening the door a crack, he took a deep sniff.

The cleaning crew had not yet made it to the stairs. But on the other hand, the Brummgas hadn't been in their rooms for very long, either. If last night's pattern still held, he had perhaps two minutes before the stairways and corridors began to fill up. Bracing himself, he pushed open the door and slipped outside.

Warrior's luck was with him. He made it down the hallway and the stairs, avoiding the traps and tripwires Jack had located last night. The entry chamber, too, was deserted.

He was crouched safely in a dark corner of the kitchen when the first Wistawk slave came stumbling tiredly in to collect his equipment.

The sorting out of buffers and sprays and cleaning cloths took only a few minutes. Then they all headed upstairs, and Draycos once again had the kitchen to himself.

The slaves' food locker was much smaller than the huge freezers and irradiators that held the food for the Chookoock family. But it was big enough, and adequately stocked. He chose several packages of pre-cooked food, then added a dozen different juice bottles to his pile.

The next step was to find a way to carry everything back to the slave compound. Fortunately, many of the packaged foods came in identical handle bags made of a rough, dark-brown cloth. A little ingenuity, and he was able to combine three of the bags into a sort of backpack. A quick check out the kitchen door, and he was bounding across the open ground toward the sports area, the thorn hedge, and the slave compound beyond.

He couldn't head directly in that direction, though. There were still the hidden guard posts to consider, scattered along the paths between the various hedge openings and the house itself. Much as he would have liked to deal with those Brumm-gas, this was not the time for it. Veering in a wide circle to the northwest, he headed for a more remote section of the hedge.

There were no guard boxes in this area. No patrols, either, at least none that had passed by recently. Apparently, the Brummgas didn't think any trouble could come at them except through the openings they themselves had put into the hedge.

Of course, once he was over the hedge, there would still be a lot of slave territory for him to search. Or maybe not. On his first night's exploration, he'd seen four small buildings off by themselves. With luck, one of them would be the isolation hut Noy had been sent to.

Ahead, the thorn hedge appeared, forming a darker patch against the dark sky. Draycos picked up speed, judging his distances; and at the right moment crouched down in his run and leaped.

Even with the extra weight on his back, the jump was an easy one for a K'da warrior. He hit the ground with a muffled rustle of dead leaves, and ducked into the shadow of a nearby bush.

There was no sign of Brummgas. No scent of them, either, as he carefully tasted the night air around him.

But there *was* something odd, he realized as he inhaled deeply. A faint scent that smelled just vaguely familiar. A scent that reminded him somehow of Noy.

Noy?

He sniffed harder, swinging his head back and forth to try to locate the source of the scent. It was there, all right. Somewhere to the north, he decided. North, and a little above him.

Above him?

He frowned upward. Surely Gazen's isolation hut wasn't built up in the trees. Besides, the scent wasn't strong enough to be coming from Noy himself.

He hesitated; but his instincts said this was worth checking out. Making sure his backpack was secure, he headed north.

Almost immediately, the "above" part began to make sense. Behind a clump of bushes the ground began to rise, and he found himself climbing one of the many low ridges he'd already noted in this area. The scent was still faint, but growing stronger with each step, and he continued on until he reached the very top of the ridge.

And there, camouflaged with dead leaves and grass, was a large mechanical device built from branches and bits of metal and wire and plastic.

It was a glider. And not just a glider, but a glider sitting on a makeshift catapult.

For a minute Draycos walked around the contraption, marveling at the ingenuity of its design. He was mostly a ground warrior, and certainly no expert at flying machines. But he was familiar enough with them to know a properly built one when he saw it.

This one was indeed properly built. All it would take would be some cranking on the catapult, a stretching and tightening of the elastic ropes already in place, and the glider would shoot off the ridge and soar into the sky.

Directly into the lasers and flame jets waiting in the white wall.

For a moment he stood there, the breeze vibrating against the straps of his backpack. Had its builders learned about the lasers and abandoned their scheme? Or were they still ignorant of the deadly dangers lurking at the top of the wall, and were merely waiting for the proper time to attempt their escape? Should he disable the craft to make sure none of the slaves took off to their deaths?

But no. He would warn Jack, certainly, and through Jack try to warn whoever had created this marvel. But it wasn't his place to destroy it. Turning away from the glider, he headed east.

The first of the small huts was empty. In the second, he found Noy.

He crept up on the hut from downwind, sampling the air carefully as he went. If the Brummgas were still looking for whoever had been digging into their hedge, they might have left a guard to watch the boy.

But there was no scent in the area but Noy's. Once again, it seemed, Gazen and his people had ignored an obvious security point. Mentally shaking his head, he eased the door open.

He had hoped to be quiet enough that the boy would sleep through his visit. But even as he pushed the door open, he realized he had miscalculated. Noy was only half-asleep, tossing and turning on his cot, muttering softly and incoherently under his breath.

And as the breeze whistled through the hut, Noy's sweaty face turned toward him. The half-open eyes went a little wider . . .

Draycos froze in the doorway, waiting for him to shout or scream. But all that escaped Noy's lips was a small whimper. "Are you here to take me?" he whispered.

The tip of Draycos's tail curled in a frown. "What do you mean?" he asked.

"Is it time?" Noy asked, his voice a little louder and trembling like a flower in an earthquake.

"Time?"

The boy took a shuddering breath. "Is it time for me to die?"

CHAPTER 26

Draycos's first instinct was to get out of there. To duck out of sight, pull the door closed with the tip of his tail, and come back later when he could deliver his package without being seen. In Noy's feverish state, surely the boy would decide afterward that this had been just a dream.

But the very unexpectedness of Noy's question had nailed his paws to the floor.

And now he was stuck. Because there was no way he could leave a sick child wondering if he was about to die. Especially not when he thought the appearance of a K'da warrior was the omen of that death.

"No," he assured the boy in his calmest voice. "It is not time. Not at all."

The boy blinked. "But—"

"I have brought you some food," Draycos explained. Coming all the way into the hut, he closed the door behind him. "Also some fruit juice," he added. "You must be very thirsty."

The boy stared as Draycos came around the side of the bed, never taking his eyes off the K'da for a moment. "You *are* thirsty, are you not?" Draycos tried again as he slipped off his backpack.

Noy nodded silently. "It is well that I brought this, then,"

Draycos went on, choosing one of the bottles and prying off the seal. "I hope you like . . . I believe this is called grappo juice." He held the bottle toward Noy.

The boy's mouth worked as if he was trying to say something. His gaze had shifted now from the K'da's face to the bottle, and the claws holding it. "Go ahead," Draycos said encouragingly, moving it a little closer to him. "It will be good for you. Drink."

Slowly, Noy took the bottle. Staring down into it, he lifted it to his mouth.

A few drops slithered down the corners of his lips. But most of that first drink made it inside where it belonged. "How does it taste?" Draycos asked.

Noy looked up at the K'da, then back into the depths of the bottle. "A little funny," he said.

"Yes, that is the way of a fever," Draycos agreed. "Foods often do not taste normal."

Noy drank again. Then, all at once, the strength seemed to go out of his arms. The bottle started to slip from his grip—

Draycos's forepaw snaked out smoothly, catching the bottle before it could fall. "Very good," he said as he set it down beside the cot where Noy could reach it. "Perhaps you should rest now. You can drink more in a little while."

"Okay," the boy said. He was starting to sag a little, and his breathing seemed more labored. "Could I have—" He paused, looking around as if searching for something.

"Another drink?" Draycos suggested, picking up the bottle. "Certainly. Allow me to hold it for you."

The boy drank deeper this time before coming up for air. "Still tastes funny," he said, panting a little. His eyelids were definitely sagging now.

"It will taste better tomorrow," Draycos said, wishing he had had more experience with human sicknesses. Too late, he wished he'd thought to bring Jack's comm clip out here with him. Perhaps Uncle Virge could have helped him know how to deal with it. "I will give you one more drink, then I shall let you rest."

"No!" Noy gasped. His hand fumbled for Draycos's forepaw, gripping it with an odd combination of desperation and weakness. "Don't leave me. Please. Don't leave me."

Draycos twitched his tail in surprise. "I must," he said. "I cannot stay."

"No," Noy said. His voice had sunk to a whisper, as if he had already used up all of his remaining strength. "Please."

Draycos reached out with his other forepaw and stroked the boy's sweaty forehead. A bitter memory floated up in front of his eyes: the dead Shontine aboard his ship, the *Havenseeker,* after the enemy ambush over Iota Klestis. Friends, companions, and fellow warriors; but there had been nothing he could do for them. Noy, in contrast, was almost a stranger.

But unlike those dead friends, there *was* something Draycos could do for him. Something small; perhaps even something meaningless. But something.

"Very well," he told the boy quietly. "I will stay with you, for as long as I can. Lie down, now, and rest."

Noy's eyes were already closed as he sank back down onto his cot. "Don't leave me," the boy murmured again. "I'm scared."

"I will wait with you awhile," Draycos promised, moving the food and juice containers aside so that he could crouch comfortably beside Noy's cot. "And do not be afraid. You have nothing to fear as long as I am here."

Noy shivered once, his eyes moving restlessly beneath the closed lids. Was he becoming delirious? Sliding even deeper into his fever?

Draycos sighed to himself, wishing even harder he'd brought the comm clip. "I will sing to you," he said, for lack of anything better to say. "A song of danger and courage, of fear and victory. Would you like that?"

"Okay," Noy breathed, his lips barely moving.

And so Draycos began to sing.

Quietly, softly, gently. Songs of encouragement, and hope, and strength. Some of them were the old ballads of the K'da that he had learned as a cub. Others were his own songs, created from the joys and sorrows of his own heart.

Songs that reminded him of his people, and of their war against the Valahgua, and of the home they had been forced to abandon. Songs that reminded him of the terrible responsibility that had been placed between his claws.

Noy lay restlessly through most of it, his face and body twitching in his sleep. Every so often he would wake up, and Draycos would give him another drink of juice. He would then lie down again, and drift back into his troubled sleep.

And Draycos would stroke the boy's forehead, or rest his forepaw comfortingly on his shoulder, and resume his singing.

The night was near its end when the twitching and muttering faded away and Noy seemed to settle into a deeper and more restful sleep. His forehead seemed cooler to the touch, too, but Draycos had no idea whether that was good or bad.

What he did know was that it was long past time for him to go.

"I must go now, Noy," he said. "I will come again later."

The boy just swallowed and rolled over. Sound asleep. Draycos moved the food and juice bottles back to where Noy could reach them, and slipped out of the hut.

The trip back to the Chookoock family side of the hedge was uneventful. He reached the frying pan just as the stars were starting to fade into a reddish glow in the eastern sky. "Jack?" he called quietly, his snout pressed to the gap beneath the door.

There was no answer. "Jack?" he called, a bit more loudly. If the Brummgas had come and taken him away . . .

"About time," Jack's voice came irritably from inside. "Come on, come on—get in."

Draycos shoved the wooden slab inside. Jack's fingers appeared beneath the door, beckoning impatiently. The K'da set his paw on the hand and shifted into two-dimensional form, sliding up his host's arm as he did so.

"Geez, but you had me worried," Jack muttered as Draycos moved to his usual position across Jack's back. "I thought for sure you'd been nailed. What did you do, take the scenic route?"

"Not precisely," Draycos said. "The errand took longer than expected."

"No kidding, Sherlock," Jack said. "You have any idea what time it is?"

"I know it is close to my six-hour time limit," Draycos said. He hadn't realized just how close, actually, until now. The strength flowing into him as he rested against Jack's skin made him realize just how weak he'd been before his return. With Noy's illness filling his thoughts, he hadn't even noticed.

"So what took so long?"

"I was with Noy," Draycos said. "He was afraid, so I sat with him awhile and—"

"Wait a minute," Jack interrupted. "What do you mean, he was afraid? He *saw* you?"

"Yes, but do not be concerned," Draycos said. "He was—"

"He *saw* you?" Jack repeated, sounding stunned. "Oh, that's terrific. That's absolutely terrific."

"It will not be a problem," Draycos insisted, feeling a little annoyed at Jack's reaction. "He was in high fever. If he remembers anything at all, he will undoubtedly conclude it was a dream."

Jack didn't say anything, but Draycos could feel the boy's hands tightening into fists. "It was necessary," the K'da continued firmly. "He was afraid, and sick, and alone. Would you not have done the same if you were there?"

"Yeah, but I *wasn't* there," Jack bit out. The words were harsh, but his tone was beginning to calm a little. "I was in here. Freezing to death, and worried sick about you."

"I am sorry," Draycos said, a flash of guilt replacing his earlier annoyance. "I did not intend to cause you concern. But it was something I had to do."

"Yeah, I know," Jack said with a sigh. "Just one of those K'da poet-warrior things, huh? Like pulling that guy Dumbarton out of the hot dirt on Iota Klestis?"

"Yes," Draycos said. "Interesting that you still remember even the man's name."

"What, you don't?"

"I remember the incident, certainly," Draycos said. "But I

had not made a point of the name. Certainly none of it was of any large importance in my mind. It was a very minor act of mercy, as such things go. One of many that a K'da warrior does as a matter of course."

"I guess maybe it's because it was the first time I saw you do something like that," Jack said. "First time I saw *anyone* do something like that, come to think of it."

"And it turned out all right," Draycos pointed out. "We escaped safely."

"I still think it was a waste of effort," Jack said. "Even if we ever run into him again, which we probably won't, the guy sure isn't going to walk up and thank you."

"Reward and gratitude are not the point of such deeds," Draycos said. "The point is to do what is right, without thought of benefit or reward. Speaking of benefits, did Lisssa ever return?"

"Oh, she returned, all right," Jack said with a snort. "Over and over again, like burps from a bad meal."

Draycos frowned. "I do not understand."

"First she brought a blanket that didn't fit under the door," Jack explained. "She took it back and brought another one. That one she managed to stuff in. Waste of time—the thing wasn't very warm."

"Where is it?" Draycos asked, looking around.

"Back there behind the mesh," Jack said. "I didn't want room service tripping over it if someone actually decides to feed me."

"So she came here two more times?"

"Actually, she came three more times," Jack said. "The third time she brought more of those pancake things. I saved some, if you want them."

"Thank you," Draycos said, lifting his head part of the way off Jack's shoulder and nudging aside the shirt with his snout. Jack offered him a pancake, and he scooped it into his mouth with a flick of his tongue. It was dry and rather chewy, but he was too hungry to care. "I am surprised she would take such a risk so many times."

"You're not supposed to talk with your mouth full," Jack said. "Yeah, I've been wondering about that, too. Especially since Her Thumbleness is probably running her ragged during the day. She ought to be dead on her feet, not scurrying around like a mouse with insomnia."

"With what?"

"Sleeplessness," Jack said. "Can't sleep, so you get up and play cards or something."

"Ah," Draycos said. "Perhaps Doloms do not need much sleep."

"Maybe," Jack said. "That doesn't explain why she wants to play hide-and-seek with Brummgan patrols. Especially after that big speech she gave me way back when about having to look out for yourself."

"Perhaps she is one of those who speak one way but secretly act another," Draycos suggested.

"Don't say it," Jack warned.

"Do not say what?" Draycos asked.

"You're talking about me, right?" Jack growled. "I talk tough, but then I send you out to get fruit juice for Noy?"

"I was not even going to mention you," Draycos protested. "Truly."

"Yeah," Jack said, not sounding convinced. "Speaking of which . . . how is he?"

"I do not know," Draycos said. "He drank one and a half

bottles of fruit juice, and appeared to be sleeping better when I left him. But I do not have any experience with human illnesses."

"I should have given you the comm clip," Jack said, shaking his head. "You could have called Uncle Virge. Well, maybe we can both get out there tomorrow night. Anyway, all that juice should have helped. Thanks for doing that."

"It was my pleasure, and my duty," Draycos said. "And speaking of food . . . ?"

"Oh, right." Jack held up another pancake. "Here."

Draycos had just finished the last one when he sensed the approach of distant footsteps. "Someone is coming," he warned Jack, listening hard. "Three Brummgas, from the sound."

"Oh, good," Jack said sourly. "Room service has finally showed up."

A minute later the door was unlocked and swung open. "You," the lead Brummga rumbled. "Come."

"Wha—?" Jack mumbled, sounding as if he had just been startled awake.

The Brummga didn't bother to repeat the order. He merely reached in and hauled Jack out. "You will come," he said, setting the boy down around the side of the frying pan and giving him a shove toward the house. "The *Panjan* Gazen wants you."

CHAPTER 27

As Jack had expected, the Brummgas took him in through the kitchen door. Also as expected, the kitchen was bustling with slaves preparing breakfast.

Not quite as expected, though, the Brummgas did not take him directly to Gazen. Instead, they turned him over to Heetoorieef. "I have been told to make you presentable," the Wistawk informed Jack coolly. "A breakfast has been prepared for you, as well. Do you wish food or a cleaning first?"

"I think I'll go with the cleaning," Jack said, watching as the Brummgas stomped their way out through the kitchen, the slaves scattering out of their path as they went. "It's okay—I know the way to the bathroom."

He started toward the stairs to the slave quarters. But Heetoorieef stepped into his path. "I have been ordered to keep you in the kitchen until you are called for," the Wistawk said. "There is a cleaning facility over here."

The "cleaning facility" turned out to be a slightly oversized sink with a spray nozzle. Standing beside it, Jack cleaned himself up as best he could, trying to keep out of the way of the hurrying slaves.

After the common shower rooms at the Whinyard's Edge

training camp, and the even more open showers back in the slave colony, he knew he should be used to this by now. But he wasn't. Here, especially, it felt like he was taking a bath in the middle of a city park.

Though again the rest of the slaves seemed to have developed the knack of turning off their eyes to such things. No one even seemed to notice his full-sized dragon tattoo. Or if they did, they didn't mention it to him.

Heetoorieef had left a pile of clean clothes by the sink. Not a clown outfit, this time, or even the artificially cheerful household slave uniform. These were normal, everyday street clothes.

That all by itself was ominous, especially coming off of a night in the frying pan. Had Gazen decided to take Jack up on his offer to do some burglary for him?

Or was this a subtle signal that Jack had already been sold?

He was nearly dressed when the outer kitchen door was again flung open. He looked over and saw a half dozen Wistawki slaves stagger inside, with two Brummgas in the rear herding them along.

His first thought was that the whole lot of them were drunk. His second thought was that they were so utterly fatigued that they were asleep on their feet.

It was only as the first one nearly tripped and turned halfway around that he spotted the bright red lines crisscrossing his back.

The bright red of fresh blood.

Jack caught his breath, his eyes darting to each of them in turn. All six of them had been savagely whipped.

Heetoorieef was just passing by. "Heetoorieef," Jack

hissed, grabbing the other's arm and jerking his head toward the bleeding Wistawki. "What happened?"

Heetoorieef looked toward the others, his alien face unreadable. "They are thieves," he said. "They stole from the slaves' food locker."

Jack felt something catch in his throat. Oh, no. "You're sure it was them?"

"The Brummgas are sure," Heetoorieef said. "That's all that matters."

"But—" Jack broke off. "Suppose they're wrong?"

"And what if they are?"

"What do you mean, what if?" Jack retorted. "They'd have beaten them for nothing."

Heetoorieef turned his eyes onto Jack. "And what if they did?"

Jack stared up at him. "Don't you even care?" he demanded.

The Wistawk looked away. "They are slaves," he said, very quietly. "I am a slave. Come, your food is ready."

Numbly, Jack followed, not even bothering to fasten his shirt all the way up. He felt sick to his stomach, sicker than he'd felt about anything that had happened since he'd arrived in this place. Sicker even than he'd felt watching two innocent bystanders get shot back on the Vagran Colony, right after he'd first met Draycos.

Because this one was his fault. One hundred percent his fault. *He* was the one responsible for that stolen food, not them. That whipping should have been his, not theirs.

In the old days, Uncle Virgil would have had a good laugh over seeing someone else get nailed for a job he and Jack had pulled off. Uncle Virge would probably be less openly cheerful, but even he would congratulate Jack on his good luck at avoiding the blame.

Draycos, in contrast, probably felt every bit as sick as Jack did.

The worst part was that there was nothing in the universe he could do to fix it. Even if he jumped up on the table right now and announced his guilt to the Brummgas, it wouldn't make any difference. The slaves would still be bleeding, the skin of their backs still torn.

For almost three months now Uncle Virge had been warning Jack against Draycos and his K'da warrior ethic. He'd told Jack over and over again that he should stick with looking out for himself, and not worry about other people.

Jack had mostly ignored him, following Draycos's lead and letting the dragon make most of the moral decisions. And up to now it hadn't really cost him very much.

But the guilt now twisting through his stomach was a cost he hadn't counted on. Maybe a cost he wasn't willing to pay.

A small table and chair had been set up near the slaves' food locker, with a bowl full of steaming breakfast stew waiting. "There," Heetoorieef said, gesturing toward it. "Your meal. The *Panjan* Gazen commands that you eat."

Of course Gazen would command it. Jack was a slave, too, after all. Commands, hotboxes, and whippings were all part of the package. "Sure," he muttered.

He sat down. Whatever appetite he'd brought in with him this morning had vanished like Alice down the rabbit hole. Even if it hadn't, he would have felt awkward helping himself to a hearty meal with the rest of the slaves still hard at work around him.

Still, this might be the only decent meal on today's schedule. Maybe on the whole week's schedule, the way Gazen played things. Whether he had an appetite or not, he needed his strength.

Besides, the aroma rising with the steam had already set his stomach growling. Giving up, he picked up the spoon and carved out a small bite.

"Wait," Draycos's voice whispered from his shoulder.

Jack froze, the spoon halfway to his mouth. "What?" he whispered back.

"Let me smell it more closely," Draycos said. He shifted lower on Jack's chest, and the end of his snout rose from the skin.

Jack moved the spoon to the protruding snout, pulling the edges of his unfastened shirt forward a little with his free hand to help hide the dragon from view. "Well?"

Draycos's only answer was to keep sniffing. "Come on, come on," Jack said impatiently. This had better not be something stupid, like the kettlespice balance not being quite right. "What, is it spoiled or something?"

"No," Draycos said. "It is poisoned."

Carefully, Jack lowered the spoon back into the bowl. "You sure?"

"I am positive," Draycos said. "I cannot identify the exact type. But I am certain it *is* a poison."

Jack took a deep breath. So that was how Gazen planned to do it. "A squatter poison," he said. "Bet you aces to deuces it's a squatter poison."

"I do not know that term."

"It's a type of poison that gets into a person's system and

then just sort of sits there," Jack explained bitterly. "Sometimes for years. They're mostly used for big-animal control, like that touring show with the reconstructed dinosaurs."

"What do you mean, it sits there?" Draycos asked. "Where does it sit?"

"All through the tissues," Jack said. "Muscle fibers, lungs, maybe the heart lining. And as long as you take a daily dose of the right antidote, you're fine."

"And if you do not?"

"Then you're dead."

For a moment Draycos was silent. "That is how Gazen plans to keep you under the control of your new buyer," he said. "But can you not find your own supply of the antidote?"

"Sure," Jack said. "Problem is, I don't know which squatter poison it is. The wrong antidote could kill me all by itself."

"What then do we do?"

"We start by going hungry," Jack said, picking up the glass of water beside the bowl and holding it close to his chest. "Take a sniff. Anything here?"

Again, the snout rose an inch out from his skin. "No," Draycos said after a couple of sniffs. "It is clear water."

"Okay," Jack said, taking a sip. It tasted a little funny, but that was probably his imagination. "I just hope there wasn't anything in those pancake things Lisssa gave us."

"There was not," Draycos assured him. "I would have smelled it."

"I hope so," Jack said, taking another sip of the water. It still tasted funny.

"The buyer will have to be told the proper poison and antidote," Draycos went on thoughtfully. "Perhaps we can overhear that information, or else learn it from him later on."

"That's the second time you've mentioned a buyer," Jack said. "You know something I don't?"

"We are expecting you to be sold, are we not?" Draycos reminded him. "These precautions would indicate that time is near. And of course, there are also those military transports to consider."

A sip of water tried to go down the wrong way. "Transports?" Jack demanded when he stopped coughing. "Where?"

"On the west end of the grounds," Draycos said, sounding surprised. "Near the vehicle parking area, between the mansion and the main gate. Did you not see them as we were being brought to the kitchen?"

"I missed it completely," Jack muttered, feeling thoroughly disgusted with himself. "How many were there?"

"At least five," Draycos said. "Possibly more. I was only able to see glimpses of them between the bushes and trees."

"That explains the nice clothes, anyway," Jack said, reaching down and fastening his shirt the rest of the way up. "Looks like Gazen's got a demonstration planned for this morning."

"But Uncle Virge said the auction would not be for three more days," Draycos objected.

"Maybe Gazen got bored," Jack said. "Or maybe all the interested buyers were able to get here early."

He grimaced. "In which case, he might end today's demo by calling for bids."

"What is our plan, then?"

Jack hissed between his teeth, trying to think. "Okay. Step one is to somehow shake ourselves loose long enough to get back to the conference room where we stashed the recorder. Assuming we were lucky enough to get a clear view of Gazen's startup sequence, the next step is to get into his office and copy the Chookoock family mercenary data."

"And then?"

"We run like rabbits," Jack said, draining the rest of the water glass. "I haven't quite got that part figured out yet."

Heetoorieef reappeared at the edge of Jack's vision. "What is this?" he snapped. "You are not eating? You were ordered to eat."

"I'm not hungry," Jack told him. "I guess the sight of shredded Wistawki spoiled my appetite."

Heetoorieef's ears twitched. "I see," he said in a more subdued voice. "I'm sorry."

"I'm sorry, too," Jack said. How sorry, Heetoorieef would never know.

Or maybe he did. "Yes," Heetoorieef said, in a voice that seemed all too knowing. "It's time. Come with me."

CHAPTER 28

Gazen was alone in his office when Heetoorieef showed Jack in. "There you are," the slavemaster said. "All rested and fed, I trust?"

"I'm fine," Jack said.

Apparently the tone hadn't been slavelike enough. Gazen's expression didn't change, but in a single movement he scooped up the extendible slapstick from his desk and flicked it at Jack.

Reflexively, Jack flinched back, banging his left elbow against the wall in the process.

He needn't have bothered. With another wrist flick, Gazen stopped the tip of the weapon a foot in front of his face. "Nervous this morning, I see," he commented. "Not too nervous to perform, I hope."

Jack felt his eyes narrowing. So this was it. The slave auction was indeed coming off early. "Perform?" he asked innocently.

"There are some men who have come to see what you can do," Gazen said. "I trust you'll make it worth their trouble."

"I think I can manage that," Jack said.

"Good," Gazen said. "Because I'd hate to see you embarrass yourself in front of such distinguished visitors."

"I understand," Jack said. "What are they, mercenaries? Other slaveowners? Oversized rodents?"

Gazen smiled slightly. "Very good," he said. "Once again, you show how quickly you grasp the realities of a situation. You've realized that I can't twitch you the way I normally would at such a disrespectful tone. After all, we can't afford to upset those delicate finger muscles."

"Not if we want me to bring a good price," Jack agreed.

"Certainly not," Gazen said. "Still, it may be that no one wants you. Tell me, did you happen to notice a group of slaves come through the kitchen this morning?"

Someday, Jack promised himself darkly, he would find a way to sandblast that bland expression off Gazen's face. "Yes."

"Good," Gazen said. "Then we can both hope that you bring a good price. I trust I need say no more?"

Jack swallowed. No, the implications were as clear as two feet of empty space. He could impress the stuffing out of Gazen's prospective buyers, or he could end up with a shredded back himself. "No, sir."

"Good," Gazen said, standing up. "I do so like a quick learner."

Picking up his slapstick, he slid it into his belt pouch. "Come. Your audience awaits your performance."

He led the way to the banquet hall where they'd held Her Thumbleness's High Day celebration a few nights earlier. But the room had been so rearranged that Jack hardly recognized it. The center had been completely cleared out, with a rug laid down and the tables and chairs arranged in concentric circles around it. Scattered through the empty center were a dozen different types of safes, door locks, and alarm systems. It was rather like a strange dinner theater set up to host a home security show.

There was also a lot of open floor between the various stations, far more than would be needed for each of the audience members to have a clear view. That probably meant the rug was loaded with traps and alarms that Jack was supposed to identify and avoid or disarm.

Fortunately, he wasn't going to have to do it bare-handed. An assortment of tools had been spread out on one of the tables at the edge of the circle, tools that ranged from standard-workman to standard-burglar to extremely non-standard-burglar. Scattered in among them, he saw, were the tools he'd used to break into the gatekeeper's house.

And surrounding it all, seated silently at their tables, was the audience.

There were at least two hundred of them, Jack noted, most of them human but with a number of aliens scattered throughout their midst. There were quite a few Brummgas present as well, mostly lounging around the rear areas of the room chatting quietly to each other. Cynically, he wondered if the auction's invitations had been slanted toward groups who had already hired some of the Chookoock family's mercenaries. A few of the guests were in expensive civilian suits—criminal bosses, most likely, or else representatives of some of the Orion Arm's sleazier governments. But most of the potential bidders were wearing military uniforms.

All sorts of uniforms, too, running the range from very elegant to just barely above shabby. Mercenaries, privateers, maybe a few pirate gangs. All the various groups who might come into possession of other people's safes in their lines of work.

All of them, apparently, looking for a way to get into those safes without the risky use of high explosives.

"Good day to you all," Gazen said, waving Jack to a halt and stepping alone to the edge of the circle. "As you know, the reason for this auction . . ."

He launched into a glowing report of Jack's skills and history, every bit of the latter completely made up. He was going for a high price, all right.

"Jack!" Draycos murmured at Jack's ear.

"Shh," Jack hissed back, glancing at Gazen. The man might be busy spinning a castle out of cobwebs, but that didn't mean he'd gone deaf. And he was only five feet away.

"To your left," Draycos whispered, a note of urgency in his voice. "Four tables back, wearing green clothing."

Casually, Jack shifted his feet and turned leisurely to look that direction. There were four tables' worth of soldiers in green combat fatigues back there. "Which one?" he murmured.

"Behind the three in ordinary clothing," the dragon said.

Jack had already noticed that particular group of civilians. Two of the three men were young and alert and dangerous-looking. Obvious bodyguard types. The third man, the one in the middle, was something quite different. He was late-middle-aged, with black-streaked silver hair, a nose like a hawk's beak, and a mouth set in tight and bitter lines. "Where?" Jack asked again, shifting his attention to the group of mercenaries behind the civilians, trying to figure out which one Draycos had found so interesting.

"Fourth from the left," Draycos murmured.

Jack focused on him. The man was reasonably big,

strongly built, with dark hair and craggy features. There didn't seem to be anything special about him.

And then, suddenly, the face clicked.

It was Dumbarton. The man who'd grabbed Jack as he and Draycos had escaped from the wreckage of Draycos's ship on Iota Klestis. The man Draycos had zapped unconscious with his own slapstick, then insisted on propping up against a tree so that he wouldn't burn to death.

Jack turned away, faking a quiet cough into his right fist. His lungs were suddenly aching, his heart feeling like it was trying to batter its way out of his chest. It was over, then. Any minute now Dumbarton would recognize him, and blow the whistle—

"He attacked you from behind," Draycos murmured in his ear. "I do not believe he ever saw your face."

Jack frowned, running the memory through his mind. The dragon was right. Dumbarton had hidden behind a tree, grabbing Jack as he ran past. Before he'd had a chance to turn his prisoner around, Draycos had knocked him out.

Of course, he must have seen Jack coming toward him before the grab. But that whole ridge had been thick with smoke from the crash and its aftermath, and the man had been careful to duck out of sight before his prey got too close.

Jack coughed again, just for show, then straightened up again and looked casually back at Dumbarton. There was indeed no sign of recognition in the man's face.

He turned back to Gazen, his heartbeat beginning to calm down again. So if Dumbarton wasn't a threat, why had Draycos bothered to point him out? Merely to show that, despite Jack's earlier prediction, they had indeed bumped into him again?

And then it hit him. Dumbarton hadn't been wearing any insignia during the looting of the K'da ship. Neither had the Brummga they'd also tangled with. Neither, for that matter, had the Djinn-90 fighters they'd had to fight their way past. Whoever had set up that attack had taken pains to make sure any potential witnesses couldn't identify them.

But here, there was no need for such caution.

And there was indeed a small red-and-yellow insignia attached to the top left of Dumbarton's green shirt. Squinting slightly, Jack could just make out the two words circling around it.

Malison Ring.

He took a deep breath. Finally. After two months of trying to dig through spacecraft records, mercenary records, and now even slave records, they had finally done it. They had found the mercenary group who had joined with the Valahgua.

And after all that work and sweat, the answer had practically dropped into their laps. All because Dumbarton had come to Gazen's slave auction.

Because he hadn't burned to death on Iota Klestis. Because Draycos had taken the time to perform a very minor act of mercy.

Mentally, Jack shook his head. Uncle Virge, he knew, wasn't going to believe this.

Gazen finished his presentation and gestured Jack toward the tool table. "All right, Jack," he said, smiling as always. But Jack could see a hint of the earlier warning in his eyes. "There are the locks. Open them."

Jack smiled back. The first smile he'd really felt since arriving on Brum-a-dum.

And it felt good. It felt really good. "Certainly," he said.

Four hours later, Gazen called a break for lunch. By that time, Jack had managed to open three of the door lock systems and four of the safes. He had also, just for good measure, disarmed three hidden floor alarms without a peep out of any of them.

He had hoped he might be able to con Gazen into allowing him to eat with the rest of the group. Mingling with them would increase the risk that Dumbarton would suddenly recognize him, but it would also give him a chance for a decent and unpoisoned meal.

But no such luck. The minute the Wistawki waiters appeared, Jack was whisked off under Brummgan guard back to the kitchen.

There, Heetoorieef had another meal ready for him. It contained the same poison as the breakfast stew.

Jack spent part of the lunch break moving the food around on his plate and pretending to eat. Occasionally, when no one was looking, he forked a few bites down behind one of the cabinets. If he could convince them that he'd swallowed enough of the poison, they might quit spiking his food.

On the other hand, at that point they would presumably also start feeding him the antidote. That could be just as dangerous; and there was no guarantee that his resident K'da could sniff it out the way he could a straight poison. All the more reason to wrap this up and get off this planet.

An hour later, with the buyers well-fed and Jack's own

stomach still growling unhappily, he was taken back into the banquet hall.

The afternoon session went as well as the morning one had. Jack finished opening the safes, popped the rest of the door locks, and disarmed the security alarms.

He also avoided two more booby-traps that Gazen had added to areas of the rug Jack had already cleared. A rather cheap trick, in his opinion, but one he'd sort of expected the slavemaster to pull.

As near as he could read his audience, that success alone made as much of an impression as all the rest of it put together.

The sky was beginning to darken outside the windows by the time Gazen called a halt. "Thank you all for coming," he said as Jack returned his tools to the table. "You have until nine o'clock tomorrow morning to submit your bids. In the meantime, the hospitality of the Chookoock family is at your disposal."

There was a general murmuring and creaking of chairs as the buyers started to gather their notes and other items. "You—come with me," Gazen said to Jack. "You—" he added to one of the Brummgan guards, pointing to the equipment table "—put those away. And make sure he didn't steal anything."

He set off across the banquet room floor. Jack followed, the inevitable Brummgan guards thudding stolidly along behind him.

Midway to the door, he managed to quietly lose the lock-pick he'd palmed.

He'd expected Gazen to take him back to the kitchen for a third try at stuffing squatter poison down his throat. Instead, the slavemaster led the way toward his office.

Toward it, but not to it. Circling past the door, he went into the small conference room around the corner from it.

The same conference room where Jack and Draycos had hidden their stolen recorder.

Gazen opened the door and went in. "Sit," he ordered, jabbing a finger at a chair near the back of the room. "There's someone who wants to meet you."

"Oh?" Jack asked, glancing around the empty room as he crossed to the seats. "Where is he?"

"He'll be along in a moment," Gazen promised. "You did very well today. Very well indeed. Even I was impressed."

"Thank you," Jack said, the hairs on the back of his neck tingling unpleasantly as he sat down. What was the slavemaster up to this time?

"You particularly impressed one of our visitors, as well," Gazen went on. "So much so that he asked for a private meeting." Behind him the door opened, and one of the civilian bodyguards who'd been sitting in front of Dumbarton stepped in. He glanced around, then nodded back toward the door. A moment later, his two companions from the demonstration joined him, first the hawk-nosed, middle-aged man, then the second bodyguard.

And there was something in the older man's eyes that sent a shiver up Jack's back.

"Here they are now," Gazen said, a strange sort of sinister amusement lurking in his tone. "This, gentlemen, is Jack McCoy. Say hello, Jack."

"Hello," Jack said cautiously.

"And now say hello to Jack," Gazen invited.

The hawk-nosed man took half a step forward. "Hello, Jack Morgan," he said quietly.

Jack felt the breath freeze in his lungs. He'd heard this voice before. Twice before. The first time was through Dumbarton's comm clip as he stood in the hot dirt of Iota Klestis. The second time was from behind glaring lights in the luxury office aboard the *Advocatus Diaboli*.

It was the man he'd called Snake Voice. The man who had framed him for robbery, and then for murder, and then had forced him into his plan to kill Cornelius Braxton.

A man who'd also been present when Draycos's advance team was slaughtered by the Valahgua.

"Well, well," Jack said as calmly as he could. "Mr. Arthur Neverlin. It's a pleasure to finally meet you, sir."

CHAPTER 29

Neverlin's face didn't even twitch. But Gazen's did. Rather strongly, in fact. "I thought you said he didn't know you," he said, flashing a glare at Neverlin.

"I said he'd never seen me," Neverlin corrected. "We have met, though, after a fashion."

"Of course we've met," Jack said, with a heartiness he didn't especially feel. So there it was, the connection he and Draycos had been searching for all this time: Arthur Neverlin, the Chookoock family, and the Malison Ring, an unholy alliance tied together with the Valahgua. "Didn't he tell you, *Panjan* Gazen? He tried to kill Cornelius Braxton and take over Braxton Universis. That's why he's on the run now, from Braxton and most of the law enforcement agencies in the Orion Arm."

"As you can see, he's also been listening to Braxton's lies about me," Neverlin said, lifting his eyebrows at Jack. "I don't suppose he bothered to mention that I've been his chief troubleshooter for over twenty years. Or that I've pulled Braxton Universis out of trouble more times than you could count or that he could remember."

He leveled an accusing finger at Jack's face. "And while I'm slaving away running *his* empire, *he's* spending his time dabbling in his little charities and getting his picture taken with Internos politicians. *I'm* the one who keeps the company running. *I'm* the one who does the work. Why *shouldn't* I have the title and the authority?"

"Gee, I don't know," Jack said. "Maybe because it isn't yours?"

"That's rich, coming from a professional thief," Neverlin said scornfully. "You've got a lot to learn about how the real world operates."

Jack grimaced. "You sound like Uncle Virge."

"No doubt," Neverlin said, turning to Gazen. "Speaking of whom, you say he's sitting on the ground at Ponocce Spaceport?"

"That's where their ship is, anyway," Gazen bit out, glaring blackly at Jack. "I *knew* there was something bent about this whole thing. What do you think they're up to?"

"No idea," Neverlin said. "But we can figure that out later. Right now, the trick will be to actually get hold of the man. He's as slippery as greased ice."

"Why don't I send some Brummgas over there, backed up by some Djinn-90s?" Gazen suggested. "He'll either come quietly, or he'll have his ship turned into Christmas tinsel around him."

Neverlin shook his head. "I want him alive and in one piece, not scattered across the Brum-a-dum landscape."

"He'll surrender," Gazen insisted. "What other choice will he have?"

"I don't know," Neverlin said. "But it's not wise to underestimate Virgil Morgan. I did that a couple of months ago, to my regret."

He shrugged. "Still, the game goes on. And we do hold an important pawn. You said he's been treated?"

Gazen looked at Jack. "Actually, we're not sure," he said carefully. "The, uh—"

"If you're talking about the poisoned food, the answer is no," Jack offered. "I didn't eat any of it."

Gazen's eyes narrowed. Neverlin merely smiled. "As I said, slippery. Both of them."

He lifted a finger, and one of the two bodyguards stepped forward. "But the time for subtlety is past," Neverlin went on. "We'll pour some of it down his throat, then call his uncle and have a little chat."

"Wait a second," Jack said hurriedly as the bodyguard got a none-too-gentle grip on his upper arm and hauled him to his feet. "You don't have to do this. Let me call Uncle Virge and tell him what you're planning. I'm sure he'll be happy to talk with you."

Neverlin smiled thinly. "Thank you for the kind offer. But I've already seen what happens when I let you set the terms of a deal." He gestured, and the bodyguard started toward the door, pulling Jack behind him. "No, you're the sort of untrained puppy who does best with a good solid leash attached."

The second bodyguard pulled the door open. "These two are going to the medical suite," Gazen informed the two Brummgas waiting outside the room, gesturing at Jack and the bodyguard. "You'll escort them there. I'll call the doctor and give him his instructions."

"And when he's ready, take him to my shuttle," Neverlin put in.

"Just a minute," Gazen said, holding out a hand. "I'm sorry, Mr. Neverlin, but you can't do that."

"Morgan won't just meekly give in," Neverlin said patiently. "He'll attempt a rescue or some other equally insane thing. We don't want him to know exactly where the boy is."

"Then we'll hide him somewhere on the grounds," Gazen said firmly. "He's still Chookoock family property."

"Fine," Neverlin said disgustedly. "Then I'll just buy him. All right?"

"I'm sorry, but I can't let you do that, either," Gazen said. He looked uncomfortable, but his voice was firm. "We've offered him for sale and asked for bids. I can't sell him—to you or anyone else—without giving an equal chance to *all* those bidding. It's strict Chookoock family policy."

"Then the Chookoock family had better learn when to make exceptions," Neverlin warned. His voice was quiet, but there was a dark menace sliding beneath it like a shark in murky waters. "Or had you forgotten what's at stake here?"

"Maybe he's just wondering if your side is really the smart one to bet on," Jack murmured.

Neverlin favored him with a tight smile. "How little you know," he said softly. "But you'll learn. As will the rest of the Orion Arm." He looked back at Gazen. "Remind your superiors of the power they stand to gain. And then I *will* take the boy out of here."

Gazen's lip twitched. "I'll give them the message," he said. "But that's all I can do."

Neverlin snorted. "Underlings," he said contemptuously. "Fine; *I* will talk to them. Take me there."

"As you wish." Gazen threw a dark look at the Brummgas. "What are you waiting for? I told you what to do. Do it."

"Yes, *Panjan* Gazen," one of them said. "Come, humans."

The Brummgas led the way back across the entryway chamber. "And here we go," Jack commented, glancing part way over his shoulder. The bodyguard was following behind him, staying a cautious three steps back. Too far away for Draycos to get to, at least not without being seen. "It might not be a bad idea for *you* to think about which side you're on, either," he suggested.

"I'm on the right side," the bodyguard countered calmly. "You will be, too, in a couple of minutes."

They reached the far side of the chamber and headed into a deserted corridor Jack had never been down. "I just thought you might want to reconsider," he went on, glancing over his shoulder again. Aside from their little group, he couldn't see anyone else in either direction. This was probably the best chance he and Draycos would have. "You too, of course," he added, turning around to look at the Brummgas on either side of him. "Lucky for you, the Chookoock family isn't the only one hiring on Brum-a-dum."

"He's a talky one, isn't he?" the bodyguard grunted.

"All you humans are talky," one of the Brummgas growled. "He is one of you. You keep him quiet."

"You hear that?" the bodyguard said. Jack held his breath; from the sound of the voice, he could tell the man was moving forward, closing the gap between them. "Shut it off, or we'll do it for you."

"Oh, come on," Jack argued. "Freedom of speech comes right after the preamble in the Internos Constitution—"

"I said *shut up*," the bodyguard snarled. He stepped up behind Jack and gave him a hard slap across the side of the head for emphasis—

And Jack was shoved forward as Draycos boiled up out of the back of his shirt. Even as he tried to catch his balance there was a *crack* of K'da scales against human skin from behind him. An instant later, out of the corner of his eye, he saw the dragon arcing overhead toward the two Brummgas.

And as the bodyguard landed on the floor with a thud, Draycos caught the Brummgas' heads between his forepaws and slammed them together. The two aliens collapsed, sprawling into an untidy heap.

"Easy," Jack warned, glancing quickly around. Just ahead on the right was a door marked *Storage*. "Those helmets of theirs aren't all *that* strong."

"I needed to make certain they were unconscious," Draycos said grimly, crouching low to the floor. "Besides, one of them helped whip the other slaves. I could smell Wistawki blood on him."

"Ah," Jack said, trying the storage room door. It was unlocked. "Is revenge part of the K'da warrior ethic?"

"We are authorized to deliver justice," Draycos said, hooking one of the Brummgas by the tunic and dragging him into the storage room.

"I know that," Jack said, crouching beside the Brummga and starting to unfasten his jacket. "So was this one justice or revenge?"

"Perhaps a combination of both," Draycos conceded, going back for the other Brummga. "Odd. I have never felt the desire for revenge before."

Jack frowned as he dumped the Brummga alongside his

companion. "Not even with the Valahgua slaughtering your people?"

"I have felt fear, and courage, and resolve," Draycos said, the tip of his tail making slow circles in the air as he added the bodyguard to the pile of unconscious bodies. "But I have never acted so strongly from revenge before."

"Probably too much time spent with us emotionally impulsive humans," Jack grunted, pulling off the first Brummga's jacket. It was heavier than it looked. "Or with Uncle Virge. Revenge and profit were Uncle Virgil's two main reasons for doing anything. Help me get this on, will you?"

"Wearing this will not allow you to masquerade as a Brummga," Draycos warned as he took most of the weight of the jacket on his forepaws.

"Not in here, no," Jack said. "But outside in the dark it might be good enough. Especially while I'm sitting in one of those cars they use to move slaves around."

"We do not need a car," Draycos pointed out. "Remember the military transports. We can send one to crash into the gate, then follow in a second."

"Sounds like a plan," Jack agreed, unfastening the Brummga's helmet and pulling it off. "But first I want to check and see if Noy's all right."

"I see," Draycos said, his voice carefully neutral.

"You think that's a bad idea?" Jack challenged.

"On the contrary," the dragon said softly. "It is a very courageous idea. One that is worthy of a K'da warrior."

"In other words, recklessly stupid," Jack grunted, trying the helmet on for size. It was way too big, of course, but in the dark it should do. "I've been spending too much time with *you,* I guess. Come on, let's get out of here."

CHAPTER 30

There were no guards watching the cars. Jack helped himself to one, and they headed across the Chookoock family grounds.

No one challenged them, either from the house or from the hidden guard posts, and soon they were through the gap in the thorn hedge. With Draycos directing, they arrived at Noy's isolation hut.

It was empty.

"He has not been gone long," the dragon said, sniffing at the air and the cot. "Four hours, perhaps five."

"The empty juice bottles are still here," Jack said, peering under the cot. "If the Brummgas had hauled him away, they'd probably have taken those along to try to figure out where they came from."

"Agreed," Draycos said. "Perhaps Noy decided he was recovered enough to return to the others."

"Maybe," Jack said. "As long as we're out here anyway, we might as well check."

The meal hall was brightly lit as they arrived at the edge of the slave colony. The evening meal, clearly, was in full swing.

"Okay," Jack said, shedding his borrowed Brummgan armor and dumping it in the back seat. "We do this nice and cool. As far as any of them knows, there's no reason why I shouldn't be back." Crossing the empty ground, he walked into the meal hall.

It was like stepping back into a bad dream. Or, more accurately, like stepping from one part of a bad dream into another. The sights, the sounds, the smells—all of it came rushing back like a multiple slap in the face.

Even in the few days he'd been away, he'd managed to forget the squalor these slaves lived in. The squalor, and the filth, and the hunger.

And the hopelessness.

"To your left, one table back," Draycos murmured in his ear. "Seated beside Maerlynn."

"I see him," Jack murmured back. Noy was there, all right, looking tired but otherwise mostly recovered. Ready to go back to picking rainbow berries and making money for the Chookoock family.

For the rest of his life.

And as Jack thought about that, he felt something stirring inside him. A strange sort of anger, of a kind he'd never felt before.

This was no place for a child. No place at all.

"You will go see if he is all right?" Draycos prompted.

"Sure," Jack said, heading that direction. The Jantri twins were there, too, sitting across from Noy and Maerlynn. They looked too tired to even talk. One of them—Grib—had a slapstick welt across his forehead.

And the stirring anger inside Jack started to burn with a white-hot glow. "Yeah, we'll check him out," he told Draycos. "And then we're going to *get* him out."

"What?" the dragon asked, sounding startled. "Are you saying—?"

"Jack!" Maerlynn exclaimed as she caught sight of him. "Welcome back. We've been wondering where you were."

"Sorry," Jack said, stepping to a spot between the twins. Greb had a fresh slapstick welt too, he saw now, angled across his shoulder. Fleck, or the Brummgas, must have been in especially good form today. "I got delayed. How are you feeling, Noy?"

"Okay," the boy said, smiling wanly up at him. "A little tired, but mostly okay."

"Good," Jack said. "Then go get your things together. We're leaving."

"What do you mean?" Maerlynn asked, frowning. "Her Thumbleness doesn't want him, too, does she?"

"I mean we're leaving this place," Jack said. "Out past the wall. To freedom."

The conversation at the nearby tables had faded away. "Jack, are you feeling all right?" Maerlynn asked, her fore-head wrinkling as she stretched out a hand toward his cheek. "Here, let me see—"

"I'm not sick," Jack told her, pushing her hand roughly aside. "And I'm not hallucinating. I'm leaving. Right now. And I'm taking Noy with me."

"Wow," Noy breathed, his eyes wide. "Just like he said."

"Jack, you can't just walk out of here," Maerlynn said carefully. "They'll whip you for even trying. They may even kill you."

"They can take their best shot," Jack said. "It won't do them a scrap of good."

"Jack, you're scaring everyone," Maerlynn said, her voice low. "Please. Stop."

Abruptly, Jack realized that the whole room had gone dead quiet. Lifting his gaze, he looked around.

They were all looking back at him. All the slaves. Sitting silently, their meager meals forgotten. Most of the faces held scorn, he could see, or simple flat-out disbelief. Some of them, like Maerlynn had said, were clearly frightened by Jack's attitude.

Scorn, or disbelief, or fear.

But no hope.

They had been here too long, he realized. Whatever hope they might ever have had, Gazen and the Brummgas had burned out of them.

No, this was no place for a child. It was no place for anyone.

And it was about time someone did something about that.

"I'm leaving," he called, raising his voice so that it could be heard throughout the whole room. "Tonight. Anyone else hate this place enough to go with me?"

"You're a fool," an Eytra growled from two tables over. "Many have tried. None have succeeded."

"Then I guess Noy and I will be the first," Jack said. "Does that mean you're not coming?"

"Jack, this isn't funny," Maerlynn said in a low voice. "Noy's parents tried to escape. They died. The Brummgas beat his father to death. Can't you see that all this is doing is bringing back horrible memories?"

"It's not bad to have memories, Maerlynn," Noy said. He was looking up at Jack, an oddly intense expression on his face. "Memories anchor us to the past, give us a sense of the present, and point the way to the future."

A tingle ran up Jack's back. That did not sound like Noy. Not at all. In fact, it sounded exactly like—

"What's that supposed to mean?" the Eytra asked with a sniff.

"It's something the gold dragon told me," Noy said. "He said that memories are what give us strength and courage."

"Noy, you have *got* to stop this nonsense," Maerlynn said firmly. "It was a dream. I told you that. Nothing but a dream."

"It was *not* a dream," Noy insisted. Abruptly, he stood up, wavering a little. "Here's what he said."

THE NIGHT WAS CALM, THE BATTLE NEAR,
THE ENEMY WAS WET WITH FEAR.
THEIR EARS WERE HEARKENED;
THEY HAD DARKENED
MEMORIES WE HELD SO DEAR.

AND NOW AT DAYBREAK CAME THE TEST.
AGAIN WE CHARGED, STRAIGHT TO THEIR BEST.
WE CUT THEM DOWN:
SWORD, GUN, AND CROWN.
THE BATTLEFIELD WITH BLOOD WAS DRESSED.

OUR VENGEANCE THUS WE HAD ACHIEVED,
THE RELICS OF OUR HOPE RECEIVED.
AND TO THE SONG,
TWELVE EONS LONG,
WE ADD THE LIVES OF COMRADES GRIEVED.

He took a deep breath and looked at Maerlynn. "See?" he said defiantly. "I didn't make *that* up, either."

Maerlynn had a stunned look on her face. "Where did you hear that?" she asked.

"You couldn't just sit with him," Jack muttered toward his collar. "You had to sing, too."

"I told you—the dragon sang that to me," Noy said. "And he told me not to give up hope. That someday I would be free."

"That day is today, Noy," Jack said. "For you, and anyone else who wants to go."

"This dragon," a Parprin from across the room said in a husky voice. "What did it look like?"

"It was all gold," Noy said. "Smaller than dragons you hear about in stories. He gave me food and juice, and he sang."

The Parprin flexed his ears and stood up. "All right. I'm in."

"What?" the Eytra demanded, turning in his seat to look at the Parprin. "Have you gone crazy, Muskrack?"

"The gold dragon is a symbol of hope and change," the Parprin said. "And what have we to lose?"

"Our lives, for starters," the Eytra said scornfully. "If you two humans want to be insane, go be insane somewhere else."

"I intend to," Jack promised. "On the far side of the wall." He looked down at Maerlynn. "Well?"

Maerlynn gave a deep sigh. "Jack . . . I can't. I have Grib and Greb and Lisssa to think about. What would they do without me?"

"So bring the twins along," Jack offered. "As for Lisssa, maybe we can pick her up on our way out."

"Pick her up where?" Greb asked. "She's—well, she *was* right here."

Jack frowned. "What do you mean, right here? She's at the Chookoock family mansion."

"No, she's not," Maerlynn said, frowning back. "How would she get there?"

"But—"

And then, the horrible truth hit him. Lisssa, stealing out to the frying pan every couple of hours. Lisssa, who had told him she only looked out for herself, coming to see how he was doing. Lisssa, risking her life with the Brummgan patrols to bring him food and blankets.

Lisssa, helping Gazen make sure Jack stayed put throughout the night.

Lisssa, a Brummgan informant.

"See?" Grib said, pointing behind Jack. "There she is."

Jack spun around. There she was, all right, slipping out the door into the night to report to her masters.

Jack snarled one of Uncle Virgil's favorite curses, his eyes darting to the floor and the tables. The floor? Too crowded. He'd never make it around everyone and catch up with her. Not with the lead she already had.

The tables, then? Leap up onto one of them, bound across to the next, and so on to the door? But there were just as many people around the tables as there were in the narrow aisles between them. And the tables were loaded with dishes and cups besides.

No, there was only one way to stop her now. Only one person who could catch her before she blew the whistle and brought the whole Chookoock family down on them.

"Draycos," he hissed. "We haven't got a choice." The dragon didn't answer, but Jack could feel him coil himself to spring. Jack braced himself, wondering dimly what all the scoffers would say when the golden dragon actually appeared.

Then, from the direction of the doorway came a sudden

squawk. There was a second squawk; and to Jack's amazement, Lisssa reappeared in the doorway. She hesitated, as if unwilling to continue; and then a large human hand appeared from the darkness and shoved her roughly all the way inside.

And stepping into the hut behind her—

"Here you go, Jack," Fleck called cheerfully across the room as he gave Lisssa another shove. "This what you were looking for?"

CHAPTER 31

Jack felt his knees go suddenly weak. Fleck. Bright red sash across his chest. Slapstick at his side. Full authority of the Brummgas at his back.

But he, Jack, had Draycos. A single command, and the K'da warrior would leap out of his collar and tear Fleck into small, bloody pieces—

"Here," Fleck said, flipping something small toward Jack.

Automatically, Jack reached out and caught it. It was a comm clip, one side colored and shaped just like a Dolom scale. "What's this?" he asked, frowning up at Fleck again.

"*This*—" Fleck shook Lisssa's arm "—is a Brummgan spy. Gazen gives them special privileges in exchange for information." He spun Lisssa around and gave her a final shove that landed her on one of the benches. "I've suspected her for a long time."

"Ask if she communicated with them," Draycos murmured in Jack's ear.

"Was she able to get off a message just now?" Jack asked.

"I don't think so," Fleck said. "But my guess is they already know something's up. If we're going to go, we'd better be quick."

Jack blinked. " 'We'?"

"Sure." Fleck smiled tightly, sending a look around the room. "Like Jack said," he went on, raising his voice. "Anyone else hate this place enough to go with us?"

"It's a trick," someone growled. "Fleck's one of them, too."

"None of the rest of us carry weapons," someone else added pointedly.

Fleck didn't even bother to glance that direction. He started toward Jack, the crowd melting away from in front of him.

And as he got within arm's length he drew his slapstick.

Jack tensed. But Fleck merely turned the weapon around and handed it to him, handle first. "I'm willing to take a chance," the big man said, looking around the room again. "How about you?"

For a moment the room was silent. Then, in twos and threes, the slaves began murmuring quietly among themselves. "If this *is* a trick," Jack said quietly to Fleck, "I'll make it my business to be sure you're the first one in the Brummgas' line of fire."

"It's no trick," Fleck said, just as quietly. "Strange things have been happening around here lately. Odd footprints in the dirt. Odd activity by the Brummgas at night. Someone carefully cutting their way through the thorn hedge."

He must have seen something in Jack's face, because he smiled suddenly. "Oh, yes, I knew about that. The Brummgas tried to keep it quiet. But I knew."

He nodded fractionally to the side. "And now we've got Noy coming back from an isolation hut with stories about gold dragons."

"What do you think it all means?" Jack asked, keeping his voice even.

"Maybe it's nothing but wishful thinking," Fleck said bluntly. "Maybe you're just a con man playing on old legends and gullible types like Muskrack who find omens in everything they see or hear. Maybe all you're doing is trying to turn us into a distraction so you can sneak out alone." He paused, his eyes steady on Jack.

"I came back to get Noy," Jack told him. "I just thought some of the rest of you would like to get out, too."

Fleck snorted under his breath. "And maybe you're such a good con man that you can sound as honest as you're sounding right now."

Jack felt a stirring of anger. Here he was, risking his own life and freedom for these people. Living up to the K'da warrior ethic that Draycos was always prattling on about. And all Fleck could think about was that it might be a con? "Look, Fleck—"

Fleck stopped him with an upraised hand. "All I know is two things," he said. "One, that none of this strange stuff happened until you showed up. And two—"

He looked at Noy. "There's no way that kid came up with that poem on his own. No way. Something big *is* going on, and I'm willing to take a chance on it."

His eyes drilled into Jack's face. "Just remember one thing. I'm the one responsible for these people. It's my job to keep them in line so that the Brummgas will stay off their backs. If you're spouting smoke . . . you understand me?"

Jack swallowed. "Perfectly."

"Jack, may I have a word with you?" Draycos murmured at his ear.

Jack took a deep breath. "I'm going to take a quick look outside," he told Fleck. "Be right back."

He could feel the slaves' eyes following him as he made his way to the door. Maybe they were wondering if he'd given up on them and was heading out on his own.

Good. A little pressure might help them make up their minds.

He'd half expected to find a ring of armed Brummgas waiting outside. But the night was quiet. "I know what you're thinking," he told Draycos before the dragon could say anything. "And I suppose it *is* stupid to trust Fleck. But as near as I can read him, he seems okay."

"I agree," Draycos said calmly. "There is no reason for him to have stopped Lisssa if he was on the Brummgas' side."

"Unless it's a setup," Jack said, as the thought suddenly struck him. "Maybe Lisssa never was a spy."

"No," Draycos said. "I had not thought of it before, but when she came to the frying pan to offer you food, I did not smell any paint on her. Yet she implied Her Thumbleness had brought her into the house for that purpose."

"Right," Jack said, nodding. Now that Draycos mentioned it, he hadn't smelled anything, either. "So she *was* a spy. Good. What did you want to talk to me about?"

"I merely wondered if you had considered the extra problems involved in bringing such a large group of slaves with us," the dragon said.

Jack looked sideways down into his collar. "I thought *you* were the one who hated slavery so much."

"I did not say I did not approve," Draycos said, a little huffily. "I merely asked if you had considered the problems."

Behind Jack, the meal hall door opened. Jack turned to see Fleck come out, a small group of slaves behind him. "All set," Fleck said. "This is it."

Jack felt his throat tighten. Of the hundred and fifty slaves inside, no more than twenty had elected to come. "This is *it*?"

"Life inside the wall is a known," Fleck said grimly. "Life outside is an unknown. What can I say?"

"Even when that known is slavery?"

"This is the group," Fleck said. "Take it or leave it."

Jack looked them over. Muskrack the Parprin was there, he saw. So were Maerlynn, and Noy, and even Greb and Grib.

His mind flashed back to Maerlynn's comment that first night in the slaves' quarters. That the Jantri twins, who had never known any life besides slavery, were quite happy under Chookoock family rule. And yet, here they were.

One of Uncle Virgil's favorite sayings ran through the back of his mind. *Unless you become like a little child, you cannot enter the kingdom of heaven . . .*

Of course, Uncle Virgil had generally used the line in regard to some job where Jack was supposed to con his way into a particularly well-stocked vault somewhere. But it applied even better here. "We take it, of course," he said.

"Good," Fleck said. "What's the plan?"

"Diversion," Draycos murmured in his ear. "Glider."

Jack frowned. He dearly wished Draycos would stop throwing these short, cryptic messages at him. "First things first," he said. "Do I understand we have a glider available?"

Fleck blinked in surprise. "You know about that?"

"Of course," Jack said, trying to sound casual. It must be something Draycos had found on one of his nighttime walks. "The question is, how do *you* know about it?"

Fleck's lip twitched. "I was the one who helped Noy's parents build it. Unfortunately, they got caught before they could use it to take him out."

"Not so unfortunately," Jack told him. "If they had, all three of them would be dead. The wall has lasers and flame jets aiming upwards to stop anyone who tries to get in or out."

"I didn't know that," Fleck said in a low voice. "So I guess that's it for the glider."

"Not necessarily," Jack said. An idea was taking shape in the back of his mind as Draycos's cryptic comment started to make sense. "Do we know how many armed Brummgas they've got in the estate?"

Fleck shrugged. "I'd guess sixty or seventy."

"Vehicles?"

"A couple dozen of those open-topped cars," Fleck said. "There are also six small airfighters—Clax-7 patrol planes, six-seaters. Those are probably armed."

"Then we're in business," Jack said. "How long will it take to get the glider ready to fly?"

"It's mostly ready now," Fleck said. "I just need to wind up the launcher and fire it off."

"And it'll go over the wall?"

Fleck grimaced. "Halfway over, anyway."

"That's all we'll need," Jack assured him. "How many people will it take to get it going?"

Fleck was eying him closely. "I can do it myself," he said.

"Okay," Jack said. "That's your job, then."

He gestured over his shoulder. "The rest of us are going to go through the thorn hedge and head for the front of the house. There are some transports there, big ones that can get us off-planet. We'll borrow one, and take it right through the gate."

"Who's going to fly it?" someone asked.

"I will," Jack said.

"How will we get through the hedge?" Maerlynn asked.

"Yeah," Muskrack agreed. "They watch that gap."

"There's another opening we can use, about a hundred yards east of the road," Jack told him. "Once you fire off the glider, Fleck, you head there and catch up with us."

"What about the guards?" Noy asked.

"Most of them should charge off to see who was trying to get over the wall," Jack said. "We'll just have to take care of whoever's left by ourselves."

"What, with that?" someone asked, pointing to the slapstick Fleck had given Jack.

Jack smiled. "Hardly," he said. "I've got a friend already on it."

There was a moment of awkward silence. "*A* friend?" someone asked pointedly.

"Trust me, he's more than able to deal with the Brummgas," Jack assured him, grimacing to himself. *Trust me,* he'd said; only these weren't fellow con men he was trying to talk into helping on some scheme. These were slaves, who'd seen every other escape attempt ruthlessly crushed by their Brummgan masters.

There was another moment of silence. "Well, then, we'd better get going," Fleck said with a hearty confidence Jack could tell he didn't entirely feel. "You have any other instructions?"

Jack took a deep breath. "You've got five minutes to gather whatever you want to take with you," he said, pointing toward the sleeping quarters. "Fleck, give us—" he paused, doing a quick estimate "—give us twenty minutes before you fire off the glider. Can you do that?"

Fleck nodded. "Sure."

"And really hustle on your way back," Jack warned.

"Once we start our play, we may not be able to slow it down. Okay; everyone go get your stuff."

The group scattered, the slaves hurrying toward the two sleeping huts. "Good luck," Jack said, nodding to Fleck.

"See you soon," Fleck said. Giving Jack one last measuring look he turned and headed the opposite way into the forest.

"What now?" Draycos murmured.

"First job is to get through the hedge," Jack told him, heading toward a wide tree twenty yards from the light pouring out of the huts. "Think you can finish that hole you were working on?"

"No problem."

"Gazen may still have guards watching it," Jack pointed out. "You'll have to deal with them."

"As I said, no problem," the dragon repeated. "And then?"

"I'm afraid you're going to get the heavy end of this one, buddy," Jack said. Reaching the wide tree, he slid halfway around it, putting his right sleeve out of sight from the slave areas. "You're going to have to clear the path for us through whatever guard posts the Brummgas have out there. *And* you're going to have to do it without letting any of our group spot you. I know that's a lot to ask."

"You have not yet truly seen what a K'da warrior can do, Jack," Draycos said. "Where shall I meet you when I am finished? At the mercenary transports?"

"Right," Jack said, his throat suddenly feeling dry. The grim confidence in the dragon's voice was just a little scary. "I'll pick the best-armored one and set it to ram the gate. We'll take the next-best-armored one to ride out in."

"You will need to alert Uncle Virge that we are coming."

Jack nodded. "I'll call him as soon as you're on your way. Any questions?"

"None." With a flicker of weight, Draycos slid out of Jack's sleeve. "I will see you there."

"Good luck," Jack called softly as the dragon bounded off into the night.

"Warrior's luck," Draycos corrected over his shoulder.

He disappeared behind a stand of rainbow berry bushes and was gone. Glancing once more around him, Jack lifted his left foot and pried back the sole.

Uncle Virge, he thought darkly, was going to love this.

CHAPTER 32

The last hint of glow was gone from the western sky. Draycos moved across the ground like a golden shadow, quick and silent.

A golden shadow that was rapidly fading to black as his pounding heart drove dark blood into his muscles and scales. A poet-warrior of the K'da, in full combat readiness.

Jack had indeed never seen what a K'da warrior could do. He probably wouldn't see it now, either.

The hidden Brummgan watcher was just settling into position when Draycos arrived at the hedge. Comfortably concealed, no doubt feeling quite pleased with himself, the guard was clearly not expecting any trouble.

He didn't so much as squeak as Draycos knocked him cold.

The hedge itself was still the tangled mess he'd found on his previous visits. But now that he didn't have to conceal his handiwork, the thorny branches retreated before his slashing claws like driftwood before an incoming wave. A few minutes' work, and he had a hole that even Fleck would find adequate.

So far it had been easy, simple tasks that even a raw K'da trainee could handle. Now came the tricky part.

The breeze was coming steadily from the west. Crossing

through the hedge, he swung wide to the east, downwind of whatever sentries and hidden guard posts the Brummgas had set up to watch the gaps in the hedge. He ran hard and open along the ground, sniffing the air as he went, trusting his now completely black scales to conceal him.

So the glider had been built by Noy's parents. At least that explained why he'd detected the boy's scent at the site.

Or did it?

Because it was clear that no one had worked on the glider for quite some time. From the way Maerlynn had talked, he'd had the impression Noy's parents had died at least a few months ago.

Which meant that whatever he'd smelled at the glider had gone through several months of wind, rain, nosy animals, and simple evaporation. K'da senses were good, but they weren't *that* good. Not by a long throw. Not by several long throws.

At least, not under normal circumstances.

The odor of distant Brummga touched his snout and tongue, and he took a quick bearing that direction. There was a stone fountain several hundred yards away, probably where the guard was lurking. Mentally marking the spot for future reference, he continued on.

For that matter, his sense of smell shouldn't be good enough for this task, either. In fact, now that he thought about it, all his senses seemed to have been gradually improving over the past couple of months.

The past three months, in fact. Ever since he'd teamed up with Jack. The question was, why?

There was one rather unpleasant possibility. Ancient legend said that as a K'da approached death, his senses often sharpened dramatically.

But that couldn't be it. Draycos had been very close to death aboard the *Havenseeker*, just before Jack showed up. He hadn't felt any dramatic surge in his hearing or smell then. At least, he didn't think so.

For that matter, he felt perfectly fine right now. Better than he had in years, actually. Certainly nowhere near close to death.

But there was also that strange incident back at the frying pan, where he'd somehow fallen off Jack's back and through the wall of their prison. Could Jack have been right about his human body somehow rejecting the K'da symbiont?

Because if that were true—if humans could only serve as temporary hosts to K'da—then it was possible that Draycos was indeed near death right now. Nearer, perhaps, than any symptoms might show.

But true or not, there was nothing he could do about it. And whatever the future held, right now he had some slaves to free.

He had circled nearly to the mansion itself before he was confident that he'd marked all the hidden guards. There were three groups in concealed sentry posts, plus four other groups who had taken up positions behind flower gardens or trees or fountains. Most likely, those latter ones had been rushed in as backup troops in response to Jack's disappearance.

Which was fine with Draycos. Personally, he liked having enemies bunch up this way. It made them easier to find.

And in this case, he even knew which direction they would be facing.

Curving back along his circle, he approached the first of the hidden sentry posts, tucked away inside a cluster of tall bushes. Staying low to the ground, he crept up and delicately pushed one of the lower branches aside.

The entire center part of the cluster had been cut away, leaving room for a cozy spy nest. Two Brummgas were inside, sitting in front of a set of Argus monitors like the ones Jack had used during his own sentry duty with the Whinyard's Edge. The aliens were armed with both the standard slapsticks and long-range laser rifles.

Cutting his way through the bushes would have been both slow and noisy. Easing himself back, Draycos crouched down and gave one last look around. Then, with a quick calculation of distance and angle, he jumped upward.

The leap was right on point. His rear claws cleared the tops of the bushes by a fraction of an inch, and he dropped squarely on top of the two Brummgas. A quick double head slam later, and this post had been neutralized.

He gave the monitors a quick check. No sign of Jack and his party yet.

For a moment he debated taking the sentries' laser rifles and hiding them where the escaping slaves could get hold of them. But even with his brief military training Jack wasn't a very good shot. The other slaves were likely to be even worse. It would be safer for everyone if Draycos did all the path-clearing work himself.

The next obstacle in line was ahead and about fifty yards to the left, two guards crouched behind the rim of a stone fish pond. Leaping back out of the bushes, he headed in that direction.

He had finished off that group and three others and was heading for the final two sentry posts when the sky to the northwest abruptly lit up like the inside of a strobe flash.

He froze in place, sinking deeper into the grass. There was a faint glow in that direction now, reddish light flickering against the low clouds.

Right on schedule, the glider had gone to its death. The only question now was whether it would succeed in the purpose they had set for it. Keeping low, he continued on toward his next target.

The Brummgan response was faster than he had expected. He had just reached the concealed sentry post when he heard the distinctive sound of lifters from behind him. He ducked under the edge of the bushes just as a group of six Clax-7 patrol planes shot past, heading for the wall.

The Clax-7s had reached their goal by the time Draycos finished with this latest group. One of the aircraft was visible just inside the wall, hovering guard above the burning glider. The others were out of sight, probably on the ground with their crews examining the wreckage for bodies.

There was one sentry post left, this one disguised as a large wooden equipment box at the back corner of the sports field grandstand beside the western flagpole. Draycos was running silently toward on it when the sky again lit up with the flash of laser fire.

His claws dug into the ground as he twisted around, fully expecting to see the hovering Clax-7 firing at Fleck or, worse, at Jack and the rest of the escaping slaves. To his surprise, though, it was the hovering airfighter itself that had been hit, trailing fiery smoke as it spun to the ground out of sight.

And taking its place in the sky, only hovering just *out*side the wall instead of inside it, was the *Essenay*.

Draycos turned away, mentally shaking his head. Whatever he might think about Uncle Virge's ethics, the computerized personality definitely had a talent for making grand entrances.

He reached the equipment box without incident. Slicing through the locking bar, he flung the door open. Once again, he'd caught the Brummgas with their backs to him. Once again, they never knew what hit them.

The *Essenay* was still firing as Draycos pushed the door closed behind him. Firing downward, he noticed, over the wall into the estate.

Was he shooting at the other Clax-7s? But the laser blasts seemed to be low-power ones, too weak for cutting through airfighter armor. Was he shooting at the Brummgan searchers, then? But there was far too much firing for that.

Curiosity got the better of him. Climbing up the back of the grandstand, he jumped to the flagpole. It was made of metal, but the material was soft enough for his claws to handle. Digging in, he headed up.

And from the very top, he could see that Uncle Virge wasn't shooting at either the Clax-7s or their crews. Instead, he was laying down a line of laser fire between the airfighters and the Brummgas, trapping them back against their own defensive wall.

"Clever," Draycos murmured, mentally flicking his claws in admiration. In the same act, Uncle Virge had both created a diversion and neutralized a sizeable portion of the enemy force. *And* he'd accomplished both without unnecessary killing.

The escaping slaves were in sight now, a ragged line of people hurrying across the sports field in the direction of the house and the mercenary transports that would take them to freedom. Shifting around on the flagpole, Draycos turned to look that direction.

The transports were gone.

CHAPTER 33

It was quiet, Jack thought as he led the way past the grand-stand. Almost too quiet, especially considering all the noise going on back at the wall. Between the *Essenay* and the Brummgas' Clax-7s, there was quite a show going on over there. He just hoped Uncle Virge was following his instructions and was pinning down the guards without killing them.

Still, sooner or later, Gazen was bound to pull his head out of the clouds and wonder what the show was for. At that point, one would expect him to check that his slaves were tucked away in their beds and not strolling around Chookoock family property without permission.

On the other hand, maybe the fact that there were no Brummgas charging at them from the house meant that Gazen thought his hidden guards were still keeping him safe. The fact that those guards weren't doing their job meant that Draycos had done his.

More impressive yet, he'd done it in silence. Jack had been listening hard ever since they'd gotten within sight of the hedge and hadn't heard so much as a gurgle.

Uncle Virge had never really believed Draycos was as good as he claimed. Up to now, Jack really hadn't had any way to prove him wrong.

After tonight, he would.

"Where are we going?" Maerlynn puffed from behind him. "We're not going to the house, are we?"

"No, just around the side," Jack told her. "Remember those transports I told you about? With luck, we'll be out before anyone in the house even knows about it."

"Hey!" Noy said, grabbing at Jack's sleeve and pointing toward the grandstand. "Over there. What's that?"

"Where?" Jack asked, peering into the darkness.

"Over there," Noy said, pointing harder. "I saw two little green lights."

K'da eyes? "I'll check it out," Jack said briskly. "Maerlynn, keep them moving. I'll catch up in a minute."

He headed toward the grandstand at a quick jog, slowing to a walk as he reached the structure. "Draycos?" he whispered.

"Here," the dragon called back. From behind a large wooden box two glowing green eyes appeared.

"You're lucky we even noticed you back there," Jack commented, stepping close and sticking out his hand. "Noy must have really good eyes."

"In actual fact, I was staring at you for over a minute," the dragon said. Putting a paw on Jack's hand, he slithered up his sleeve. "If you had not seen me, I would have moved farther along your path and tried again."

"I was hoping you'd come up with some clever way to reconnect," Jack said, starting back toward the group. "What do you think of Uncle Virge's light show?"

"Most impressive," Draycos said. "Jack, we have a problem. The military transports are gone."

Jack nearly tripped over his own feet. *"What?"*

"Most of those who came for the auction have left," the

dragon said. "The only vehicle still there is a single civilian craft. I suspect it belongs to Arthur Neverlin."

Jack hissed between his teeth. If he hadn't stopped to go back and check on Noy . . .

He shook the thought away. "So Neverlin's still here," he said. "Makes sense. He's probably in there raining fire and brimstone on Gazen over my disappearance."

"Very likely," Draycos said. "However, our problem still remains. From the view I had of his vehicle, I do not believe it will be strong enough to destroy the gate."

"Even if it was, we'd be left with no way to get out ourselves afterward," Jack agreed grimly. "Unless we walked, and there are a whole bunch of Brummgan guard posts along the way."

"And most likely better protected than those I eliminated near the slave areas," Draycos said. "They would of course be alerted now, as well."

"So a stroll down the driveway is out," Jack said, slowing down. They'd better work this through before they rejoined the rest of the group. Reaching to his left collar, he tapped his comm clip. "Uncle Virge? How's it going?"

"Just fine, Jack lad, just fine," Uncle Virge's voice came back. "I've got them pinned down nicely. And with this overhang, they can't even shoot back."

"How many are there?" Draycos asked.

"Twenty-five," Uncle Virge said. "Mostly Brummgas, though I spotted three humans in the group."

"And you are certain they are still there?"

Jack felt his lip twitch. "Oh, boy," he muttered.

"What?" Uncle Virge demanded. "What is it?"

"The overhang," Jack told him. "Sure, they can't see you;

but you also can't see *them*. They could be sidling their way along the wall back to the house right now."

"Or are moving toward the gate to cut off our escape," Draycos added.

Uncle Virge muttered a very rude word. "I will be—"

"It's too late to worry about it now," Jack cut him off. "Anyway, you're still keeping them away from the Clax-7s. That's worth a lot."

"The value may be about to drop," Uncle Virge said, his voice suddenly tight. "I'm picking up a signal from the mansion. Gazen is ordering two Djinn-90 fighters to lift from Ponocce Spaceport."

Jack squeezed a hand into a fist. "How soon till they get here?"

"Depends on how ready they are to fly," Uncle Virge said. "Ten minutes, maybe fifteen. Twenty if you feel especially lucky today."

"I don't," Jack said, running some quick estimates through his mind. If he hurried, and if there was no opposition along the way, five minutes ought to get him to Neverlin's shuttle. Another five to run his sewer-rat program on the computer and get it started . . .

"I might be able to blast open the gate from out here," Uncle Virge suggested doubtfully.

"Don't even try," Jack warned. "They're bound to be ready for something like that."

"What do you want me to do, then?"

"Might as well keep those Brummgas pinned down as long as you can," Jack told him. "But the minute those fighters show up, take off."

"Take off where?" Uncle Virge demanded. "Jack, lad—"

"The frame of life is rigid," Draycos spoke up. "The time of life defined."

There was a short pause. "Understood," Uncle Virge said. "Watch yourself, lad."

He clicked off. "What was that?" Jack asked Draycos as he turned off the comm clip from his end. "More of your K'da poetry code?"

"Yes," Draycos said. "It is part of a saga about the siege of Colthin. In that action, the attackers continued to circle the fortress, evading the defenders' weapons and gradually running them out of ammunition."

"Not exactly the situation here," Jack grunted. "But close enough. I guess."

"The point is that he will remain in the area, and merely evade the fighters' attacks," Draycos said.

"That's the theory, anyway," Jack said, breaking into a run again. "Okay, here's the plan. We get back to the group, tell them to follow, then hoof it full-speed to Neverlin's shuttle."

"And then?"

Jack shook his head. "We'll figure something out."

He caught up with the rest of the escaping slaves, delivered his instructions to a reluctant and increasingly nervous-looking Maerlynn, and continued on ahead of them. Two minutes later, he was crouched beside an incredibly ugly sculpture at the edge of the landing area.

And there was still no response from inside the mansion. It was as if the Brummgas had completely missed what was happening, or were huddling deep inside their stone fortress, trembling with fear.

Or were simply waiting patiently for the slaves to walk into their trap.

"Well, there it is," Jack muttered to Draycos as he studied the shuttle squatting fifty yards away. It was a fancy one, all right—not much smaller than the *Essenay*, all steel and molded high-strength plastic and hand-polished chrome, with quadruple drive engines and at least that many lifter panels. Apparently, Neverlin was one of those who believed that the more backup systems, the better.

Or maybe he just liked loading his vehicles with expensive extras. In the shadows under the shuttle, Jack could see a set of fold-in, heavy-duty landing skids, the kind that guaranteed landings so soft that Neverlin wouldn't spill even a drop of whatever drink he was holding at the time. "Nice-looking parlor," he murmured.

"Pardon?"

"Literary reference," Jack told him. " 'Come into my parlor, said the spider to the fly.' I don't suppose there's any way for you to tell if they're waiting inside." He snorted. "Let me rephrase that. Is there any way for you to tell how *many* of them are waiting inside?"

"I am sorry," Draycos said regretfully. "I can smell Brummgan scent, certainly. But the wind has faded, and I cannot identify any direction for the odors."

Jack rubbed his chin. "Let's do a numbers game, then. Uncle Virge said he had twenty-five of Gazen's troops pinned down, at least until they can sneak their way around to the gate. How many did you take out clearing the path for us?"

"Fifteen."

"Making forty in all," Jack said. "Fleck's top estimate was that Gazen had seventy armed thugs. Figure at least six more in those hidden guard huts between the house and the gate, plus another ten inside the house to protect the Chookoock family in case we take it into our heads to charge the place. Any of those figures sound too high?"

"Possibly even a bit low," the dragon said slowly. "With an attack coming from a ship as well-armed as the *Essenay,* and with the gate the only clear way inside, I would post at least ten guards along that approach."

"Especially since they have no way of knowing if we have other backup waiting outside," Jack said, nodding.

"Correct," Draycos said. "In addition, with a slave of your skills and reputation on the loose, I would leave at least fifteen to protect the Chookoock family."

"I'll take that as a compliment," Jack said dryly. "Which leaves only five Brummgas to make direct trouble for us. If we instead go with my numbers, we could end up with as many as fourteen."

"Either way, those are not very good odds," Draycos pointed out.

"Either way, those are lousy odds," Jack countered. "But there's not much we can do about it. We need that ship to get out of here."

"You have a plan, then?"

"I'm working on it," Jack said, trying to sound confident. "But there's nothing to be gained by hanging around out here."

Jack straightened up from his crouch; hesitated. "By the way," he said. "I don't think that you—I mean if it *is* a trap—"

"I will most likely not be able to keep my existence a secret any longer," Draycos finished calmly. "Yes, I know."

"Maybe we should try something else," Jack offered,

though at the moment he couldn't imagine what that something else would be. "Surrender to Neverlin, maybe, and figure on escaping once we're out of here."

"They will not let you leave without putting poison into your body," Draycos reminded him. "And even if we found a way to avoid that, the slaves we lead would have to remain."

Jack sighed. "You're right."

"Do not be discouraged, Jack," Draycos said. "Even the most precious secret must sometimes give way to a higher purpose. A true warrior must learn when and how to make sacrifices. This is a gamble worth taking."

"Okay." Jack took a deep breath. "Let's do it."

He half expected Gazen to spring the trap while he was still outside the shuttle, on open ground with nowhere to hide. But he made it to the hatchway without anything happening.

For a moment he crouched beside the entry ramp, catching his breath and peering inside. Unlike the military transports of this size he'd flown in, Neverlin's shuttle seemed to be built along the same lines as a miniature spaceship. Instead of opening into a single large cabin, the hatchway led into a small entry/airlock chamber, with another door leading out of the entryway into the main body of the shuttle. Bracing himself, he went up the ramp.

The trap wasn't waiting in the entry chamber. It wasn't waiting in the corridor that led out of it, either. Jack headed forward through the gloom of the ship's nightlights, listening to his own footsteps whiffing softly through the thick carpet. Could he have been wrong about Gazen's strategy? Could the slavemaster really have missed such an obvious bet?

A few yards ahead the corridor opened into a larger cabin,

furnished with three rows of well-spaced, comfy-looking seats. First class all the way. Stepping inside, he continued forward.

And as he reached the middle of the room, it abruptly lit up like a Sirian noon.

CHAPTER 34

Jack threw his arm up to protect his eyes from the light. But even before the arm was in position, his wrist was grabbed and twisted roughly behind his back.

"I told you he couldn't resist the temptation," Neverlin's smooth, snake-like voice came over the scuffling noises of heavy feet suddenly on the move. More hands grabbed at Jack's arms and shoulders, pinning them in place. Bodies smelling like sweaty Brummga pressed against him from all sides, preventing him from using his feet to either run or kick.

"And I told *you*," Gazen's less civilized voice retorted, "that he was working with that Tubman Group."

Cautiously, Jack eased his eyes open against the glare. Gazen and Neverlin were standing just inside the door at the far end of the cabin, with Neverlin's two bodyguards on either side of their boss. The one Draycos had clobbered earlier had a pressure bandage on his head, a scowl on his face, and a nasty-looking gun in his hand.

"Don't be absurd," Neverlin scoffed. "The Tubman Group? Nonsense. Virgil Morgan and his nephew don't do charity work."

"Then how do you explain all those slaves skulking

around out there?" Gazen demanded. "I tell you, he's trying to stir up a revolt."

Slowly, carefully, Jack turned his head. He got only about halfway around before one of the Brummgas noticed the movement and twisted his head to face forward again. But he'd seen enough to figure there were eight Brummgas crowding around him.

Closer to Draycos's estimate than his. Still very lousy odds.

"He just brought them to spread a little chaos in case he needed a diversion," Neverlin said. "As far as he's concerned, they're expendables." He cocked an eyebrow at Jack. "Or hadn't you noticed that he didn't actually bring any of them aboard with him?"

"So you don't think they're of any use as bargaining chips?" Gazen asked.

"Not a chance," Neverlin said. "Take them back to their huts, or burn them where they stand. Your choice."

Gazen nodded and reached to his collar—

"Wait," Jack said.

The instant the word was out of his mouth he wished he could call it back. Gazen surely wouldn't simply kill Maerlynn and the others, at least not here and now. Even if he decided their actions deserved that, he would more likely have them whipped to death as an object lesson for the rest of the slaves.

But Jack hadn't thought it through quickly enough. And now it was too late.

"Well, well," Neverlin said, smiling smugly. "So he really *does* have some feeling for those dirty little zeros out there, does he? This is one for the record books."

"Or else he's just squeamish," Gazen rumbled contemptuously. "You should have seen his face after those Wistawki passed him in the kitchen this morning."

"You didn't need to whip them," Jack ground out. "They didn't steal the food. *I* did."

Gazen snorted. "Don't make me laugh. You were in the frying pan all night."

"Forget the food," Neverlin said impatiently. "Tell me, Jack. How much do you really care about that riffraff out there?"

"And decide quickly," Gazen added. "I've got a squad at the upper windows with sniper rifles trained on them."

Jack swallowed. The trap had been sprung, and here they were, with all of the Brummgas clustered close around him.

But Draycos was still lying quietly against his skin. What in space was he waiting for?

And then, as he focused again on the group by the door, he suddenly realized what the reason was.

"Oh, yeah, that's real brave," he said, putting as much scorn into his voice as he could. "Shooting unarmed slaves from windows. That's the way a *man* does business."

"As opposed to whatever you did to my guards out there?" Gazen countered.

"You should be happy I didn't kill them," Jack said, hoping he was right in guessing that Draycos *hadn't* killed them. "*Or* Mr. Neverlin's hoppy-pop bodyguard there," he added. "How's your head, pal?"

The bandaged guard made a sound deep in his throat. "Easy, Jondo," Neverlin said. "You'll get your turn."

"Yeah, it's always *their* turn, isn't it?" Jack said contemptuously. "Bodyguards and Brummgas. You two ever do any of this stuff yourselves? Or do you always hide behind other people?"

Gazen took a step forward. "Listen, kid—"

"Stop it," Neverlin said. His voice was quiet, but there was something in his tone that brought Gazen to a sharp halt. "Don't let him goad you. He's finished, and he knows it."

"*He* doesn't think I'm finished," Jack said loftily. "He's still afraid of me. If he wasn't, he wouldn't always be hiding behind his Brummgas. He's a coward; pure, simple, and unfrosted."

He cocked an eye toward the Brummgas in his line of sight. "You know, if *I* were you, I'd find a better boss to work for."

"Shut up," Gazen snarled.

"Make me," Jack challenged.

Gazen's glare shifted over Jack's shoulder. He sensed a slight movement behind him—

"I said *stop*," Neverlin snapped. "Are you insane, Gazen? We need him conscious to talk to his uncle."

"Oh, right," Jack said sarcastically. "I'm supposed to talk him into surrendering. Suppose I don't feel like doing that right now?"

"Then your friends outside will die," Neverlin said softly.

Jack gave him a smile he wasn't particularly feeling. "And you think I care?"

For a long minute Neverlin studied his face. Jack met the gaze evenly, his heart pounding in his chest. If they called his bluff—if Gazen started shooting the slaves out there—

"With all due respect, sir," the unbandaged bodyguard murmured, "I don't think we have time for this. Those Djinn-90s could be here any time."

"He has a point, Jack," Neverlin agreed. "We don't want your uncle getting himself killed in a firefight, now, do we?"

"I'm not going to tell him to surrender," Jack said stubbornly. "We've got time on our side. And you don't dare hurt me."

Neverlin shook his head. "For a clever boy, Jack, you have some amazing memory failures. Castan?"

The unbandaged bodyguard slid his gun back into its holster and pulled out a small, flat box. Opening it, he pulled out a hypospray. "The squatter poison," Neverlin identified it. "Remember?"

Jack pressed back against his captors, as if trying to cringe away from the hypospray. One of the Brummgas tightened his grip on his arm—

"Ow!" Jack gasped, as if it had really hurt.

"Don't hurt him!" Neverlin snapped.

"I didn't," the Brummga protested, sounding bewildered. "I just—"

Jack hissed again in imaginary pain. "Stop it," Gazen ordered. "You heard Mr. Neverlin."

"Back off him," Neverlin said. "Just *back off*."

Reluctantly but obediently, the Brummgas let go of Jack's arms and shuffled a step backward. "Last chance, Jack," Neverlin said. "One way or another, you're going to cooperate."

Jack took a deep breath, straightening as tall as he could. "I don't cooperate with losers," he said.

Neverlin shook his head. "You young fool," he said softly. "Do it, Castan."

The bodyguard started forward again, shifting the hypospray into working position in his hand. Jack hunched down, raising his fists into a boxer's stance. "You keep away from me," he said tightly. "You hear?"

"This is ridiculous," Neverlin said, the smooth coating of

his voice cracking with exasperation. "Jondo, go and hold him."

"Yes, *sir*," the bandaged bodyguard said, taking a couple of quick steps to catch up with his partner, his gun pointed squarely at Jack's stomach. Side by side, the two men approached, the Brummgas backing off another step as they approached.

"Very good, Jack," Draycos murmured.

"You're welcome," Jack murmured back, smiling in satisfaction.

Because now, instead of there being two armed men out of easy reach at the far end of the room, the whole group of enemies were nicely clustered together. "There you go, buddy," he added as Jondo and Castan stepped up to him. "Have a good time."

And with a K'da battle scream, Draycos burst from the front of his shirt.

He took out the two bodyguards first, one forepaw slapping hard against their heads in a quick one-two punch. Twisting in midair, he caught Castan in the chest with his rear paws and shoved off him to reverse direction. Almost as an afterthought, his flicking tail sent Jondo's gun sailing across the room to bounce off the side wall.

Jack dropped into a low crouch. He'd had a vague plan of slipping out of the center of the fight and trying to get one of the bodyguards' guns so he could give Draycos some help.

But there was no need for a plan. Draycos was way beyond any need of help.

Once before, Jack had seen his new partner in combat, fighting a group of scavenger heenas in the Vagran Colony

Spaceport. He had thought then that he was seeing the dragon at his full potential.

He'd been wrong. He'd been terrifyingly wrong.

It was as if someone had dropped a black-scaled threshing machine on top of the Brummgas. Draycos was everywhere, leaping and diving and twisting across their heads and shoulders like an insane cat on hot metal. He never seemed to touch the same Brummga more than once. But each time he did, his claws slashed, or his paws slammed, or his tail whipped.

And when the Brummga fell, he didn't get up again.

They never had a chance. This kind of fighting wasn't in any of their training manuals, and there was no time to improvise. Drawn slapsticks were knocked aside; hastily drawn guns were ducked beneath.

And the attack went on. They didn't know how to stop him, or how to get out of his way. They never even knew which direction he would be coming from next, as he shoved randomly off their fellow soldiers or the ceiling into each new attack.

It was over almost before Jack could catch his breath. Certainly it was over before he could move. The last Brummga slammed backward to the deck; and with a final spin and leap, Draycos again shot past overhead. Jack spun around, suddenly remembering Gazen and Neverlin.

He needn't have worried. Both men were still by the door, frozen in place like a pair of well-formed ice sculptures. Draycos was standing on the deck in front of Gazen, stretched up on his hind paws with his head so close to the slavemaster's that his snout nearly touched the other's nose.

One set of claws pressed against the side of Gazen's neck.

Jack cleared his throat. In the sudden deadly silence, the noise sounded like distant thunder. "If I were you, gentlemen," he advised, "I'd be real careful right now."

"Mother of . . ." Neverlin whispered, the words trailing off as he stared at Draycos. His eyes flicked to Jack, back to the K'da. "But it's . . ."

"It's a poet-warrior of the K'da," Jack confirmed. Stepping over to Castan's limp body, he pulled out the bodyguard's gun. "You and the Valahgua missed one."

Neverlin twitched violently at the name *Valahgua*. He threw another look at Jack, then focused again on Draycos.

And suddenly, the stunned and disbelieving panic vanished. "So it was *you*," he said, his voice almost calm again. "*You* were the boy who escaped us on Iota Klestis."

"Right again," Jack said, stepping up and pressing his borrowed gun into Neverlin's stomach. "Either of you carrying any weapons? Or shall I ask Draycos to search you?"

"What *is* this?" Gazen hissed. Unlike Neverlin, he was trembling visibly.

But then, Neverlin didn't have K'da claws pressing against his throat. "This is your life in your hands," Jack told him, taking the slavemaster's extendable slapstick from its holster. "How badly do you want to live today?"

Gazen swallowed hard. "What do you want?"

"Let's start by telling your snipers to back off," Jack said. "I want those slaves out there free to join me without getting shot."

Slowly, Gazen reached toward the comm clip on his shoulder. He stopped short as Draycos gave a soft warning growl. "It's all right, Draycos," Jack soothed. "Gazen wouldn't try to pull a fast one by using code words or anything like that. He'll give the right order, and all the Brumm-gas will go away, and everyone will live through this. Isn't that right, Gazen?"

The slavemaster's eyes flicked past Draycos to the Brumm-gas lying in crumpled heaps on the deck. "Yes," he whispered.

"There, you see?" Jack said. "Okay, Gazen, go ahead. Oh, and you *will* make it sound like everything's all right out here, won't you? Like this is just a simple, minor change in the plan?"

Gazen took a deep breath. "Of course."

The performance was not exactly up to Stellar Award standards. But it was probably good enough. Especially since most of those on the far end would be Brummgas.

"Good," Jack said after he'd shut off Gazen's comm clip and slipped it into his own pocket. "Now, I guess the question is what exactly to do with you."

Beside him, Draycos's ears twitched. "Listen," he said.

Jack strained his ears. "What is it?"

"The sound of weapons fire," Draycos said grimly. "The fighters have arrived."

CHAPTER 35

Like the rest of the shuttle, the cockpit was a miniature version of a larger spaceship's flight deck. It was a three-seater, too, with copilot and system monitor stations in addition to the usual pilot's chair.

"Have a seat," Jack ordered his two prisoners as he closed the cockpit door halfway and slid into the pilot's station. "This'll only take a minute."

"You really think you have that long?" Neverlin asked.

Jack peered out the canopy, a tight knot in the pit of his stomach. The two Djinn-90s had indeed arrived, and were engaged in combat with the *Essenay*.

And for all the *Essenay*'s speed and Uncle Virge's computerized skill, it was clear the ship was fighting for its life. It wove and dodged madly through the sky, trying to stay out of the fighters' sights while at the same time having to keep from straying over the deadly wall.

And for the moment, at least, there was nothing Jack could do to help. Tearing his eyes away from the view, he started keying in the sewer-rat program.

"I say we let them take him out," Gazen said blackly. "The kid and his uncle have become way more trouble than they're worth. There has to be another safecracker some-where you can use for this job."

"I'm sure there is," Neverlin agreed. "But I have no inten-tion of letting Virgil Morgan die before he's told us who else knows about this."

"What do we need Morgan for?" Gazen argued. "We've got the kid, right?"

"You've got a really strange definition of ownership," Jack put in, keying the last part of the sequence. Now it was sim-ply a matter of waiting for the program to do its job.

"You can't escape, you know," Gazen warned. "Sooner or later, they'll come out here and close you down."

"Like your other Brummgas did?" Jack asked pointedly.

"Sheer weight of numbers will eventually take you down," Neverlin said calmly. "Even a K'da warrior can only do so much."

"You might be surprised," Jack said, trying to match the other's confidence. The computer locking system was start-ing to waver now under the sewer-rat's attack. Should be any minute. "But no matter what happens here, you're still in big trouble."

"Really," Neverlin said. "How do you figure that?"

"Because your bid to grab control of Braxton Universis has gone smokers," Jack told him. "That means that when you go up against the main K'da and Shontine refugee fleet, you won't have the Braxton security forces to draw on."

He nodded toward the mansion. "Or do you think the Chookoock family and their ten-thumbed Brummgas can do the job all by themselves?"

Gazen snorted. "Look, kid—"

"What's your point?" Neverlin cut him off.

"My point is that you're finished," Jack said flatly. "You're a sinking ship; and *you*, Gazen, are going to go down with him if you're not careful. But if you call off those Djinn-90s and open the gate, that'll be the end of it. StarForce never has to know you were ever involved with this."

Neverlin actually laughed out loud. "*StarForce?* You expect us to believe Virgil Morgan would go to *StarForce* for help?"

"Gazen?" Jack asked, ignoring him. "Last chance to join the winning side."

"*Your* last chance to surrender and maybe live through this," Gazen countered.

Abruptly, Draycos's head twitched toward the half-open door. "Footsteps," he warned.

Jack nodded. "And that ends the negotiations," he said, pulling out the slapstick he'd taken from Gazen and keying it to full power. Whether the newcomers were Maerlynn's group or more Brummgas, he didn't want his prisoners blurting out anything about Draycos. "Nighty-night."

He flicked the tip at Gazen, then at Neverlin. A pair of brilliant sparks later, both men were down for the count.

Draycos touched Jack's hand as he retracted the slapstick, sliding up his arm out of sight. Jack could hear the pounding feet now in the corridor. Hiding the slapstick behind his back, he waited.

The door slid the rest of the way open, and Fleck burst into the cockpit, a laser rifle gripped in his hands. "Easy, Fleck," Jack said hurriedly. "It's under control."

"I guess so," Fleck said, his voice sounding a little strangled.

He threw an odd look at the sleeping prisoners, then another one at Jack. "That pile of Brummgas back there. Your work?"

"I had help," Jack told him. "Where's the rest of the group?"

"I told them to strap in," Fleck said, slinging the rifle over his right shoulder.

"Wow!" Noy breathed from the doorway as he peeked in. "You really know how to fly this?"

"If he doesn't, we're crushed berries," Fleck said. "At least we've got a couple of hostages now. You want me to move them back into the main cabin?"

"Yes, thanks," Jack said. "And be sure to strap them in."

"If we've got enough seats," Fleck said, grunting as he hoisted Neverlin over his shoulder. "We've picked up a few extra passengers. A Wistawk named Heetoorieef and a few of his buddies were waiting outside when I came by."

"Really," Jack said, frowning as he turned to the control board and keyed in the startup sequence. The main controls looked pretty standard. But where were the weapons controls? "How did he even know anything was up?"

"He said word had gotten out that you were missing and that the Brummgas thought you were trying to escape," Fleck said. "He pulled together all the household slaves who would come and sneaked them outside. I hope that was okay."

Jack shrugged. "The more the merrier."

"And I have to tell you that that private army you've got running blocks is really something," Fleck added. "I was falling over sleeping Brummgas every other step out there."

"We aim to please," Jack said. "That where you picked up the rifle?"

"Thought it might come in handy," Fleck said. "I guess I didn't have to bother."

He disappeared out the door, Neverlin's dangling feet clunking against the corridor as he headed aft. "What are we going to do about the wall?" Noy asked, coming up to Jack's side.

"Don't worry, we'll get through," Jack promised. "Go back and strap in, okay?"

"Okay," Noy said. He took one more lingering look at the controls and left.

"Blast it, where are the weapons?" Jack muttered, still searching the control board. "This is one of Neverlin's ships. It *has* to be armed."

Draycos leaped from his collar and landed beside the copilot's seat. "They are here," he said, bounding up into the chair and flicking his tongue toward a section of the control board. "What do you wish done?"

Jack peered out the canopy at the running battle. "The Djinn-90s aren't expecting an attack from inside the wall," he said. "If we can nail one of them, that'll give Uncle Virge a better chance."

"Understood," Draycos said. He arched his back over the board, his claws skating delicately over the controls.

"Holy *fra*—?" came a gasp from behind them.

Jack spun around to see Fleck trying to fumble the rifle off his shoulder. "It's all right," he said quickly. "He's a friend."

Fleck took a shuddering breath, his hands freezing on the rifle sling. "A friend," he said as if trying the word on for size.

"And an ally," Draycos added, swiveling his long neck to stare back at him.

"And it talks, too," Fleck muttered. "You the one who took out all the Brummgas?"

"Every one of them," Jack said. "And we're a little busy right now. Just get Gazen out of here, okay?"

"Sure," Fleck said. "Okay. What do you want me to do then?"

"Stand by the hatchway with that weapon," Draycos said. "There may be a way of opening it from the outside, and they may try to rush us as we lift."

Fleck looked questioningly at Jack. "Do it," Jack confirmed. "Trust me, he's the military expert on this team."

"If you say so," Fleck said, hoisting Gazen over his shoulder. "Good luck."

"And don't say anything to the others," Jack added, nodding toward Draycos. "We're sort of trying to keep him a secret."

"Yeah, I figured that," Fleck said dryly. "Don't worry."

He left, this time shutting the door behind him. "I am ready," Draycos said. "When shall I fire?"

"The minute you get a clear shot," Jack told him, peering back at his own board. "I don't want to risk tipping them off by lifting until you've—"

He broke off as a triplet of brilliant blue sparks flashed out from the shuttle's nose. He jerked his head up, just in time to see one of the Djinn-90s buck violently to the side. Trailing a plume of smoke, it rolled away from its pursuit of the *Essenay,* dropping like an injured duck.

"Was that what you wanted?" Draycos asked calmly.

With an effort, Jack found his voice. "Yeah, that should do it," he managed. Crabbing sideways, the damaged Djinn-90 dropped over the wall into the slave area and disappeared behind the trees. A second later, there was a second burst of fire, and a fresh red glow added its bit to the light from the glider fire.

Jack caught his breath. The fighter had gone *over* the wall, without drawing any fire from the hidden weaponry. "Did you see that?" he asked.

"Yes," Draycos said. "Do you think they have shut down the wall defenses?"

"Not with a battle going on," Jack said, thinking hard. "It must be a localized thing, probably running off transponders in the fighters. The wall senses when a Chookoock vehicle is heading across, and holds its fire."

"The Clax-7s," Draycos said, his neck arching suddenly. "They are still on the ground by the wall."

"And they should have the same transponders," Jack said, feeling a surge of excitement as he threw power to the lifters. "That's our way out. Come on, let's get this thing moving."

CHAPTER 36

Gazen hadn't been bluffing about the snipers at the windows. Even as Jack lifted the shuttle off the ground, the hull began rattling with the impact of rapid-fire machine-gun bullets. He twisted the vehicle up and away from the mansion, folding the landing skids in against the shuttle's underside to protect them and hoping Neverlin had gone as heavy on the hull's armor plating as he had on the shock absorbers. Turning toward the glow of the burning glider, he tapped his comm clip. "Uncle Virge?" he called, searching the sky. Wherever the *Essenay* was, it was somewhere out of his line of sight.

"I'm here, lad," Uncle Virge came back. "Thanks for the assist."

"You're welcome," Jack said. "How are you doing?"

"Not too well," Uncle Virge admitted. "They've just ordered another two Djinn-90s into the air."

"How soon?"

"No more than five minutes, I'd guess," the computer said. "And to add insult to injury, it seems that the local law enforcement agencies are scrambling patrol craft of their own."

Jack grimaced. "I guess they don't like firefights over their cities."

"Law enforcement agencies are like that."

"Right," Jack said, putting the shuttle into hover mode over the burning glider and Clax-7s and peering out the side of the canopy. No Brummgas were in sight. "Can you take out that other Djinn-90 before the reinforcements arrive?"

"Just between us, I wish you'd taken out this one instead of the other," Uncle Virge said, his voice sounding strained. "This pilot is definitely the smarter of the two."

"Tell him to try a *kom treeta* maneuver," Draycos called from the copilot's seat.

"What was that?" Uncle Virge asked.

"He says to try a *kom treeta*," Jack told him.

Uncle Virge grunted. "Hold on."

Jack clicked off the comm clip. "Something from your late-night poetry sessions, I assume?" he asked Draycos.

"Yes," the dragon replied. "It is similar to the maneuver we used over Iota Klestis."

"Let's hope it works," Jack said, easing off the lifters and keying the landing skids to unfold again. "Looks like the Brummgas Uncle Virge had pinned down took off as soon as he left."

"Yet they did not take the aircraft with them?"

Jack frowned in sudden uncertainty. Why *hadn't* they taken the Clax-7s away with them?

The shuttle was still descending. Kicking in the lifters, he got it moving up again.

Half a second later, the Clax-7s blew up.

Jack fought the controls as the shock wave bounced the shuttle around like a hooked fish, throwing them perilously close to the wall. "Check the monitors," he snapped. "See if we've lost anything vital."

"Right," Draycos said.

With an effort, Jack backed the shuttle away from the wall and swung it around. The controls were suddenly feeling sluggish, he noted. That was a bad sign. "Status?"

"We have lost the rear section of lifters," the dragon reported. "The underside has also been holed near the drive engines. We will not be able to escape into space in this craft."

"Terrific," Jack growled. "Anything else?"

"Minor sensor and navigational damage. Otherwise, we appear mostly intact."

"At least now we know why they didn't take the Clax-7s away," Jack said as he again clicked on the comm clip. "Uncle Virge? You still there?"

"*I* am, yes," the computer said tightly. "What about *you?*"

"Just a little singed," Jack assured him. "Their little booby-trap wasn't quite as successful as they probably hoped. What's happening out there?"

"The *kom treeta* worked perfectly," Uncle Virge said, a note of satisfaction in his voice. "I dropped him just past the outskirts of town, and I'm heading back to meet you."

"Great," Jack said. "Unfortunately, my plan for getting out has just gone smokers."

"How about ramming the gate?" Uncle Virge asked. "Give me another couple of minutes and I can be there to pick you up."

"It's a little more complicated than that," Jack warned. "We've got passengers along."

"You've got *what?* How many?"

"About thirty."

There was dead silence from the other end. Apparently, none of Uncle Virge's large repertoire of curses was up to this one. "Jack, lad, have you taken leave of your senses?" the other demanded at last. "Where in the Orion Arm do you intend to put them all?"

"Don't worry, I've got that part covered," Jack told him. "The only sticking point is how we're going to get out of here."

"Well, you'd better come up with something fast," Uncle Virge warned. "I've got those new Djinn-90s coming in now from the east."

"From behind us," Draycos murmured. "Perhaps they think our sensors have been damaged."

Jack frowned over at him. The dragon was using that tone again. "Hang on," he told Uncle Virge, clicking off the comm clip. "You have an idea?"

"Perhaps," Draycos said slowly. "Tell me, how maneuverable is this craft?"

"It was better before we lost the rear lifters," Jack said. "Probably still pretty good, though."

"And those landing skids are hinged to the outer sides of the hull, opening outward from the center like standard cabinet doors?"

"Right," Jack said, frowning. "Why?"

Draycos bounded backward out of his chair and padded to Jack's side. "Do you have the incoming fighters on sensor yet?"

Jack checked his displays. There they were: two blips on the screen, approaching the wall on the far side of the Chookoock family grounds. "There," he said, pointing.

For a moment the dragon peered over his shoulder in silence. "Here is what you must do," he said. "Swing around so that you are facing them. Then drive straight toward them."

Jack blinked. "Straight *toward* them?"

"I will tell you when to turn," Draycos said, jumping up onto Jack's shoulder and melting down his shirt. A quick slither, and he was back in his usual position. "Go now," he ordered, the top part of his head rising up from Jack's shoulder.

"This is stupid," Jack warned as he threw power to the drive and sent the shuttle curving around toward the approaching Djinn-90s. "I mean, *really* stupid."

"So they will think, as well," Draycos agreed. "Trust me."

Jack shook his head. "I hate it when you say that."

He turned the shuttle's nose east and sent it speeding across the darkened landscape. Another minute, and he spotted the Djinn-90s' running lights as they flew toward him.

"They are crossing the wall," Draycos said.

Jack glanced at the displays. "Right," he confirmed.

"And again no attack from the wall's defenses."

Jack frowned. "Is that all you wanted to know? Whether the wall would still let them through?"

"Partially," Draycos said. "Now; come around a quarter circle to the right and head south."

"That'll open up our port side to attack," Jack warned.

"They do not seek our destruction, but our capture," Draycos assured him. "Go now."

"Right," Jack said, turning the shuttle's nose to the right. He braced himself; but aside from altering their own course slightly the Djinn-90s didn't react. "Now what?"

"Hold course until you are five seconds from the wall, then turn right again and head toward the gate," Draycos instructed.

The wall was looming ahead. Jack took them to within three seconds, then twisted the control stick over again, turning his tail to the approaching fighters. This time they opened fire, short pulses that burned chunks of metal and plastic off the shuttle's hull. "Trying to take out the engines," Jack shouted as the wail of warning alarms filled the cockpit. "What now?"

"Keep heading for the wall," Draycos said, his head lifting a little higher from Jack's shoulder. "And slow down to two-ten."

"Slow *down*?" Jack peered at the display. "They're gaining fast enough as it is."

"Slow down," Draycos repeated, his voice making it an order.

Jack clenched his teeth and complied. "I hope you know what you're doing," he bit out. "The rate they're coming, they'll be on top of us in no time."

"Again, they do not wish to destroy us," Draycos repeated. "Aside from your own value, we also have Gazen and Neverlin aboard. As you pointed out, they are merely trying to disable us."

"Great," Jack muttered. Ahead, he could see the pale white of the wall rapidly approaching. "So what are we going to do? Spite them by getting ourselves vaporized?"

"Prepare to turn again, this time a quarter-circle to the right," Draycos ordered, his head stretching close to the displays.

Back toward the slave areas. "Ready," Jack said. The wall was coming up mighty fast—

"Now."

Jack twisted the stick again, and again the safety straps pressed into his chest as the shuttle cut hard over. He straightened out—

And ducked involuntarily as one of the Djinn-90s shot past overhead.

"Geez!" he hissed. "When did they get that close?"

"On our last turn," Draycos said calmly. "They know now that you are aware you cannot fly safely over the wall. They see you as racing around inside the estate like a frightened rodent in a cage, trying to escape capture while searching hopelessly for a way out."

"Yeah, that about sums it up," Jack growled as the dark landscape flashed by beneath them. "So what *are* we doing?"

"Lulling them into carelessness—watch out!"

Jack twisted the stick to the left as the other Djinn-90 flashed past overhead. "Excellent," Draycos said with grim satisfaction. "With no further concerns that we will attempt to fly over the wall, they will now attempt to force us down."

"They'll need more than two of them for that," Jack said, looking cautiously up through the top of the canopy. The first fighter had returned and was pacing him directly overhead. "They don't have nearly enough mass to push us to the ground."

"They probably have more ships available," Draycos pointed out. "And time is on their side." He shifted position, pulling his neck back so that only his eyes were poking off Jack's shoulder, and Jack felt his sleeves swell as the dragon's forelegs rose from his wrists. "Or so they think," he added. "Open the landing skids."

Jack frowned. But this was no time to argue. Reaching over, he touched the switch. "Landing skids opening," he reported, glancing at the indicator. "Locked in place."

"They see it," Draycos murmured. Jack could feel the dragon's forelegs tensing against his skin, his claws stretching out to rest on the control board. "They believe they have won."

"Here he comes," Jack warned as the Djinn-90 overhead began to drop toward them. "Trying to make sure we don't change our minds."

"Yes," Draycos said. "Brace yourself." There was a muffled clink of metal against metal as the fighter bumped firmly against the top of their hull. Draycos jabbed at the controls—

And Jack gasped as the shuttle rolled a hundred eighty degrees on its long axis, flipping him over to hang upside down against his restraint straps.

"Draycos!" he yelped as the drive began to screech with the sudden strain of holding the shuttle in the air without the aid of the lifters. "What are you *doing*?"

"Landing skids closed!" the dragon shouted back over the noise. There was another muffled grinding of metal on metal— "Now!" Draycos snapped. "Full speed to the wall!" The shuttle bucked like it had hit a sudden crosswind—

And then, suddenly, Jack understood. When he'd flipped the shuttle onto its back, Draycos had put the Djinn-90 crowding above them squarely between the shuttle's big landing skids. By then closing the skids, he had caught the smaller fighter like a bug inside the spines of a Venus fly-trap. They were flying as a single big ship now: the shuttle, the fighter . . .

And the fighter's handy wall-defense transponder.

"Got it," Jack said, feeding as much power to the drive as he dared. The shuttle was bucking harder as the fighter pilot belatedly woke up to the scheme and fought to free his trapped ship.

But he was too late. Seconds later, the combined ship shot smoothly over the double breaking wave of the white wall.

They'd made it.

"Let him go," Jack snapped.

"Releasing now," Draycos called back. The bucking ceased as the dragon opened the landing skids again and the trapped fighter darted free. "Turn us over again and I will go back to the weapons board."

"Forget the weapons," Jack said, rolling the shuttle and dropping thankfully back into his seat as the vehicle righted itself. He got his bearings and made a hard turn to the left. "We won't be in the air long enough to bother with that."

"But there is yet a long way to go before we are free," Draycos objected.

"Not really," Jack said, tapping his comm clip as he fought the shuttle's controls. "Uncle Virge?"

"Here, lad," Uncle Virge said. "Shall I come get you?"

"No," Jack said. "Head off-planet—Station C. I'll catch up with you there."

"Right. Good luck."

Jack clicked off. There was his target, straight ahead. "Draycos, can you find the ship's intercom?"

"There." A K'da foreleg rose from Jack's arm again, pointing.

"Thanks." Jack hit the switch. "Brace yourselves, everyone," he called to the passenger section. "As soon as we're down, unstrap and make for the hatchway. We aren't going to have a lot of time."

He keyed the intercom off and twisted the nose high. An instant later, the shuttle hit the ground, sliding along on its skids with a tortured squeal of stressed metal. It made maybe another fifty yards before finally grinding to a halt.

"Everyone out," Jack shouted back toward the door as he

untangled himself from his straps. "Nice landing, huh?" he added to Draycos.

"Very similar to the *Havenseeker*'s final flight," Draycos said, a little too dryly. "What now?"

Jack smiled as he made for the door. "We take them to the one place in this part of Brum-a-dum where escaped slaves will be safe."

The Djinn-90s were circling overhead as Jack sprinted along the street. "Where are we going?" Fleck asked as he caught up with him, the borrowed laser rifle held ready.

"There," Jack said, pointing ahead past the glowing sign on its decorative post. "Get ready to blast the door open if we have to."

The weapon wasn't necessary. Not only was the door not locked, but it even opened as Jack ran up the steps. "Yes?" asked the thin woman standing in the doorway, goggling at the crumpled shuttle behind him.

"My name's Jack McCoy," Jack panted, braking to a halt. "I have some escaped slaves with me. We claim sanctuary with the Daughters of Harriet Tubman and the Internos government."

The woman lifted her eyebrows, her gaze flicking along the line of ragged slaves coming uncertainly up her walkway. "Well," she said calmly. "You'd all better come inside."

"Thanks." Brushing past her, Jack headed down a darkened hallway.

He was halfway along it when someone caught his arm. "Hold on," Fleck's voice murmured in his ear.

"Fleck, I have to go," Jack protested, tugging uselessly against the big man's grip. "Right away, before the cops and Gazen's people get here."

"Yeah, I know," Fleck said. "I just wanted to say thanks to you and your friend. For all of us."

Jack looked down the hallway, a sudden lump in his throat. "You're welcome," he managed. "Take care of them, will you?"

"Absolutely," Fleck promised, letting go of Jack's arm. "Get going. I'll say good-bye to the others for you."

Jack nodded, not trusting himself to say anything else.

His vision seemed a little blurry as he made his way down the hallway.

CHAPTER 37

The *Essenay* was waiting at their prearranged Station C rendezvous when he and Draycos arrived. Not on some distant world, as the Brummgas monitoring their transmissions would hopefully assume, but in the last spot anyone would ever think to look: nestled snugly beneath the overhang of the Chookoock family wall, barely half a mile from the gate.

How Uncle Virge had managed to sneak the ship in Jack couldn't guess. All he knew was that that it was lying quietly now, its power output near zero, its chameleon hull-wrap blending perfectly with its surroundings.

"Welcome aboard, Jack lad," Uncle Virge greeted him cheerily as he slipped in through the hatchway. "Good to have you back."

"It's good to be back," Jack said, feeling suddenly tired all over as he sealed the hatch. Tired, but immensely satisfied. "How badly were we hit?"

"Oh, they never laid a finger on me," Uncle Virge scoffed, his voice following Jack's progress from the various ship's speakers as the boy headed to the galley. "One or two very tiny things we can fix once we're out of here. I imagine you're hungry."

"Starving," Jack said, going straight to the food synthesizer. "And Draycos is even worse."

"I am all right," the dragon said, leaping out from Jack's collar. He landed on the deck and stretched in all directions. "You did well, Uncle Virge."

"Thank you kindly," the computerized voice said with only a hint of sarcasm. "The compliments of a lunatic K'da are so very gratifying."

"That's not fair," Jack objected, keying the food synthesizer.

"I'm merely quoting the comments and opinions of the Chookoock family," Uncle Virge soothed. "You should have heard the radio traffic as you charged the wall that last time."

"Oh?" Jack said as the synthesizer popped out two servings of Draycos's hamburger/tuna fish/chocolate/motor oil specials. "A bit perturbed, were they?"

"It was more like group heart failure," Uncle Virge said dryly. "They'd already seen my little *kom treeta* maneuver—"

"*My* little *kom treeta* maneuver," Draycos murmured as Jack set his meal down on one end of the galley table.

"Whatever," Uncle Virge said. "That was bad enough; but when you then pinned that Djinn-90 like a wrestler with a leg-lock, they about fell apart."

"I'm sorry we missed it," Jack said, returning to the synthesizer and punching up a double cheeseburger for himself.

"Don't worry, I made a recording," Uncle Virge said. "First they were screaming at the pilot to get himself loose, then screaming at him *not* to get himself loose because you were too close to the wall and Gazen and Neverlin would get fried. Then they were screaming at the other Djinn-90 to get there *now* even if he had to fry his engines to do it—"

"You *did* say we had an actual recording, right?" Jack interrupted him.

"The joy is in the telling," Uncle Virge said. "But that was nothing compared to the mass conniption fit they threw when you dropped the shuttle right on the Tubman Group's doorstep and led the slaves inside. Like Moses heading toward the Promised Land. How did you get out through all the local police, anyway?"

"Nothing to it," Jack shrugged, collecting his cheeseburger and carrying it to the table. "Like you said, all the attention was on the slaves filing in the front. I just went straight through the house, out the back door, and disappeared into the night before they got themselves organized."

Uncle Virge make a clucking noise. "Simple, but elegant. And a nice stick in the nose for the Chookoock family, too."

"That wasn't why I did it," Jack reminded him, taking a big bite of his sandwich.

"No, of course not," Uncle Virge said. "So are we finally ready to go to StarForce with this?"

"Not quite," Jack told him around his mouthful. "We now know it's the Malison Ring mercenaries that Neverlin is using."

"Excellent," Uncle Virge said. "Fine work."

"But we still don't know where the rendezvous with the incoming refugee fleet is going to be," Jack continued. "If we can get into the Malison Ring records and dig that out—"

"Wait a minute, Jack lad," Uncle Virge cut him off. "Just wait one minute."

"I am afraid I have to agree," Draycos put in, licking a bit of tuna from the end of his snout. "Infiltrating yet another mercenary group would be highly dangerous, especially now that Neverlin knows you were the one on Iota Klestis."

"Not really," Jack said, smiling tightly. "You see, Neverlin doesn't know we know about the Malison Ring. He'll never think of looking for us there."

"Unless he remembers our previous run-in with Dumbarton," Draycos warned.

"He'll never put it together," Jack insisted. "Look, we know there are three groups involved in this. That means only three places we can get the rendezvous location from. The Chookoock family is out. Neverlin is *definitely* out. That leaves the Malison Ring."

"So let StarForce go in and get it," Uncle Virge urged.

"You put StarForce on this and Neverlin will fold the game so fast it'll make your feet dizzy," Jack told him. "They'll fade into the woodwork and come up someplace where no one will look for them. And then the refugee fleet will die. No, Draycos and I are the only ones who can do it."

Uncle Virge sighed. "Draycos, you talk to him. I don't seem to be able to get through anymore."

"We will speak about this later, Jack," Draycos said. "Perhaps there is another way."

"You find it and I'll do it," Jack promised.

"I shall work on it," the dragon assured him, tonguing the last bite of food into his mouth "In the meantime, do you suppose I could have another one of these?"

Cornelius Braxton looked up from his breakfast cakes and coffee and the usual stack of morning reports as his wife walked into the room with a sheaf of papers of her own. "Good morning, Cynthia," he greeted her. "You're up early."

"I wanted to check the mail," she said, sitting down at the table across from him. "We got a note from Kelly. Daryl's got a quick job on Happenstance in two weeks, and he'll be dropping her and the family off for a visit on the way."

"Wonderful," Braxton said approvingly as he poured her a cup of coffee. "A man can go only so long without seeing his grandchildren. How long will they be here?"

"She says the job should only take him a month or so," Cynthia said. "He'll pick up Kelly and the children on his way back."

"That means another trip to Great Galaxy Romp, you know," Braxton warned. "Maybe even two or three. Those kids are impossible to wear out."

"As long as I don't have to ride the roller coasters," Cynthia said. "Now for the darker side of the news. Harper got a ping on Arthur Neverlin."

Braxton set down his fork. "Where?"

"Brum-a-dum, of all places," she said. "A long-range shuttle from the *Advocatus Diaboli* was apparently involved in a slave escape from one of the big families."

Braxton blinked. "*Arthur* was helping slaves escape?"

"I don't think the break was his idea," Cynthia said dryly. "He was found unconscious in the shuttle afterward. Or rather, what was left of the shuttle—it was pretty badly banged up."

"But the police *did* detain him?"

"Briefly." Cynthia made a face. "Unfortunately, the slave family—the Chookoocks—pulled some weight and got him out before any serious police could get there."

"Sounds like Brum-a-dum," Braxton said sourly, picking up his fork again. "So Arthur's been playing with the Chookoock family. That must be where he got the Brumm-gas Jack Morgan told us about."

"Very likely." Cynthia lifted her eyebrows. "But here's the *really* interesting part. The escape was apparently engineered by a young boy named Jack McCoy."

"Doesn't ring any bells," Braxton said. "Do we have a photo?"

"No, he managed to disappear even before Neverlin did," Cynthia said, selecting one of the papers on the stack and handing it across the table. "But take a look at the description."

Braxton ran his eye over the paper. He paused, read it again more closely. "Are you suggesting Jack McCoy is actually Jack *Morgan*?" he asked, looking up at his wife.

"The description certainly fits," she pointed out, handing over another handful of sheets. "Especially when you read some of the slaves' statements."

Braxton's coffee reheated itself twice before he finished reading through the pages. "Well, well," he said at last, laying them aside. "Sounds like our young friend's had a very busy month. And involved with Arthur, too."

"I'm not sure *involved* is exactly the word," Cynthia warned. "After all, he *did* wreck Neverlin's shuttle on his way out of the Chookoock compound."

"Yes," Braxton mused. "That's at least twice now the two of them have bumped into each other. Arthur must be getting very annoyed. Did anyone track Jack off Brum-a-dum?"

"Not as far as I know," Cynthia said. "But he has to surface sometime. And we *do* have the description and parameters of his ship, you know, from when he used our fuel credits at Shotti Station. We could have Harper put out the word for our people to watch for him."

"That might not be a bad idea," Braxton murmured, selecting a sheet from his own stack of papers and handing it to his wife. "Because I've just been looking over Chu's report on the mark Jack scratched into my cylinder back on the *Star of Wonder*."

Cynthia frowned as her eyes flicked down the paper. "He must be joking," she said, looking up at her husband again.

"Chu doesn't have that kind of sense of humor," Braxton said. "At least, not in writing."

"But an *animal* claw?" she protested. "What would Jack have been doing with an animal claw?"

"I don't know," Braxton conceded, picking up the report on the Brum-a-dum slave escape. "But I think it's about time we found out."

He looked across the table at his wife. "Let's go find Jack Morgan."

ABOUT THE AUTHOR

Timothy Zahn is the author of thirty original science fiction novels, including the very popular Cobra and Blackcollar series. His first novel of the Dragonback series, *Dragon and Thief*, was named a Best Book for Young Adults. Jack Morgan's adventures continued in *Dragon and Soldier*, and most recently, in *Dragon and Herdsman*. Zahn's other recent novels include *Night Train to Rigel, The Green and the Gray, Manta's Gift*, and *Angelmass*. He has had many short works published in the major SF magazines, including "Cascade Point" which won the Hugo Award for best novella in 1984. He is also author of the bestselling Star Wars novels *Heir to the Empire* and The Hand of Thrawn duology, among other works. He currently resides in coastal Oregon.

DRAGON and SLAVE

The Third Dragonback Adventure

TIMOTHY ZAHN

ABOUT THIS GUIDE

The information, activities, and discussion questions that follow are intended to enhance your reading of *Dragon and Slave*. Please feel free to adapt these materials to suit your needs and interests.

ABOUT THE AUTHOR

Born and raised near Chicago, Timothy Zahn earned a B.S. and an M.S. in Physics from the University of Michigan and the University of Illinois, respectively. He began writing science fiction as a hobby while pursuing his physics doctorate, slowly devoting more and more time to this endeavor. In 1980, after selling two short stories and with the support of his wife, he began writing full time, penning eighteen stories in that first year. By 1984, he had accomplished his goal of earning a living as a writer. Known for his acclaimed Star Wars Hand of Thrawn series, the popular and prolific Zahn is the author of more than thirty science fiction titles, including the bestselling Star Wars trilogy *Heir to the Empire, Dark Force Rising,* and *The Last Command*; novels *Night Train to Rigel, Angelmass, Conquerors' Pride, Conquerors' Her-*

itage, and Conquerors' Legacy; three collections of short fiction; and the Hugo Award–winning novella "Cascade Point." He lives with his family on the Oregon Coast.

ABOUT THE DRAGONBACK BOOKS

The Dragonback books are epic mysteries in which Jack and Draycos, an orphan boy and his alien companion, must find their way through a turbulent interstellar world. The art of Zahn's series is that woven into each fast-paced adventure is also a complex, compelling moral tale. For, beneath the layers of exotic aliens, technology-laden landscapes and inter-planetary action, lies an intensely human question: Is it possible to trust another as completely as you trust yourself?

QUESTIONS FOR DISCUSSION

1. What errand brings Jack and Draycos to Brum-a-dum at the beginning of *Dragon and Slave*? Why does Jack feel he must help Draycos?

2. Who is Uncle Virge? What is Uncle Virge's opinion of Jack and Draycos's mission? As a reader, how do you relate to this computerized character? How do Jack and Draycos each relate to Uncle Virge?

3. Does Brum-a-dum remind you of any earthly place about which you have read, a scene from history, or anywhere you have been? If yes, describe this place and its similarities to Brum-a-dum.

4. Who is Gazen? To what species does he belong? What is Gazen's relationship with the Brummga? What does he think of Jack?

5. Who are the Chookoock family? Describe their compound. Who occupies the Chookoock family quarters? What is the source of the Chookoock wealth?

6. What is the "slaves' hotbox"? What happens to Jack on his first night in the hotbox? Why do you think Gazen chooses this punishment for Jack?

7. To what alien species do Maerlynn, Grib and Greb, and the other slaves Jack meets belong? What human slave does Jack encounter?

8. As Jack changes his clothes, he realizes that the slaves do not even look at him—perhaps do not even notice the "tattoo" on his back. What other disquieting discoveries does he make about the behavior and attitudes of the slaves on Brum-a-dum?

9. Describe the barriers around the slave quarters. What weaknesses do Jack and Draycos find in the barriers? How do their plans evolve as they live in the slave quarters?

10. At what task do the slaves spend much of their time? Who is Fleck? Who is the Klezmer? How does Lisssa treat the Klezmer? How do the other slaves treat the Klezmer? How might you explain this behavior?

11. Who is "Her Thumbleness"? How does she treat slaves? What would you do if you were treated in this way? How does Her Thumbleness figure into Jack's plans? Compare Jack's attitude toward Her Thumbleness with the attitudes of the other slaves.

12. How is Jack responsible for getting Noy into trouble? How do Jack's and Draycos's actions toward Noy reflect changes in their own behavior and ways of thinking?

13. Who does Jack recognize in the audience when he is called to demonstrate his skills for the slave buyers? What urgency does the slave auction bring to Jack's situation?

14. What is wrong with the food Gazen tries to have fed to Jack? What is the most upsetting aspect of Gazen's character?

15. What surprising allies does Jack discover when he plans his escape from Brum-a-dum? What do these alliances reveal about slavery and those forced to be slaves?

16. How does Lisssa betray Jack? If you were called upon to defend her actions to Fleck and to Jack, how might you do so? How do Fleck and Jack feel about Lisssa?

17. At various points in the novel, Uncle Virge proposes that Jack and Draycos give up their mission on Brum-a-dum and leave their errand to legal authorities. What arguments do Jack and Draycos make against Uncle Virge's proposals and why?

18. How do Jack's enemies feel about Virgil Morgan at the conclusion of the novel? How does Draycos feel about Uncle Virge? What last-ditch maneuver does Draycos employ to engineer his escape with Jack? How does Jack save his slave passengers?

19. As Jack struggles to stay alive amidst cruel slave traders and downtrodden slaves, he faces a question more challenging than hacking into a Brummgan computer: How can you truly tell your

enemies from your friends? How does Jack answer this question?
How would you answer this question?

20. At the end of the novel, how might Jack define the term
"slave"? In what ways has Jack's brief life as a slave changed his
understanding of freedom?

21. Does Jack's experience as a slave on Brum-a-dum affect his
feelings towards Draycos? How do his thoughts about slavery help
recommit Jack to helping Draycos with his mission to help the
K'da and Shontine refugees?

22. In the final pages of the novel, Cornelius and Cynthia Braxton discuss Arthur Neverlin, the identity of Jack McCoy/Morgan,
and the scratch mark left by Jack on the *Star of Wonder.* What
conclusions do they draw? Do you think the Braxtons are allies or
enemies to Jack? How does this final chapter affect your understanding of Jack and Draycos's mission?

WRITING AND RESEARCH ACTIVITIES

I. WRITING ABOUT ALIEN WORLDS

A. The author describes the smells, sounds, sights and sensa-
tions of his interstellar landscapes, bringing each place alive for
earthly readers. With classmates or friends, make a list of favorite
descriptive passages from the novel. Discuss how these passages
create a vivid picture of Brum-a-dum.

B. After completing section I, exercise A, above, write a description of your classroom, bedroom, favorite restaurant, local
ball field or another location. Describe the sights, sounds, and
smells of the place as well as the way being there makes you feel.

C. Beyond description, Timothy Zahn gives Jack and Draycos their own sets of unique expressions and mottos. For example, in Chapter 2, Jack notes that a certain risk gone wrong might leave him ". . . toast. Jelly side down." Keep a list of such phrases from the book for each character. Put a star next to phrases similar to those you use, or that you could apply to situations in your own life. If desired, make a list of your own favorite expressions.

D. Imagine you are responsible for describing the planet Jack and Draycos will visit on their next Dragonback adventure. Write a paragraph describing the planet from the point-of-view of Jack or Draycos. Make a drawing of the *Essenay*'s approach to this new planet. Give your planet a name.

E. Who governs the planet you imagined in exercise I, exercise D, above? What types of aliens inhabit the planet? What types of industry, entertainment or military installations exist there? Are there any particular expressions, anthems or mottos unique to the planet? Write a short outline covering some or all of these details.

II. EXTINCTION

A. The idea of extinction pervades *Dragon and Slave*, from Draycos's mission to save the last of his kind to the dismal plights of the Brum-a-dum slaves whose families are destined for death within the confines of the slave quarters. Go to the library or online to find a definition of the term "extinct." Write a paragraph, poem, or original song lyrics exploring the concept of extinction and what it means to you.

B. Uncle Virge and Draycos are both dependent upon Jack. Each, in his own way, would face extinction without Jack's help. Create a chart comparing and contrasting these two characters' relationships with Jack. Then, writing as if you were Jack, compose a short dramatic speech, journal entry, or other composition describing how it feels to be responsible for the existence of these other beings.

C. Learn more about an animal facing extinction in the real world. Make an informative poster describing the animal, its habitat, the threats to its survival, and ways to help save this animal. Display the poster in your school or community.

D. At moments in the novel, Draycos considers the possibility that his existence may be coming to an end. Writing as if you were Draycos, tell about these thoughts and what your survival means for the rest of your K'da and Shontine kind.

III. SLAVERY

A. Jack is deeply moved by his experience as a slave. Go to the library or online to learn more about types of slavery that have existed in the history of our world, such as slavery in ancient Rome, "coolie" labor in the British Empire, or African slavery in America. Share your findings with classmates or friends in a short oral report.

B. Imagine you lived in the slavery era of your report from section III, exercise A, above. Write a political speech decrying slavery and encouraging your government to abolish the practice. Perform your speech for classmates or friends.

C. Imagine you are one of the Chookoock slaves from the novel, who has somehow learned to read and write. Write a series of journal entries describing your life, your feelings about servitude, and any changes in your thinking brought about by the actions of Jack Morgan.

D. Go to the library or online to learn more about the real historical figure Harriet Tubman. Who was she? What did she do? Why did Timothy Zahn choose to use her name as he did in the novel? Answer these questions in a short essay.

E. Create a painting, clay sculpture, short play script, cinematic storyboard, or other artwork highlighting the aspects of freedom that are most important to you. With classmates or friends, create a Freedom Display incorporating your artwork, short biographies of some champions of freedom, lists of books and films celebrating freedom, and other materials you think appropriate. Invite other students, family members, or community members to tour your display.

QUESTIONS & ACTIVITIES FOR THOSE WHO HAVE READ MORE THAN ONE BOOK IN THE DRAGONBACK SERIES.

I. THIEF, SOLDIER, SLAVE

"Thief," "soldier," and "slave" are terms applied to Jack in the titles of Timothy Zahn's Dragonback books. Go to the library or online to find definitions for each of these terms and brief biographical information for historical figures given each of these labels (at least one famous (or infamous) thief, soldier, and slave). Use this research as the basis for a discussion of the similarities and differences between these terms, and what lessons Jack learns as he experiences each role.

II. DRAGON

In the title of each novel, Draycos is referred to as "Dragon." Create a brainstorm list of words you associate with "dragon." Research the topic of dragons online. Cut pictures from magazines, create your own drawings, or find other visual materials that support your understanding of the concept of "dragon" and how it applies to the character in the novel. Incorporate these words and images into a small collage or other artwork.

III. ALIEN FORMS

Make a list of the diverse alien life forms encountered by Jack in the Dragonback novels. Use this list as the basis for a dictionary-style booklet entitled "A Guide to Timothy Zahn's Aliens." For each entry, include the alien's name, a physical description, and other available information. If you like, include aliens from other Timothy Zahn novels. Create a cover illustration and other graphics for your booklet. Share your completed booklet with classmates or friends.

Look for

DRAGON
and HERDSMAN

0-765-34041-1

by **TIMOTHY ZAHN**

Now available from
Tom Doherty Associates